Montana 1948

"A beautiful novel about the meaning of place and evolution of courage. . . . A wonderful book."

—Louise Erdrich

"This story is as fresh and clear as the trout streams fished by its narrator. . . . As universal in its themes as it is original in its peculiarities, *Montana 1948* is a significant and elegant addition to the fiction of the American West, and to contemporary American fiction in general."

—Howard Frank Mosher, *The Washington Post Book World*

"*Montana 1948* stands out as a work of art. . . ."

—Susan Petro, *San Francisco Chronicle*

"A real page-turner. . . . Very thoughtful, very artistic, beautifully written. In short, it has everything."

—Dave Wood, *Minneapolis Star Tribune*

"Wonderful. . . . Be prepared to read this compact book in one sitting. Start at 10 P.M. By 11, you're hooked. You finish in the wee hours, mesmerized by the fast-moving plot, the terse language, uncompromising characterization, and insights into life."

—Mike Bowler, *Baltimore Sun*

Justice

"Though not sentimental, and certainly not simple, [*Justice* is] bound to touch a nostalgic spot in readers who equate small towns and wide-open, wild spaces like these with a simpler time. . . . That Mr. Watson is able to capitalize on this myth—and the yearning that attends it—even as he gives the lie to it is further evidence of his subtlety and skill."

—Ellen Akins, *The New York Times Book Review*

"A worthy collection, filled with rugged prose sometimes as biting as a northern plains wind, the next page as inviting and lyrical as a well-stoked wood stove. . . . *Justice* explains much of the history of *Montana 1948*."

—Tim McLaurin, *Washington Post Book World*

"Gracefully constructed. . . . With prose as unassuming and a narrative style as authentic as a Montana landscape, *Justice* will inevitably have a reservation at the select table set for only the very finest . . . fiction."

—Jo Gilbertson, *Minneapolis Star-Tribune*

"Beautifully written. . . . Some of the stories about men in *Justice* evoke the feeling of *A River Runs Through It*, but it's Watson's description of the Hayden women that gives the reader the sweetest gift."

—Carol Knopes, *USA Today*

"This fine book is billed as a 'prequel' to Watson's earlier book, *Montana 1948*, but don't be fooled—[*Justice*] stands quite well on its own. . . . From the way fresh snow illuminates a moonless night, to the way a gun feels in a man's hand, to the way a baby rolls and moves inside a pregnant woman, Larry Watson makes us feel Montana life."

—Laurie Hertzel, *Minnesota Monthly*

Books by Larry Watson

In a Dark Time
Leaving Dakota
Montana 1948
Justice
White Crosses

Larry Watson

In a Dark Time

A Novel

WASHINGTON SQUARE PRESS
PUBLISHED BY POCKET BOOKS

New York   London   Toronto   Sydney   Tokyo   Singapore

WSP

A Washington Square Press Publication of
POCKET BOOKS, a division of Simon & Schuster Inc.
1230 Avenue of the Americas, New York, NY 10020

Copyright © 1980 by Lawrence Watson
Originally published in hardcover in 1980 by Scribner

ISBN: 0-671-55164-7

First Washington Square Press trade paperback printing April 1998

10 9 8 7 6 5 4 3 2 1

WASHINGTON SQUARE PRESS and colophon are
registered trademarks of Simon & Schuster Inc.

Cover design by Brigid Pearson
Front cover photos: faces by Leigh Wells;
    school courtesy of the Curt Teich Postcard
    Archives/Lake County (IL) Museum

Printed in the U.S.A.

To Susan

"In a dark time, the eye begins to see."

—THEODORE ROETHKE

In a Dark Time

2 April 1973, Monday

*T*he third body was found this morning. At seven forty-five a janitor found her in the boys' lavatory on the third floor across from the Biology Lab. Like the other two girls, she had been strangled, and she was found naked, her clothes, cut into strips, piled neatly beside her. It has been only three weeks since the last murder, and there were six weeks to the day between the first and the second. Numbers one and two were spaced, I remember noting, at report-card intervals. And now, if the mathematics of it work out, the next one will occur in a week and a half. After three murders, these are the kinds of observations that one is reduced to making.

The first girl was found in one of the small practice rooms in the music wing. She was in the school early to practice her cello, and she was also found by one of the janitors. The second girl was discovered by a student. Her body was behind one of the flats on the stage in the old gym. She had apparently been in school early as well (despite the warnings that were issued after what had happened to the first girl), but she was not found until after eleven thirty A.M., and the office had already called her home to find out if the girl was absent for a legitimate reason.

I should have started from the time the first girl was killed to make some sort of a record. Ordinarily, I think of a journal as something of a self-indulgence, as a place where one records those things that the memory doesn't see fit to save. I have a student in my senior English Literature class who keeps a journal. Every time I come into the classroom, he is there, in the first desk in the row next to the window, his long hair held back with a blue bandana, and he is writing feverishly in the journal which he knows every writer must keep. He writes in his journal, he says, his poems, his insights, and his innermost thoughts—whatever is "going on in his head." He is continually trying to foist his journal on me, to force me to share with him something of which I want no part. I tell him that it is probably best that he keep these private things to himself, that his journal will be more useful and meaningful to him if he does not make it indiscriminately public. But what is happening here and now, in Wanekia, Minnesota, in this spring, is an extreme situation, and I think to make a record of it is less a business of self-concern, of contemplating one's navel, and more an act of simply keeping one's eyes on what is happening here and now. And I want to hold onto it all, to know always not only that it happened, but to know who was here and what they said and how they dealt with all this. Someone has to watch things closely. Right after I left the school, I bought a black loose-leaf notebook and two hundred sheets of narrow-lined paper. I use a black felt-tip pen, and I print carefully, keeping vertical lines as straight as possible and making the circles and semicircles as round as I can.

When I drove into the parking lot this morning and saw the three police cars, I knew immediately that it had happened again and the feeling came over me again. It is a throat-tightening, adrenaline-pumping feeling. The only thing I can compare it to was when I was in high school and would come home late at night. I would drive the car into the dark garage, and before I got out I would sometimes get the sudden feeling that someone was in the garage, pressed against the wall and waiting in the shadows for me. But rather than remain afraid in the car (or backing out of the garage), I would get a rush of power and leap from the car, any of the quavering of fear all gone into the tightening of muscle, ready to confront whatever was there. And when nothing was there, my shoulders would drop, and I would go slack. That was the way I felt this morning—afraid of what was going to be there but at the same time excited about being at the scene. And I probably will not go slack for a few days.

The three police cars were parked at the wrong angle, and one of the cars still had its red light on, beating in a quick circle and flashing dully in the early sunlight. The ambulance was backed up to the stairs that led down from the central doors. The new sections of the school have been tacked onto the north and south ends of the original building, and the new wings jut out to form a block-shaped U with the older section. The faculty parking lot is in the back in the center of the U, and the three sections make something of a courtyard for the teachers' cars. The courtyard faces the east, and the sun was shining into the lot so that everything was cast in a harsh and unreal light. The bright colors of the cars, the chrome on the ambulance and the police cars all reflected the light. I looked up at the rows of classroom windows to see if I could see anyone inside, but it was impossible to see through the windows—the sun made them look like sheets of gold foil.

It's strange, but when I drove in I don't think it was the presence of the police cars that signaled that something was wrong as much as it was the way they were parked. Yellow lines have been painted diagonally on the asphalt for the cars, and the police cars were parked the wrong way across the yellow lines, as though they were all crossing X s.

People were standing around in small clumps. Closest to the ambulance, lined up by the stairs, were the students who had already arrived at school, all of them straining to see over someone else's shoulder. The rest of the people in the lot were policemen and teachers, and for the most part they both stayed with their own groups. Across the street people had begun to come out of their houses and were standing on their lawns and sidewalks, staring over at the school. The people across the street were still in the shade because of the angle of the sun and the high trees, and many of the women were wearing housecoats and had their arms folded as if they were trying to keep warm in the cool, damp morning air. The cars that drove by slowed automatically as if they were pulled up short by strings as soon as the drivers saw the police cars and the ambulance. Before I left, the news must have been on radio and TV because a steady caravan of cars began to circle the school slowly.

Another small thing, like the police cars parked the wrong way, that said that something was wrong was Mr. Proctor, the principal. He was smoking, drawing nervously on a cigarette cupped in his hand and talking to a detective who was writing something in a small notebook. Mr. Proctor is fifty-five years old and has been a principal for nine years, and he had set his sights on that position from the time he got into "the education business" at the age of twenty-three. (All these things, his age, his ambitions toward "principal-dom," he confessed to the faculty and staff at a general meeting right after the second murder, the same meeting at which he began to cry and uttered what Roger and I agree is one of the most astounding understatements of all time; he said, "Nothing like this has ever happened at any of the schools I've been associated with.") Mr. Proctor believes, I think, that he became a principal and has been so successful as one, because he never walked through the front door of a bar (all bars in Wanekia have back doors), and because he has never smoked in public.

I parked at the east edge of the lot and stayed by my car. When crowds gather, when traffic accidents occur, when buildings burn, when drunks fall to the pavement, I stay away from the people who cluster like ants around some sweet thing dropped in the dust. I stay away because I don't want it to be thought that I am as morbid as everyone else. (Perhaps I am too harsh—it may only be curiosity.) When I was ten years old, I was on vacation with my parents in

4

Los Angeles, and one night my aunt and uncle took us to Chinatown for dinner. As we were leaving, a fight broke out between a man in a blue Hawaiian shirt with yellow parrots on the back and a man in a white jacket. They circled each other like real boxers, but when they exchanged punches, they came together in a rush and flailed at each other like schoolboys. When blows did land, they didn't sound like the sharp cracks of movie fist fights; instead they thudded and splatted, and they ended up punching each other in the chest and on the side of the head with the flat of their fists. I hung back to see the fight, thinking all the time that since we were in a large city one of the men might pull a knife or gun. Suddenly my mother grabbed my arm and yanked me away. She shook me and said, "That's not for you to see—you don't have to watch like those other rubberneckers," taking in with a sweep of her arm the whole crowd of people now in a circle around the two men. So I stay back from the crowds and resist the impulse to get up close. I stay away so it cannot be said of me that I am just like the rest of them—those who have to see it all. But it takes an effort to keep back, because what I really want to do is to see if anyone is still in the burning building, if they are going to jump from the third-floor window or be consumed by flames, to see if someone is in the wrecked car, folded into the back seat or pinned behind the steering wheel, to see if the drunk has broken his teeth in his fall, if he is aware of his own blood on the sidewalk. And what I really wanted to do was to join the students by the ambulance, and to know, once and for all, if the eyes of strangulation victims truly bulge as they did in that Alfred Hitchcock film, if you could actually see the finger-shaped bruises on her throat. But I kept my distance, leaning against my car as casually as I could, trying to pretend that I wanted to be somewhere else, that I was only there because I might be needed.

John Turner came across the lot toward me. The morning was cool, but he was wearing his short-sleeved white shirt and his narrow striped tie. Most teachers no longer feel any compulsion to wear a tie, but Turner is never without one. I think he does it as sort of a holding action; he's slovenly, his tie is awkwardly knotted, his large belly hides his belt buckle, and his white shirt refuses to stay tucked in, but his tie must be his way of keeping his appearance from complete disorder. He was smoking too.

"Did you just get here?" he said.

"Just a couple minutes ago."

"Jesus, it's bad."

"Same thing as before?" I realized that we were both speaking in hushed voices.

"Same as before. One of the janitors found her in the boys' can. I heard him talking to a cop. He said he was cleaning bathrooms, and when he came in he saw a bare foot sticking out from under the door of one of the stalls. I guess she was propped up on the toilet."

"I don't suppose they caught anyone?"

"No, hell no. The cops have closed off the school, but they haven't got anybody. They're not even close, I bet."

I noticed that Turner's face was suitably somber; beneath all the slack flesh of his face I could see his jaw knotting. It struck me that everyone must be watching everyone else's face—to see if anyone is smiling when he should be frowning, laughing when he should be crying.

"Who's the victim, do you know?"

"I don't know. They're not going to release any information until they notify the next of kin. Some of the kids might know who she is, and I'm sure Proctor knows too."

I began to feel sorry for the girl. Already she was being talked about in that jargon that surrounds all this—"victim," "next of kin"—those oddly neutral television news terms. Her chances of ever being remembered as herself, as the girl who received the Kiwanis scholarship or the girl who married the boy from St. Paul or even the girl who threw up at the Prom were all gone now. From that point on she was going to be remembered as one of the girls who was murdered in Wanekia High School.

"Have they canceled classes yet?" I asked.

"Not yet. But they will." Turner was a good person to be talking to because he always knew what was going on. I don't think he asked questions, and I don't think people offered him information, but he knew everything. If a student was in trouble or if someone wasn't going to be offered a contract for the next year, Turner knew about it. I suspect he's the type of person who overhears things, and from the bits and pieces that are dropped within his earshot, he's able to construct whole stories. And since he sees himself as a semiofficial dispenser of information, he is very easy to question. But it would have been easier still for me to talk to Roger, or if Alexandra had been there, I think I could have used the excitement of the situation (and the information from Turner) to talk to her. I kept looking through the lot for either of them.

Not far from me, a girl in a navy blue sweater was standing alone by the doors to the gym. She had her hands pressed against her face and she was crying. Black streaks from her mascara ran down from her eyes and suddenly she began to sob audibly. I watched her, and her eyes started to get wider and her shoulders were jerking up and down as if she were trying to catch her breath, and the cries that came from her sounded like the yelping of a dog hit by a car. Bonnie Jacobsen, one of the guidance counselors, must have heard her, because she walked quickly across the lot to the girl, put an arm around her, and walked her toward the largest group of policemen. Turner drifted away from me; I assume he was going to overhear what he could overhear.

I have always had trouble understanding death on anything but a very abstract level; it has little reality for me until I have some sort of stimulus, usually meaningful only to me, some sort of small shock to bring it all home. When my grandfather died when I was ten, I couldn't comprehend his death until the day of the funeral when I saw my mother and my uncle with their arms around each other crying. A friend of mine killed himself when we were in high school, and I was one of the pallbearers at his funeral. The notion that I would never see him again, that he was truly dead, did not come fully to me until we were at the cemetery. It was a bitterly cold March day, and we were standing inside one of those wall-less tents in which they conduct graveside ceremonies and the canvas was flapping in the wind. While I was standing there a corner of the drape they had over the hole came up and I saw the scraped sides of the freshly dug grave and I knew then. Not long ago I saw a documentary about the Nazi concentration camp at Dachau. In one of the scenes a bulldozer is shown pushing scores of bodies into a pit. Now for years I have been as outraged as anyone at the slaughter of millions of people by the Nazis, but it wasn't until I saw that film and in that one scene, despite the grainy quality of the film, among the welter of all the white arms and legs sticking out at odd angles, I suddenly saw someone's face. That face made the horror of it real to me. After the first murder, I had to go to the school library and get a copy of last year's annual and look at the picture of the girl, at her awkward smile, her long dark hair, and, more than anything else, the cast she had in one eye, to know that someone was truly dead. With the second girl, it came to me when I was walking down the hall the day it happened and I saw the girl's father. He was the owner of the garage where I have my car serviced; he's a tall, heavy, red-faced man, and whenever I had any business dealings with him, his size and his loud voice always intimidated me. But on that day, he was walking down the hall crying, and a police officer was holding him gently by one arm as if the big man were hurt. He had a handkerchief pressed to his face, and his head was bowed. When he walked by me, he looked up, and I saw that his tears had dripped onto his glasses. So the sound of the girl in the navy blue sweater this morning meant to me that someone was dead.

From merely a practical point of view, it's remarkable that this can keep going on. This school is a very different place since the murders began. (Understatements do not belong exclusively to Proctor.) All before- and after-school activities have been canceled. There are no more intramural sports;

no track, band, orchestra, or choir practices; no students held after school to make up exams or to receive extra help; Student Council meetings are held from twelve to one. Students are discouraged, unless it is absolutely necessary, from being in the halls during the day. Mr. Proctor has issued few specific directives to teachers; we have simply been cautioned to be "watchful" and to "use good judgment" in all things. There was a great deal of talk, after the second girl was killed, that the school would be closed indefinitely, but the police apparently advised against it and the school board voted such a proposal down. (I think they both think that it would be a sign of weakness to close down.) After this morning, the proposal will probably come up again. A policeman, Sergeant Bush, has been stationed in the school since the second girl. He spends most of the day at a chair in the central hall right next to the trophy case.

The ambulance finally left the parking lot. The crowd halved itself to make room for it, and as soon as it pulled out onto the street, its siren began, first a low whine like a record played at the wrong speed, then it wound itself to its full wail. I noticed that it did not appear to be driving away at much more than a normal rate of speed, and I wondered if they had a particular policy about proceeding with occupants already dead. One of the police cars followed the ambulance out of the lot.

Mr. Proctor was up on the steps with the police chief, and both of them were motioning for everyone to come closer. The crowd made a ragged circle around the steps, and when everyone quieted down, Proctor began to speak.

"I suppose all of you know by now what's happened. Another one of our girls has been murdered. We can't give you any of the details now, and there's nothing more to be done around here by us, so let's just go on home. The police are handling everything. School is closed for the day, but so far as we know now, classes will meet tomorrow as usual."

He started to turn away, then it seemed as though he must have thought he should say something more, because he faced us again and said, "I'm sorry. I know this is a bad

9

business." His voice sounded as if he were going to say more, but he quit there and came down the steps.

While he was speaking I stayed at the back of the crowd. There was something about the quality of his voice, thinned by my distance from him and diffused by the morning air, that reminded me of the first time that I heard his voice. It was in August, 1971, and I was staying at my parents' house, had just finished summer school, had gotten a masters' degree, and had been admitted to a PhD program and I didn't want to go. One afternoon I was lying in the backyard in the sun reading Walt Whitman. I remember I was reading "Song of Myself," the "it shall be you" section, the part I think I know almost by heart. My mother called me to the telephone, and it was C. W. Proctor. They were looking for someone to teach senior English, had found my name in the placement-office files, and wanted to know if I would be interested in the job. I said yes so quickly I surprised myself. At first Proctor tried to persuade me to think about it for a while and get back to him, but once I had him convinced I was certain about the position, he told me I could have it. Then he said he was glad to "have me aboard." When I went back out in the yard my copy of *Leaves of Grass* was lying open, and the wind was causing the pages to flutter gently like the lift and fall of a dead bird's wing. I remembered why I had been reading Whitman; I had been thinking that I might like to write my dissertation on him someday. But abandoning graduate school and all that went with it and going out into the world seemed at that moment very right to me, as though I were obeying a Whitman command to put the book down and hit the road. It never seemed quite right to be reading Walt Whitman to find dissertation topics anyway. I thought Walt would be proud of me.

The people began to leave slowly, as if they were all in that sluggish and numb state of first waking. Just as I was getting in my car, I saw Dick Croom standing by his car. He took off his sport jacket, shook it as if he were trying to air it out, and then carefully and methodically spread it out on the front seat of his car. I know Dick Croom, and nine weeks ago he would have quickly and simply gotten into his car and driven away. But I knew exactly what he was doing. He has a new ritual, and it's one of the small, insignificant, meaningless actions that many people have recently developed. These actions are like tics, and they are ways of dealing with what is happening here.

I am going to watch these things closely.

3 April 1973, Tuesday

A large number of students were absent today. In my eight-thirty study hall attendance must have been barely fifty percent. A woman called the school office saying she represented a group of concerned parents and that none of their children were going to return to school until this business was cleaned up. As it turned out, only ten students are children of "concerned parents," but I'm sure many parents are keeping their children out of school, at least for a time. After the first murder, school was closed for two days while the police searched for clues, but when classes began again you couldn't keep them away. Attendance was down after the second murder (although not as drastically as today), but they all returned gradually, and I'm certain they will now too.

Just last week someone said that the school board was still insisting that those two days be made up.

In the office, tacked up over the teachers' mail boxes, was a freshly mimeographed notice that said the funeral will be held at two o'clock Thursday afternoon at Zion Lutheran Church. Classes will be canceled for the afternoon (to be made up later?), and the faculty is "strongly encouraged" to attend the services. We weren't strongly encouraged the first two times—I wonder why this situation is different. I didn't attend the first two funerals and felt guilty about it both times (even though I didn't know either of the girls), and I think I'll go this time.

The toilet seat is missing from the lavatory where the girl's body was found. Someone said that he saw the police carry it away in a clear plastic bag. Half of the third floor is blocked off with those black-and-white-striped barricades that look like saw horses, and I imagine the police have to look everywhere for clues, for whatever clues they can find. I can understand that. I think I, as much as anyone, want to know who the murderer is. But I want to know more than his identity. I want to know *why*. I would like to be able to look into his eyes and see what is there, to see how that person is different, how he came to the point in his life when he began, for what reason, to strangle young girls to death. I remember a few years ago there was a television special about two murderers who were serving life sentences in a Utah prison. I don't recall their names, but the two of them, high on amphetamines and wine and beer, killed a number of people one night in Salt Lake City. One of the people they killed was a taxi driver who had given them a ride to the airport. And I think they had been in a bar that same night, and they suddenly began shooting at everyone in the bar. I watched them being interviewed in prison, and when the program was over I felt, along with a sense of horror and revulsion, a sense of frustration. They talked calmly about what they had done, and even discussed, in detail, how they had committed the murders. They joked about how one of their victims had begged for his life. When they were finally asked why they had done what they did, they only looked at each other; one of them smiled and the other one shrugged. They seemed smug, almost as if they were taunting their questioners by not answering. I'm almost afraid of that happening here; the murderer being caught but no one ever being able to understand how or why it ever happened. And I want to know why.

4 April 1973, Wednesday

My parents called me tonight. As usual, my mother asked if I knew to whom I was speaking. And when I guessed, she seemed, as she always does, slightly hurt, as if there were something wrong in my knowing the gravelly voice of my own mother. Actually, I was surprised—surprised they had not called last night or the night before.

When they called I felt perturbed. I was tired, I had papers to grade, and the day had not been a good one. In my afternoon English Lit class, we were talking about Donne's "Valediction: Forbidding Mourning," and they didn't understand the first goddamn thing about it. I should have known it was going to happen and prepared for it; most of them thought the compass in the poem was of the directional, magnetic variety. Once I convinced them that it was supposed to be like a drawing compass, they seemed a little less bewildered. But even then they were distracted; they sat through the hour slumped in their desks and stared out the window at the parking lot. I suppose I could understand; tomorrow that class is going to be canceled for the funeral, and most of them were probably thinking about that.

But if they were thinking of murder in this, or in any other class, I was not to blame. By common, unspoken, unwritten consent, none of the teachers discuss the murders in class. Not indirectly. Not by sidelong references. Not at all. And unlike the college students of the sixties, these students do not demand more relevance in their classes. And cowards all, we happily comply. As a result, in Sociology, they do not discuss the social conditions that are apt to produce a mass murderer. In Psychology, they do not talk about the mentality of the psychopathic killer. In History, they pay no attention to the violent past of this country. In math classes, they learn nothing of their odds to survive to voting age. In Phys Ed, they receive no instruction in self-defense. In Shop, no one teaches them how to build a fence high and secure enough to keep murderers from the door. And in English, no one encourages them to write down their impressions of their most impressionable age. And no one points out to them how a poem like Donne's can help to mitigate the grief that all of them must feel. No one disturbs them in their classes with such matters as these.

I made small talk with my mother, talk about the weather, about the health of her friends, about my sister and her husband, and then she got to the real reason for her call.

"Peter," she said, "*what* is going on there?"

"Another girl was murdered . . ."

"We read about it in the *Tribune,* and we heard about it on the news, but we just couldn't believe it. How many is that?"

"That's three."

"My God, how much longer do you suppose this is going to go on?"

"It can't go on indefinitely. There's only so many people here."

"Stop that! You know what I mean."

"I don't know, Mother. The police have no idea who did it."

"Well, if they're anything like the police department here, they'd be the last ones to know. Do you have any ideas? Does anybody?"

Do I have any idea who is doing it? I do, and so does everybody who lives here. In fact, a day does not go by when I fail to see someone on the street whom I consider to be a likely candidate to be the killer. Fortunately, I'm always able to dismiss these suspicions. So far. What I did not tell my mother about was my trip to the grocery store last night. It was about eleven thirty, and the store was practically empty—more employees were there than customers. (Only males work in this supermarket after nine.) I was trying to remember what I needed besides bread and milk. I was alone in the aisle where the soup and other canned goods are kept when I smelled something—or I should say, I smelled someone. The smell was distinct, and though no one was standing near me, I kept looking around to see if someone had suddenly appeared. The smell was of sweat, but sweet and stale, not the smell of someone perspiring heavily from strenuous activity, but the smell of someone who had not bathed in a long time, someone whose clothes had become permeated with his body odor. As I moved down the aisle, the scent remained as strong as ever. I thought for a moment I might have been wrong, that perhaps the smell came from food, from a bag or jar or can that had come open. But the odor was unmistakable; it was human. I began to move more quickly through the store, up and down every aisle, trying to find the person who belonged to the smell. What had happened was this: for some inexplicable reason I had become convinced that whoever smelled like that was the murderer. It's quite true; I believed that, and I searched the store for the killer. This kind of thing happened once before. Shortly after the second murder, late one Sunday night, a car drove by my apartment going so fast that I was sure I would soon hear sirens and see the police cars in pursuit. The driver of the car, I was certain, was the killer trying to make a getaway. I became convinced of these things. So I could hardly say to my mother, yes, I believe I know who the killer is—I smell him in the grocery store, and I see him speeding by my home late at night. (I never did find the owner of the smell, although I did check out before I was through shopping so I could get in line behind a man in a red wool shirt to see if I could get close enough to find out if the odor came from him.)

"No, Mother, I don't have any idea who the killer is. And nobody else does either."

"Just tell us what you know. The newspapers don't give any information."

"I'm afraid I don't know much more."

"You must know more than the newspapers. After all, you're right there. Let me get your father on the extension."

And so I told. My telling was, after all, the reason for the call just as it was the reason for the calls after the first two murders. And my knowledge of that no doubt added to my irritation. Because I am, for my mother and father, the one who *knows*, the one who is right there, and because the feeling of authority is not altogether unpleasant, I told them what I knew and told it as vividly as I could. I took them through the halls of the school, let them feel the rough stucco walls, smell the freshly waxed floors, hear the whispers of the students, see the white, tear-streaked faces. I mentioned all the details I could remember and hoped more would come to me in the re-creation. I even mentioned the missing toilet seat. I felt like a camp counselor telling ghost stories to children around a campfire. The only sound as I spoke was the disparate rhythms of their breathing. When I finished, when I had related all the details I could remember, there was a long silence, uncomfortable across the long-distance lines. I felt as if I had been punishing them with the brutal story.

"Peter," my mother said, "do you want to come home?"

When she asked that I could hear my father mutter something, something like, "Oh, Margaret."

"No, Mother," I said tolerantly. "I couldn't come home even if I wanted to. You forget—I work here. I have to be on the job every day, five days a week."

"I didn't mean necessarily to stay," she said. "But maybe just for a visit. For a weekend. Wouldn't you like to get away, even for a couple days?"

"Even if I'd like to, I couldn't. I have to be here. For a number of reasons."

"If you change your mind, you know you're welcome."

"I know, Mother. I know I can always come home, and I appreciate it."

My mother hung up, and my father stayed on the phone, as he usually does, for some man-to-man talk.

"Don't let your mother get to you, Pete. You know how women can be. Especially about something like this."

"Sure, I understand."

"And that's a mighty ugly business that's going on there. Mighty ugly."

"I know." He was beginning to lecture. I let him go on.

"Your mother worries about you. Hell, *I* worry about you. We both do. You know that."

"You don't have to. Since I'm not a teenaged girl, I'm out of danger."

"Well, take care of yourself. And you call us if anything new develops. Collect. All right?"

And I promised I would. And I will.

5 April 1973, Thursday

*P*erhaps I should have been a policeman. I know that I'm noticing things that the police are missing. This afternoon at the funeral, when the minister began to speak he first said the girl's full name, and then he paused for a long time as if the words, Debra Helen Spencer, should have a special significance. And in that long pause, something occurred to me: two of the three girls have been named Debra. The first girl's name was Deborah Ann Munson. How could anyone overlook that similarity? And yet, no mention has been made of it.

I've always been good at that sort of thing—at noticing small details and building constructs from them. For a long time, I was something of a Kennedy-assassination buff. I read books about how the Warren Commission was sloppily handled, about how it was impossible for Lee Harvey Oswald to be the lone assassin. And I read an abridged version of the Warren Report. I finally lost interest when it became apparent that I was never going to know the truth; it was like doing a crossword puzzle with the wrong clues and never being able to fill in all the letters. But I still got some use out of all the reading and studying I did about Kennedy.

When I was working in Minneapolis during the summer a couple years ago, I used to go to singles' bars with a friend of mine. My opening line with girls was, "Do you remember what you were doing when John Kennedy was killed?" It never failed; they would always remember, and they always wanted to talk about it. They would remember that they were sitting in Chemistry class when it was announced over the public-address system; that they were lying in bed with the chicken pox; that they were walking to school, scuffing their feet through the piles of leaves stacked on the lawns. They would remember first, and then I would remember. I would remember that I was traveling to Duluth with my mother, father, and sister to my grandparents' golden wedding anniversary, and I was bored with the long car ride. I sat in the back seat with my head pressed against the cool glass and watched the trees and the telephone poles and the fence posts slip by, and I pretended they were all moving as fast as we were in the opposite direction. The first announcement over the car radio said only that the President had been shot in Dallas, but the report was unconfirmed. From the first bulletin, I imagined President Kennedy standing on some sort of reviewing stand that was hung with red, white, and blue bunting and suddenly a man burst from the crowd and opened fire with a machine gun. But in the scene I imagined, Kennedy received only a flesh wound in the arm, and he walked away from the stand, clutching his arm, a small trickle of blood coming out between his fingers. When they finally said that the President was dead, I remember that my parents didn't say anything, but my father did pull the car over for a few minutes, and my mother kept looking over at him with a fearful look in her eyes, and I thought she might cry from fright.

Even though the funeral was only this afternoon, I remember very little of what the minister said. There was some talk about how an occurrence (that was the word—"occurrence") like this could make us wonder about the sort of world we live in and what is God's place in this world. But, he cautioned, these are questions to which we could never find satisfactory answers ("fully" satisfactory, he said) and that faith is more than just a word—it is an important and complex principle by which we must live our lives. When he came to the part about faith, I stopped listening and secretly looked around at the other people in the church.

I envied the minister his position up on the altar behind the pulpit. From there I'm sure he could see virtually every face in the church. I sat over to one side toward the back, and I couldn't see much at all. Occasionally I would catch the white flutter of a handkerchief as it moved up to someone's eyes or nose, and I could hear sniffs and whimpers and sobs and nervous coughs coming from different corners of the church. It seemed as if people were trying to communicate with each other by code. But Reverend Bain could see it all. I imagined a small play in which the police would know, for some reason or another, that the murderer would attend his victim's funeral. Then, just at the end of the service, the minister would say, "All right, we know you're out there somewhere. I want each one of you to stand up, one by one, stare first at the cross and then look me in the eyes and say, 'I'm not the one. I did not murder Debra Helen Spencer.'" And the killer, because he was a religious fanatic, would not be able to do it, and, like a vampire confronted by daylight or a cross, would collapse and cower and finally sob out a confession. But through most of the service, Reverend Bain seemed to be looking out right above the tops of everyone's head.

Paul Mazzeo sat with the Spencer family. (Mr. Spencer has already contributed a thousand dollars to the steadily growing reward fund.) He had been going with Debbie, and he has been something of a celebrity around school since the murder. One of the chief reasons for his fame has been his anger. He has been very vocal about what he considers to be the police's ineptitude in handling the case, and he has said that he would like to conduct his own investigation. And, he said, when he does find out who the murderer is, he plans to kill him with his bare hands. I have no doubt that he means it, and I'm sure that he's capable of doing it.

But it seems curious to me that his only emotion is rage. I should think that sorrow would come first and that anger would follow only when the sadness began to subside. However, I have my own notion about what is going to happen to Paul. He is very popular in school—Student Council, basketball, track, and all of that—and as the angry and bereaved lover his stock as romantic figure is sure to rise. Anyway, I see one of Debra's friends—perhaps her best friend—offering to comfort him in his hour of need, him shedding tears on the pillow of her breast, one thing leading to another . . . Should he wish to take advantage of it, I'd wager that throughout his life Paul will be able to use Debbie's death to help him with women. Sort of an automatic sympathy-getter. I know exactly how I'd work it.

After the funeral Roger and I went out for a beer. We agreed it might be a good idea if we were not seen going into a bar in town right after the funeral, so we went to the Red-Ray Lanes, a combination bar and bowling alley right outside of town. The place was virtually deserted. One person was bowling somewhere. We couldn't see him, but at regular intervals we would hear the long rumble of the ball, the clatter of pins, the rumble of the ball being returned. The only other sign of life, besides the barmaid and the bartender, was a table next to us that had been recently used by what must have been a large group. It was covered with empty beer pitchers and glasses with patches of foam still clinging to the sides, ashtrays stacked with butts, and crumpled balls of empty cigarette and peanut packages.

We each went through three drinks pretty fast, and we talked rarely. I know I had the uneasy feeling that since it was so quiet whatever we said could surely be overheard by someone. (Although the bartender and the barmaid showed no interest in us at all. They were involved in their own conversation, and he was doing most of the talking. She was pretty and had a good figure, and from the bored way she seemed to be listening to him I imagined that he was telling her that his wife didn't understand him.)

An old man in overalls and a Sherwin-Williams painting

cap came in and sat at the bar. When he came through the door, the dark room filled suddenly with sunlight, and the brightness made everything harsh and even slightly incongruous. The drinks and the darkness and the quiet made it seem like midnight, and it wasn't even five o'clock.

Roger was sort of tilted in his chair, and I could tell by the way he was staring at the toes of his shoes and smiling faintly that he was a little tight. I guess I was too, because when I looked at him all I could see was circles. His black, bushy, curly hair ringed his head like a halo, and his beard kept the circle going. Inside the dark corona of hair and beard his steel-rimmed glasses made two more circles, and in the middle of it all his small red nose (which he said had been circumcised at his birth) made the smallest circle of all. He began to move, and I said, "Sit still, goddammit. You're making me dizzy."

Roger slowly put his finger to his lips and nodded his head furtively toward the old man at the bar.

"Loose lips sink ships," he said softly.

"What the hell are you talking about?"

He just nodded his head toward the old man again.

"Have I missed something?" I said. "Do you know something I don't know?"

Roger leaned over the table and motioned for me to meet him in the middle. "I think," he whispered, "that the old man is the one."

"The one what?"

"The One! The Bad Guy—the Villain! The Killer!"

Roger is what I guess you might call compulsively funny. Because of the particular nature of his personality, he is unable to be serious about anything; no matter what the occasion he has only one behavioral recourse—to be funny. Or at least to try to be. This penchant of his is especially refreshing at faculty meetings or stuffy cocktail parties, but today it seemed to me to be inappropriate if not actually in bad taste. And I am not easily offended. Most of the time he causes me to be as light about everything as he is; he inspires me to personal high levels of funniness, and we've often spent great lengths of time trying to top each other's lines. But today I didn't feel very funny. Not about this.

"What makes you say that?" I acted as stern as possible so he would know that I didn't approve.

He looked from side to side, leaned further over the table, and whispered, softer than ever, "The paint on his coveralls—I think it's really blood."

I stared at him the same way I stare at Grant Torgerson and Teddy Birch when they sit at the back of the room and talk through class. "First of all," I said, "blood is not blue, which is the color of the spots on his overalls. Secondly, strangulation victims do not bleed. Thirdly, I think that's in bad taste."

"Why isn't he at the funeral then?" He wasn't going to let this go easily.

"The funeral was over long ago."

"But he wasn't there, was he?"

"No, he wasn't."

"So we haven't completely ruled him out as a suspect."

"Who said anything about suspects? Why is he a suspect?"

"Because he looks suspect-like. Not suspicious—everyone looks suspicious—suspect-like."

This conversation was held entirely in whispers. If anyone else was trying to overhear what we were saying all they would be able to hear would be the breathy little expulsions of air that were coming from the direction of our table. And in our dark suits it occurred to me that we probably looked like the two gangsters in that Hemingway short story, "The Killers." All very suspicious. And silly, and I could feel my seriousness slipping away.

"That suspect of yours," I said, "looks like a Grampa. Grampas have never, in all of recorded history, ever killed anyone. Never."

"So. Who are we left with for suspects?"

"What were you doing at seven thirty A.M. on April second?" As soon as I said that I was sorry, and I was afraid that that might be the one thing that Roger couldn't be funny about. And something else too, and, Christ, I'm sorry for thinking it but a small part of me did: I was afraid he might say, "At seven thirty I was busy with my hands around the neck of Debbie Spencer." That's true; I feared that my best friend might secretly be a murderer and might suddenly decide to confess everything to me.

"At seven thirty on the morning of the second of April in the year of our Lord nineteen hundred and seventy-three," Roger said, "I was having a bowel movement. And I have twelve witnesses who will verify, under oath, my testimony."

"I give up," I said. For some reason I was bothered by the fact that he didn't ask me what I was doing at seven thirty; it seemed like a bad sign. Was he afraid to ask also?

We were both quiet awhile and ordered another drink. The old man left, the phantom bowler stopped, and everything was silent.

Finally Roger said, "You seem very grim about all this."

"The occasion seems to call for it. People are dying, you know."

"So? People die every day."

"They don't live in Wanekia."

"Dead people don't live anywhere."

We both laughed over that line, and I said that was a good title for a novel.

"But remember," Roger said, "those are not just words . . ."

"But important and complex principles by which we must live our lives."

I took a nap when I got home, and when I finish writing this I'm going to have a bowl of soup and go back to bed.

6 April 1973, Friday

I had lunch with Carl Becker today. Carl has lived in Wanekia all his life (with time out for the Navy and college) as did his father and his grandfather, and Carl is something of an expert on local history. Carl has supplemented his own memories of growing up here with extensive reading of Minnesota history. And he has a storehouse of stories that he remembers hearing from his relatives and other lifelong residents. At a party last year he told me that one of the things he's always wanted to do is to go on to graduate school and write a thesis on the history of Wanekia. Appropriately enough, Carl teaches history. Anytime that I've spoken to him it seems as though I've picked up some information about the region, usually about the Indians, mostly Chippewa, who originally inhabited the area or about the railroad men or early politicians. Anyway, I asked him today if Wanekia had a very extensive history of violent crime. I don't know what I expected to hear—something, anything that might help to explain the craziness that's going on here. Clues maybe. Carl said that as far as he knew, and he was sure he was correct, there have been two, possibly three, other murders in this century prior to this.

The stories Carl told me he told in the same quiet, deep voice that he always uses. While he talked he folded his napkin into different geometric shapes.

In 1933 Bobby Wald killed his father with an axe. Bobby would have killed his mother as well, but when he attempted to bring the axe down on her head she managed to cover her forehead with her arm. Everyone in town knew that Bobby was odd; his parents had said that they would wake up during the night and find Bobby standing over them. Bobby was walking along the highway not far from town when he was arrested by a deputy sheriff. Bobby said that it wasn't his fault "because the gangsters from Chicago made him do it." Bobby was seventeen when it happened; he was judged to be insane, and he has been in the State Hospital ever since. Carl said that the community was perfectly satisfied that Bobby was committed because everyone knew that he was "crazy as a loon."

In 1948 Warren Gadd, a cab driver from St. Paul, killed Carol Lesser, the wife of Harold Lesser, a Wanekia merchant. She was shot once through the head with a chrome-plated Smith & Wesson .38. Carl said he remembered the gun so well because in the lobby of the police station they have a display case filled with weapons, blackjacks, brass knuckles, knives, and guns which the police have taken from criminals, and the .38 is right in the center of the case. It seems that Mrs. Lesser was, as Carl put it, "a regular nympho," and that she and Gadd had been having an affair. Less than an hour after her body was found in Gadd's room in the Carlton Hotel, he was arrested in the Silver Dollar Bar. Gadd was sentenced to life imprisonment in Stillwater State Penitentiary.

The "questionable" murder occurred in 1956. One morning in December a man was found in the driveway of the home of Dr. W. C. Bradley. The man was a businessman from Seattle who was registered at a local motel. The man had a fractured skull and other injuries about the head, but no one was ever able to determine whether he had been in some sort of an accident or if he had been beaten. No one knew how he happened to die in the snow in the Bradleys' driveway—if he was trying to get a doctor, if he had been dumped there, if it was simply happenstance. For a week afterward cars steadily cruised by the Bradley home. Carl said that there were five Bradley children and each of them left town after graduating from high school and never returned.

The something that I hoped would emerge from talking with Carl certainly hasn't come clear yet. I thought I might learn that there was something peculiar about this place that would account for what has happened here. Just as I've heard that there are a large number of suicides by knife in Duluth, Minnesota, because of the large Finnish population there, and apparently Finns have a fondness for knives. Maybe I even expected a suitably exotic science fiction sort of explanation. That once every fifty years a green fog insinuates itself into Wanekia, and for a month everyone behaves crazily, then everything returns to normalcy for another fifty years. Or until the next Presidential election. But I wanted to find out something. Something more than the observation that all six (or five, depending on how one wishes to interpret the strange case of the Bradleys' driveway) of this century's murders have been the result of head wounds or injuries (if we may fairly say that strangulation occurs about the area of the head).

One thing has stayed with me from my talk with Carl. I can't seem to shake the image of axe-wielding Bobby Wald. Carl said Bobby was a tall, fat kid, and I keep imagining him walking along the highway after killing his father. I was going to drive over to St. Cloud tonight to see a nurse whom I've taken out a few times. I was going to go for two reasons. Because I just wanted to get the hell out of town for a while. But mostly because of her. Jane is about five feet tall, and she has the most wonderful short, thick, tan-the-year-around legs. She says that she can do such wonderful things with her legs because she was on the tumbling team in high school. When I was first trying to get her into bed with me I told her (as sincerely as I could make it sound) that I thought I was in love with her. She said,

"Don't. I don't need to hear that kind of shit." And I've been driving to St. Cloud every few weeks ever since.

But I've decided not to go, and I think Bobby Wald has something to do with it. The road between here and St. Cloud is particularly dark. Pine trees grow thickly along the road (which is deserted except for the St. Cloud Reformatory—its black stone walls and towers always seem to rise up suddenly and crowd the highway), and the only relief from the blackness are the bright yellow highway stripes illuminated by the headlights of your car. For some reason, that stretch of road seems especially well suited for coming across the Bobby Walds of the world weaving in and out of the pines and the high grass. I don't know why he should affect me so strongly, especially considering that someone is murdering girls in the place where I work. But I have decided to stay home.

Although I grew up in a town three times the size of Wanekia, I can only remember two crimes. Once when I was ten years old thieves cut their way through the roof of the Super Valu and cracked the store safe. The police said it was a "professional job." When I was sixteen someone threw a car battery through the glass door of Vic's Sporting Goods and stole money and some guns. Certainly there were other crimes, but for some reason these are the only ones that remain in my memory, probably because they occurred in a shopping center three blocks from my home. But as best I can remember, nobody ever killed anyone in the eighteen years I lived there. Which means what? That sometimes in some places people aren't murdered and at other times people are killed as they lie in their beds or they are dragged into school lavatories and strangled.

My apartment is on the west edge of town. The street that runs by my home turns into a highway at the end of the city limits. Usually on a Friday night I can sit by my window and watch the procession of cars drive in and out of the country. The cars are filled with teenagers who go into the country to pull off onto the dirt and gravel side roads and park by groves of trees. There they sit in their cars and drink beer or wine or smoke dope. Or they try to get bras undone or jeans unzipped. Tonight the only vehicle that ever goes by is an occasional pickup driven by a farmer who has had business in town and is returning late to his farm. The school calendar listed a dance scheduled for this evening, and it has, of course, been canceled. (Probably the first time since its inception that the "April Foolishness Dance" has not been held.) But tonight nothing goes by but farmers. Perhaps everyone who normally would drive by is spending the evening the way I am. Sitting at home, embedding a history of crimes into their memories, and looking out their windows and watching their streets remain as dark as the road between here and St. Cloud.

7 April 1973, Saturday

When I look at a map, a globe, any designation of territory, I automatically try to locate the place where I live. Usually, on any map larger than state or region, my city is not listed. Communities of this size seldom are. But still I try to locate myself. I measure the distance inward from Minnesota's western and southern borders, from Minneapolis–St. Paul, and I find the approximate area of my present home. Then I imagine how the area must look from the air. Around the city would be the green and gold and brown geometry of the farmland, and the city would appear to be little more than the leafy puffs of treetops, interrupted by the ragged path of the river and the straight lines of the main streets and avenues. Then that aerial view would come down to the ground and, like a camera tracking, would move slowly through town until, at the western edge, it would stop at my apartment building.

But lately I have been doing more than simply calculating my position. Lately, I have wondered why I am here.

When I was a child, each summer, as regularly as the arrival of the season itself, Uncle Julian would visit us. One day—it seemed to be often at lunch time—someone would look outside and see him shambling up the front walk, shifting with the weight of his suitcase from side to side as if he were walking down the aisle of a moving train. Then the call would go out, "Uncle Julian's here!" My mother and father would curse simultaneously, and my sister and I waited to find out where he was coming from this time. To the best of my recollection, and I'm sure I'm forgetting some, Julian lived in the following places: Biloxi, Mississippi; Benton Harbor, Michigan; Pomona, California; Rockford, Illinois; Norman, Oklahoma; Laurel, Maryland; Great Falls, Montana; Pocatello, Idaho; Lima, Ohio; Janesville, Wisconsin; Omaha, Nebraska; Mobridge, South Dakota; Winnemucca, Nevada. These are only the ones I remember. The concentration was in the Midwest; the cities were usually small. If there was any other pattern I was not aware of it.

Julian would stay with us until my father tired of hinting and came out directly and asked him to leave. Four or five days seemed to be about the limit. Julian was my father's brother, but there were no hints of any brotherly love between them. Julian possessed a multitude of the qualities my father disliked. He was unmarried, rootless, lazy, slovenly, physically weak and clumsy, well-read, and alcoholic. For my father, Julian seemed to have nothing more than a mild, somewhat patronizing tolerance. My mother spent all the time of Julian's visit with a sour expression on her face; she stayed out of his way and waited impatiently for him to leave.

But Uncle Julian always fascinated me. For one thing, I never knew when he ate or slept. When I went to bed, Julian would still be up, usually sitting on the front porch, and no matter how early I got up, Julian would already be awake. He never took his meals with us. However, I was most interested in him because of the dark, vague mysteries that seemed to attend him, mysteries of crazy things that he was rumored to have done during drunken rages. I knew, for instance, that he owned a gun. I knew that because one winter, I think it was when I was nine or ten, my father had to send bail money to Julian because he had been arrested for shooting out the plate-glass window of a bar when the bartender tried to close the bar. This happened, in true wild West fashion, in Wibaux, Montana. So I was always alert for any telltale bulges in Julian's clothes. That was the only violent incident I was certain of; there were hints of others. One morning my father showed up for breakfast with dark bruises on his upper left arm and shoulder; Julian showed no visible signs of violence, but he seemed to be favoring his ribs. I never knew exactly what had happened during the night, but I was, at the time, sure of two things: Julian had started it, and my father had come out on top. And of course, I wanted to know, as I suppose everyone did, why Julian kept moving from one place to another. Was he running from something? Someone? Was he continually being driven out of these towns?

So the summer when I was thirteen, I asked him. He and I were in the backyard. He was doing a crossword puzzle, a cigarette dangled from his lips, the ash falling onto the same rumpled gray tweed suit that he always wore. (I could never tell which dark spots were supposed to be part of the tweed fabric and which were cigarette burns.) I was probably pounding my fist into my baseball glove. I was the only person who willingly talked to Julian, and this was largely because I found out that among all the knowledge he possessed, he knew as much about baseball as anyone I knew. Who was the greatest ballplayer of all time? Julian said that some believed it was Ty Cobb, but for his money it was Babe Ruth because Ruth had been a first-rate pitcher before he became a great hitter. *Ergo,* Ruth was the best *all around.* A debatable position, but not without merit. Anyway, one afternoon I asked him, and it took some courage to put forth the question.

"Julian," I said (Mother had asked us please not to refer to him as "Uncle," that designation apparently being reserved for her brothers and the husbands of her sisters— *real* uncles). "Why do you move around so much? From town to town, I mean."

He filled in another answer on the puzzle before responding to me. "Why do you want to know?"

That was an attempt to intimidate me, to make me withdraw the question. But I hadn't come that far to be put off so easily. "I just want to know. It seems sort of funny."

"It doesn't seem funny to me. It makes perfect sense to me."

"Then why do you do it?"

He paused a long time, not as if he were formulating an answer, but as if he were debating whether or not to give one.

"Because I'm looking for my place."

"What do you mean?"

"Everybody has a place, one place where they should be, where they should spend their life. Someplace where, for better or worse, they're meant to be. Where the locale and the person match up just right. There's a place for everyone. The problem is finding it."

"A place where a person can be happy?" Since Julian lived such a wretched life, this question seemed perfectly logical to me. If you are unhappy, you search for the place where you can be happy.

"Not necessarily," Julian said. "Maybe you're meant to be miserable. If that's the case, you belong in the place where you can best be miserable. Where you can be *perfectly* goddamn miserable."

When Julian began to swear it was clear he was not to be bothered further. But there was something about the way that Julian put forth his theory, as crazy as it sounded even to a thirteen-year-old, that made me believe in it. And I believe in it still, even if I do believe in it in the same way that I mark the importance of black cats, broken mirrors, and spilled salt. Certainly I know, intellectually, that people seldom choose where they're going to live. They settle in New Jersey because the insurance company transfers them or in Iowa because their father bequeaths the family farm to them or in Detroit because they just never got out. But I thought I *chose* to live in Wanekia; when the offer came for the job here I accepted it not because I had to—there were options—but because I wanted to. And now I have a persistently nagging fear that *this* is my place, that in all the world this is where I'm meant to be, and here the locale and I match up just right. And it frightens me.

Uncle Julian died when I was a sophomore in college. He collapsed and died of a heart attack in a bus depot in Bakersfield, California. My father had his body shipped back home, and Julian was buried in the family plot right next to his father. An overly romantic way of summing up Julian's life would be to say that he is now in his "place." But I don't say that. The impulse is there, but I don't say it.

8 April 1973, Sunday

Roger called at noon today. He sounded so excited that he was almost shouting, and I had to hold the phone away from my ear.

"Get dressed," he said. "I've got to show you something. It's beautiful, it's goddamn beautiful!"

"I'm dressed already. Show me what?"

"I can't tell you. I've got to show you. You've got to see it. You won't believe it."

"Give me a hint."

"Shut up. I'll pick you up in twenty minutes. Be outside."

While I waited in the bright April sunlight, I watched the birds perching on the garbage cans outside the apartment building. They were starlings, sparrows, and wrens—winter birds, all in shades of brown and gray. The spring and summer birds must have started to arrive by now, but I still hadn't seen any. Nothing of bright plumage appeared yet. Every year, no matter where I have lived, I always read in the paper, hear on the radio, see on television, the announcement that Mrs. Jones has spotted the first robin of the season in her backyard. No announcement yet this year, and it's past time. And today it felt like spring; the sun was warm, the ground was no longer damp, and on certain trees and bushes you could see the hints of buds beginning to come forth. But nobody around here allows himself to become very hopeful about conditions like these. You enjoy it while it's here, but you know it's too good to last, that tomorrow could as easily bring snow as higher temperatures. But today I was going to enjoy it.

Roger's red Volkswagen came into the parking lot so fast that a cloud of dust and gravel followed him. As we pulled onto the street, he began to drive slowly, as if he were trying to prolong whatever it was he had in store for me.

"Are you going to tell me what it is you want to show me?" I asked.

"Nope. You're just going to have to suffer. And wait."

"Okay. Have it your way. It's your show." I said nothing more but rode silently and stared out the window. I did not care to give him the satisfaction of having me beg to be let in on the secret.

"Aren't you curious?" Roger asked. Apparently, I wasn't sufficiently excited about his surprise.

"Not particularly. I know whatever you're going to show me isn't going to come up to the buildup you're giving it."

His own excitement was beginning to dwindle a bit by now as well.

"You're probably right," he said. "Maybe it isn't all that spectacular. But shit, I thought it was interesting. You could show some enthusiasm."

"Give me a chance, will you? I don't even know what I'm going to see. But if it's the Second Coming of Christ, I still don't think I can get as worked up about it as you."

We were falling easily into one of the games, if you could call it that, of our relationship. Since we've become friends, we take turns lecturing each other about our respective personalities. He chides me about my "Midwestern" lack of enthusiasm and passion; I, in turn, ride him about his "big-city" ways, about his overabundance of both enthusiasm and passion. But it is all good-natured. Or it is on my part. I would not want him to be without his intensity, his constant high energy level. And I am sure that I do not truly bother him. And if I do, it's certainly no more than a faint annoyance.

And the truth was, I was curious, even if I wasn't going to let Roger know. And I was curious because, I guess, I knew whatever he wanted me to see had something to do with the killings. It was difficult to resist speculating. The thing I kept imagining we'd see was a scene at the county courthouse. (The county jail is housed in the same building.) I thought, for some reason, that perhaps someone had been arrested, and we were going to see a clamoring mob gathered on the courthouse lawn—a crowd waving pitchforks, rakes, and baseball bats in the air, and screaming for the blood of the murderer. I don't know why I imagined that scene; I guess I've seen too many movies about lynchings and mob justice.

We turned onto Wanekia's curving main street and drove toward the downtown area. At a stop sign, with the main part of the town business district, the "heart" of Wanekia, visible before us, Roger took in the scene with a wave of his arm and said, "This is it. What do you think?"

All I saw was Main Street, the Woolworth's, Rexall's, Penney's, the Carlton Hotel, Engel's Ace Hardware, and the small shops, the bakeries, cafés, bars, dress shops, and shoe stores wedged between the large stores and buildings. The street was lined with parked cars, all pulled neatly up to the curb in front of the parking meters that hadn't been used in fifteen years. I could see nothing but dirty red and brown brick, gray concrete, glass, the bright colors of the cars, and the empty neon signs, and over the intersections the traffic lights, all blinking yellow for Sunday.

"What the hell am I supposed to see?" I said.

"You'd better look again. Carefully."

I looked and still nothing seemed to me out of the ordinary.

"Okay. You got me. Just what is out there that I'm too blind to see?"

"The cars!" Roger said exultantly. "The street's full of cars."

"So?"

"It's Sunday. Nothing's open, but there's cars all over. You've got to admit—this is not usual."

I agreed it was not usual, and Roger put the car into gear and drove slowly down the street.

"There's more," he said. "People belong to these cars. Watch."

He turned left at the corner of Main and First Avenue, the "busiest" intersection in town, the intersection that everyone calls Four Corners. He double-parked in front of the First National Bank, one of the corner buildings, and finally I could see what it was that Roger had wanted me to see.

There they were. There must have been at least three hundred people on the sidewalks, all of them pushed over toward the curb in long, straggling lines as if they were waiting for a parade or a bus. Small children were hoisted onto the shoulders of fathers, men and women looked over the people standing next to them, everyone seemed to be up on his toes, all to look up and down the street to see—what? Many people seemed to have come from church. Men were still in their dark suits and ties, women were in their best dresses, and children squirmed in their stiff, once-a-week clothing. Across the street from the bank, in front of Toomer's Department Store, a group of students from the high school, looking like a delegation, leaned against the basement railing that led down to the barber shop. The scene was one I might have expected to see on the Fourth of July or on Veteran's Day but not on a mild Sunday in early April.

"What the hell," I asked Roger, "is going on?"

He didn't say anything but pointed down the street to the roof of the Elks Building. I looked and saw children on the roof; they peered over the edge and occasionally one of them floated a scrap of paper down the three stories to the sidewalk.

"I came downtown this morning to buy a paper," Roger

said. "And this is what greeted me. Although I think there's a considerably larger crowd now. I asked Ronnie Dell, who has, by the way, brought his whole family, what this shit was all about. Are you ready for this? There's a rumor that CBS News is in town. And these asses are out on the street to see if they can get on Walter Cronkite."

It was a far cry from a lynch mob on the courthouse lawn, but a mob it was. I asked, "How did it get started?"

"Someone said they saw a big white motor home—like one of those Winnebagos—with 'CBS' lettered on the side. Who knows—maybe a film crew is here."

"CBS. Carload of Bull Shit."

"Yeah, well, here they are. Your friends, neighbors, colleagues. I'm not saying they wish anybody ill, mind you, but if people *are* going to be murdered, and as a result someone's going to be on national television, it might as well be them."

"Christ, aren't they embarrassed?"

"Why should they be? They've got all their neighbors out there to keep each other company. Who's going to say anything about how ridiculous it all is? Just smug bastards like us who won't take part. And who gives a shit what we say?"

"Safety in numbers, I guess."

"Absolutely."

We sat in silence and watched the crowd. Everyone seemed happy. They chatted amiably with whoever stood next to them; they stood aside if they were blocking someone's view; they took turns holding each others' babies. It reminded me of some old-fashioned ritual, group activity, like a quilting bee or a (what are they called?) gathering to husk corn—some convocation called for some purpose when everyone came together with an abundance of good will and high spirits. This area still has a strong rural flavor; few people who have always lived here are very far from the farm or long off it. And these people *do* love a parade. (I notice that when I write of "them," I always set myself apart. Not the way it was supposed to be when I came here. But the way it is.) What will we call this new tradition, this gathering in the desperate hope that one's face will appear on national television?

I asked Roger, "If the news is here, who's going to be the official spokesman?"

"I don't know. The chief of police, I suppose."

"Proctor? Don't you think he's a logical choice?"

"God, you're right. Can you see him? He'd launch into his long spiel about how difficult it is to persist in the face of adversity. 'But we can do it if we just reach back for that something extra, that strength we didn't know we had.' "

"I don't care for the idea of Proctor representing me. Of speaking for me," I said.

"I don't care for the idea of Proctor at all."

"What about the mayor? Maybe they'd want to interview him."

"He'd be worse than Proctor," Roger said.

It occurred to me then that I didn't even know who the mayor was. "Who is he?"

"What! You've been living here for two years, and you don't even know your mayor? You don't know Smiling Ray Haley, the pride of Wanekia *and* your local State Farm Insurance representative?"

"I'm sorry, I don't."

"Don't pull that humble shit. You're proud of it. You're proud of the fact that you don't even know the name of your mayor. Peter, my boy, you're nothing but a fucking snob. Love of Whitman aside, you're an aristocrat at heart. It's useless to deny it."

"I guess I won't try then. But I do think you're mistaken." Whatever waning of enthusiasm Roger was suffering from earlier, he was recovering fully now.

"Maybe they'll try to interview you." Roger thrust his hand in front of my mouth as if he were holding a microphone. "Tell us, sir," he said in a low, mock-serious voice, "what is it like trying to teach students not to dangle their modifiers or split their infinitives when these same students are, in fact, worried about being strangled in the halls?"

Even the pretense of a microphone before me made me freeze up. "It's not easy," I said.

"No, sir, 'easy' I'm sure it's not. And thank you for sharing those thoughts with us. Just a man on the street, ladies and gentlemen."

Across the street, an old man in a shabby overcoat tried to walk through the crowd. If someone failed to step out of his way, he simply shuffled around them.

"There's Broomie," Roger said, and pointed to the old man. "I wonder what he thinks of this scene."

"Who the hell is Broomie?"

"Jesus. I can forgive your not knowing who the mayor is, but you've got to know Broomie."

"So sue me. I still don't know who he is."

"Maybe you know him by another name. Does 'Summertime Joe' mean anything to you?"

"Afraid not."

"Unbelievable. Where have you been keeping yourself?"

I looked at the old man again, and as he stepped out toward the curb, I could see him clearly. He wore a winter cap with the earflaps pulled down and carried a long-handled push broom. His overcoat, dirty and tattered and too large for him, hung down far below his knees. His face was so sharp and thin it looked as if it had been pinched in a door. His mouth was open slightly, and his expression was blank and stupid.

"So what's the story on Broomie?" I asked.

"He's a millionaire. And he's got all his money hidden around his house. Or so the story goes."

"He looks retarded to me."

"I think your judgment is probably closer to the truth. But awfully harsh. How about just 'bum'? Not too demeaning but not too noble either."

"That seems accurate."

"Do you want to go talk to him? See if he wants to be on the evening news? Or if he knows what the evening news is?"

"I'll pass. Not today." The old man seemed more pathetic to me than anything else, but I also felt something of an old worry and fear about being in the presence of the mentally aberrant. When I was growing up, there was a boy who lived down the street from us. He was mentally disturbed or retarded, but, I guess, harmless enough since he was never institutionalized. He had to wear a football helmet constantly to protect his head, and when he was outside he always kept to the backyards and alleys. Like a wild animal, he ran whenever anyone approached, so it seemed you could do nothing more than catch glimpses of him before he jumped fences or ducked into bushes. Although I was at least four years older than he and much bigger, I was afraid of him. I suppose it was because I knew he was crazy (I knew exactly what it meant then), and therefore capable of anything. Perhaps it was some of this old feeling that came back when I watched Broomie. The feeling is especially strong here and now, knowing what deeds a certain kind of person is capable of.

Roger pointed again to the children on the roof of the Elks Building. "Let's go up there," he said. "I know where the ladder is. And we can find out once and for all whether CBS is in town. We can see it all from up there."

We drove down an alley lined with garbage cans and empty oil drums and parked behind the Elks Building. Roger went ahead, and I climbed the steel ladder behind him. When we stepped onto the tar and gravel of the roof, the children who were up there, boys who must have been grade-school or junior-high age, began to run. I don't know how they found a way down, but after they took off, I never saw them again. I was perfectly willing to share the roof with them, but I suppose they weren't supposed to be up there and were afraid we were there to tell them to get down.

Standing on the roof, three stories above the street, I could feel what was making the weather so warm and pleasant. The wind—I couldn't feel it at all down on the street—was blowing strongly from the west. It tugged at our clothing and pushed the high white clouds across the sky. When the wind blows from the west here it is usually warm; in the winter these winds, warm and dry, are called "chinooks," and they blow down the east slope of the Rockies onto the plains and can melt snow and raise the temperature thirty degrees.

It is very curious, I know, but standing by the edge, looking down at the crowd, I felt the way I did when I played American Legion baseball. Sometimes when a pitcher was doing well, keeping the ball low and making everyone ground out to the infield, and the game slowed to a steady, monotonous rhythm, I felt myself apart from everything, that from left field I could see sharply all that happened, but that I saw it as a spectator. Then, to become a participant, it seemed that all I would have to do would be to take two small steps forward. To anyone watching, nothing could have appeared as inconsequential as those two steps, but to me they were as fraught with meaning as any human movement could be. That was the way I felt today, on the roof, as if I were close to the edge that separated spectators and participants. And, of course, to pursue this line of thinking, the two small steps forward today would have had me falling to my death.

But as I looked down at the people on the street, on the men, women, and children in their Sunday clothes, I did not have, as I did when I was a child, an urge to spit from the roof, to watch my saliva trail to the sidewalk, but I began to feel a tenderness toward them; they no longer seemed so ridiculous, so clownish, so absurd. Would I like to appear on national television, introduced by Walter Cronkite? Yes, I suppose I would. And did I forget, in the excitement and circus atmosphere of crowds and rooftops, about killings? Yes, I suppose I did. But I always remember in the evening, and I always remember when it is time to write in this journal. Indeed, I recall the purpose of this journal.

"Come on," I said to Roger as I turned away from the edge of the roof. "Let's get out of here. I think I'm beginning to like it up here."

9 April 1973, Monday

I gave Alexandra a ride home after school today. Her car was in the garage getting a new alternator. The building I live in is called Mt. Vernon Apartments; an adjoining building houses the Williamstown Apartments. The colonial names are earned by the red brick and the three thin, silly white columns at the entrance of each building. Alexandra lives in the Williamstown building, and I have been trying, since she moved in last fall and began teaching French at the high school, to take advantage of our status as neighbors. But no luck. The first time I asked her out, I was turned down but not, I thought, discouraged. The second time, months later, her "no" was almost rude, and I quit trying. But it seems she has been friendlier since then.

But oh, I have not given up entirely. Alexandra Bench is of rare beauty, possessor of wonderful high cheekbones, eyes the green color of something natural, alive, and growing, teeth so perfect that they cannot be real, and should there be a danger that perfection could perhaps become boring or bland, lips a shade too thin, a band of freckles across her nose and cheekbones, and in profile it is apparent that the smooth line of her nose (suitably upturned) is disturbed very slightly by a bump at the bridge. *Very* slightly. Reddish-brown hair. In profusion. She is tall and slender. And because she is very probably the most beautiful woman I have ever known, I have, since I met her, wanted her. However, let there be no misunderstanding, my desire for her has not been wholly sexual (though certainly there is that too), but I want her as one wants to possess a beautiful object. I want her to appear with me in public, so that when she and I enter a room, heads will turn and people will be awed and whisper, "My God, look at who is on his arm." And if this is a childish wish, a clear sign of immaturity, the mark of male egotism of the worst order—so be it. For many years, this is what I have wanted—to be in the company of a woman truly beautiful. ("Cute" is not enough.) When I broke off my engagement to Peggy Dahl, one of the reasons (not the primary cause, but nevertheless involved in my decision) was that she was not beautiful enough; furthermore, marriage to her would have meant that a woman like Alexandra would never be at my side, that was something that would be lost to me forever. I was not ready to face that. But like all beautiful women, I must admit, Alexandra is to me somewhat frightening, and I do feel some uneasiness in her presence. But since she has been in Wanekia, I haven't heard of any instances where she has used her beauty, as beautiful people often do, to her advantage. Or to someone else's disadvantage.

As I drove, she stared distractedly out the window, tapped her finger on the window, and gnawed at her lower lip. The picture of preoccupation. As badly as I wanted to use the occasion to try to lead up to something, I could think of nothing to say. Any conventional leads that came to mind I dismissed because I could imagine her giving only a one-word, withering reply. So I gave up, drove, and let her stare out the window.

The silence may finally have embarrassed her, because she said, "Have the police questioned you yet, Peter?"

"A couple of weeks ago. Nothing since then. Are they doing it again?"

"I guess so. They called Mary in this morning. She said it was just like last time."

After the second murder, the police questioned, ineptly, all the faculty. In alphabetical order. My own questioning took place in Proctor's office, and I had never been in his office before. (I had gotten as far as June's, his secretary's, office but had never been in the inner office.) I was surprised that it was as tasteful as it was. I expected to see the walls hung with war souvenirs, the bookcases stacked with bowling trophies, and the corners of the room adorned with state and federal flags. Instead, I found tidy, well-stocked bookshelves, a large (*too* large) modern desk, an IBM typewriter (I'm still sure Proctor never uses it), comfortable chairs, a large fern hanging in front of the window, and Proctor's diplomas (two of them) and a picture of Nixon on the wall. The officer who questioned me, a plainclothes detective named Bell, sat behind the desk and a uniformed officer stood beside him. I think that the other cop was there as a witness in case I should blurt out a confession. Detective Bell also tape recorded the interview. He had a great deal of difficulty operating the machine. I remember being almost eager for the session. Since I was innocent, since I could not be guilty of anything in the eyes of the police, since all I had to do was answer questions (to which there were no wrong answers), I had nothing to be apprehensive about. The experience reminded me of going to the optometrist when I was a child. He was the only doctor who caused me no pain or embarrassment. In fact, with his vision-altering machines and multicolored charts, a visit to him was almost fun. Similarly, my meeting with Detective Bell was another harmless institutional confrontation. I don't remember many of the questions, and the session did not last long. I do remember, however, that if I *had* been guilty, I would have been able to spot the questions as being so obvious that I could easily have dodged self-implication. I also remember Bell's last question. He asked if there was anything I wanted to say "off the record." And at that point, he *pretended* to turn off the tape recorder. He pushed a few buttons, but the machine continued to whir. I said no, there was nothing. I felt sorry for them. But Since Mary Platt has already been in, they must be proceeding in no particular order. Or in an order known only to them.

"You haven't been back in?" I asked.

"Not yet, but I expect I will be soon. I'm sure they're covering everyone."

"Yeah, I'm sure they'll hit us all." Although I did wonder briefly if there might be some reason why Mary Platt would be singled out for questioning.

"Did they ever ask you about your past?" I said, and as soon as the words came out, I wished I hadn't said anything. Since Alexandra has lived here, there has accumulated a sort of "woman of mystery" legend about her and her past, a past which no one seems to know anything about. Precious little is known about my life before I came here, but I suppose the arrival in town of someone in a beat-up Ford station wagon, someone scheduled to teach English to the community's sons and daughters is less interesting, less mystifying than the appearance of a lovely young woman wearing simple, well-tailored clothes that never hung on a rack in any J. C. Penney's. And scheduled to teach *French*, of all things! And what sort of name is "Alexandra" anyway! Besides, I no doubt have about me a Midwestern look, a look that says to the people here, "Well, he may not be *from* here, but he looks all right—probably got folks nearby." And no one has probably ever been bewildered about why I am here; I came, after all, for the job. Though their suppositions are wrong, and they would never guess someone like me would come to a place like this out of a desire to simplify, and most of all, to gain control of one's life, and to stand close to thirteen thousand people like them—if they would never guess any of those things—well, what the hell, I'm here no matter what the reason. But Alexandra would be another matter in the eyes of these people. If anyone were ever to speculate that she was from the Midwest, they would have to guess Chicago, Omaha, Minneapolis, Milwaukee. No traces of cow shit or wheat stalks about that lovely frame. So the stories have sprung up. A sample: she married and divorced a gangster from Chicago, and she is hiding from him in Wanekia. A variation: she was the mistress of a famous politician and had to run away when his wife found out. In most stories, however, she is divorced, and it is usually mentioned that she is "older than she looks." As far as I know, and I know little else about her, she has not dated anyone since she has been here. And I don't know if anyone, besides myself, has asked her out. Roger, oddly enough, has not. "Chemistry is not right. Bad vibrations," he says. So when I asked her about the police questioning, I was sure she would think that I was trying to "get at the truth" about her. But my question was without guile. When the police questioned me, they asked, rather transparently I thought, if any of "this" (meaning murders of young girls) had ever happened in any other place I lived. I did not even act offended; I simply said no. And I wondered if they had ever asked Alexandra a question like that, if it were a part of their questioning technique, or if only certain individuals were asked. I was always afraid to ask Roger or anyone else out of the fear that he might say no, they were never asked that.

But if the ill-chosen question did bother Alexandra, she did not show it. "The only thing they asked," she said, "was where I lived before I came here."

Notice, however, that she did not tell *me* where she lived before. Perhaps there is a gangster lurking in her past.

I debated whether I should try to make something out of this closeness between us, this distance of the width of the car seat. Maybe, I thought, I should ask her out for dinner or for a drink. But I finally decided not to make anything more of it than simply a ride home. If some progress had been made, no need to risk it. I may have told myself that to excuse my timidity, but it was probably the right decision anyway. Still, I wanted to say something to open things up a bit.

I waited until we were parked in front of her apartment

building, then, as she was getting out of the car, I said, "You know, I've never had an Alexandra in my car before."

She leaned down, smiled sweetly and condescendingly at me in the manner she must reserve for smiling at small children, and said, "In grade school they called me 'Al.' Thanks for the ride, Peter."

She walked away, and I noticed that she moves quickly, taking long strides. That strong, sure gait seems to me a sign of purpose and direction, and it is very attractive to me. I, on the other hand, step slowly, and I watch the ground as I walk.

10 April 1973, Tuesday

*R*oger, Gary Clubb, and I went out for a beer after school today. We went to Candy's, the bar you go to for only one reason—to drink. If you do not want to be bothered by music, either live or from a jukebox, be distracted by men and women trying to pick each other up, or be annoyed by the click of pool balls, the flashing and ringing of pinball machines—you go to Candy's. You go there to sit in the dark and to stare into your drink, to draw patterns on the bar by pushing your finger through the wet ring your drink makes on the wood. In Candy's no one will sit next to you without an invitation; they will not ask you for the correct time or a match unless they want to know the time or want a light for their cigarette. I'm not sure, I'm going to check the next time I'm there, but I don't think there are any mirrors, any reflective surfaces that force you to look at yourself, in the place. And Candy's is classless. Though the number of customers is usually small, they are as likely to be from Wanekia's upper class as its lower. We sat at a booth in the back, and Roger and Gary, sitting next to each other, got into an argument.

"I don't care what you say," Roger said. "It's just not normal."

51

"And rape *is* normal?" Gary said.

"In this case, yes. It would make me feel a bit easier anyway."

What they were discussing, as earnestly as the debate on a political issue, was the fact that none of the murdered girls were sexually assaulted. Correct that—they are certain that none were raped, and there has been no evidence of sexual physical assault. The whole discussion began when Gary said something to the effect that the girls were "lucky" not to have been raped. "Considering what did happen to them," Roger said, "it's hard to see just exactly how they could be considered to have had any good fortune."

"You know what I mean. At least they didn't have to go through that."

"We don't know what they went through. Besides, it's weird."

"What's weird?"

"Not raping them."

"Jesus Christ," Clubb said, shaking his head. "I've heard you say some far-out things, Weiss, but this takes first-fucking prize. You're unbelievable."

"Maybe you think so," Roger said. "But at least it would fit some kind of pattern of craziness if this guy would rape the girls. That would be a kind of 'normal' lunacy. And you'd know what you're dealing with."

"It's a good thing none of the parents of these girls can hear you talking now."

Roger looked up at the ceiling and sighed. "You know, Gary, I can always count on you to refuse to take anything in the spirit it's intended. What the fuck do you think? I'm coming out four-square in favor of rape?"

"What the hell am I supposed to think? Didn't you say it was weird?"

Roger stared into his beer and shook his head. He acted as if he were trying to deal with a child.

I stayed out of it. Although I knew what Roger was talking about—and I agreed with him to an extent—I didn't care to become involved in the discussion. First of all, I knew Roger wasn't finished, that he was going to continue to argue, no matter how frustrating it might be, until he made his point. Also, I did not care to argue anything, much less this subject, with Gary Clubb. Gary teaches phys ed, coaches wrestling, and is the assistant football coach. Roger calls him one of the great, timeless, mindless Americans of the age. Gary went to high school in Wanekia (took second in the state wrestling tournament), went to St. Cloud State College, and beat it back here immediately upon graduation. And, Roger says, he shows no signs of having lived in the outer world, much less through the turmoil of the sixties. ("Turmoil of the sixties"—did I say that?) Knee-jerk conservative is how I once characterized him. Gary believes in America, in discipline and hard work, in beer, in right-wing politics, in sports, in being unfaithful to his bride-of-less-than-one-year (a lovely girl). He is about five feet six inches and though his hair is now short and carefully groomed, when I first came here he still wore it in a crew cut. He is many things that I dislike, yet I find him likable, because he is, despite his faults, one of the friendliest, most outgoing people I have ever met. So, in spite of his narrow-mindedness, his politics, his simplistic view of the world, I find him pleasant to be around. In small doses. But I will not argue with him. I ignore him and will not allow myself to be baited into argument; it is an exercise in futility. Roger, however, will argue.

"Look," Roger said, and tapped his finger on the table, "rape is not normal. Sick people rape women. It is not a natural act. But it does happen. And sometimes these sick people not only rape women—they kill them as well. This happens less often, but it too happens. Many times these people are called sexual perverts or psychotics. All I'm saying is that if these girls were raped, it would probably mean that a certain *type* of criminal is involved. Maybe it would be easier to understand."

"If he raped them you could understand him?" Gary asked.

"Sure. It might mean that there's some poor slob whose nuts are so swollen that he's got to get some, and he's such

53

a loser that the only way he can manage it is to pull a girl into the can or into a practice room and stick it to her. Then, to keep her from talking, from identifying him, he's got to strangle her. See? A nice, normal, All-American pervert."

"Be serious, Weiss. I guess you'd be a lot happier if they found out the next girl was raped."

When Gary said that, he committed a real violation. Since the second murder, and more pointedly since the third, one of the things that just isn't done is to refer to the next. To do that is to say out loud what everyone is afraid of: there are going to be more murders. Everyone may believe that, but believing it and saying it out loud are two different things. And talking about it is very bad. Gary must have realized what he said because he became more subdued immediately, and his face seemed reddened with shame rather than with the excitement of anger.

"I think I know what you mean," I said. I felt sorry for him at that moment and wanted to see him off the hook.

Roger wasn't feeling as generous. "The only thing that would prove," he said slowly, "is that the killer isn't a woman."

When he said that I had a sudden chill of fear, the same kind that sometimes comes over me at night when I get into my car and feel that someone is crouched on the floor behind me. It wasn't the idea that the murderer could be a woman that bothered me—although I admit, it took me by surprise—rather it was that a new dimension had been added. Just when I was beginning to be accustomed to these crimes being enacted within certain boundaries, those boundaries were unexpectedly and hugely expanded. No longer could I pick out of crowds of potential killers only the men as likely candidates. Now the strange woman in the imitation leopard-skin hat had to be watched as closely as the man in the black raincoat. Perhaps there's no such thing as boundaries.

Gary was not as stunned as I was by Roger's theory. "You're shitting us. You got to be."

Roger got up to get another pitcher of beer, and as he

stood by the booth, he looked down at Gary and said, "Nope."

"He's not kidding," I said. "He's perfectly serious."

"He can't be! A woman! Shit, why would a woman do it?"

Just then Roger returned and began to defend his theory. "Why wouldn't a woman do it? Or a girl? Females have committed murders before, you know. Sixteen times, in fact, down through the ages. Seventeen, if you count a poisoning done by a hermaphrodite from Schenectady. That's probably sixteen and a half."

"Here we go again," Gary said.

"You really mean it, though, don't you?" I asked Roger.

"Sure. It's a possibility. All three of the girls were good-looking and they were popular. Popular people always have lots of other people hating them. That's what it means to be well-liked. Maybe some girl gets pissed off because it's always the same girls who are going out with the football team captains or with Wesley Warnock or whomever. And the same girls getting elected class treasurer or Barn Dance Queen. Believe it or not, these things really matter to some people. So this kind of shit finally gets to some girl out there, and she starts killing off the competition. Or maybe it's a real dog, and she's tired of being put down by all the Homecoming Queens of the world. And she strangles them. Simple—no?"

"She'd have to be pretty strong, wouldn't she?" I said.

"I don't know. How much strength does it take to strangle someone?" Obviously, Roger didn't feel he had to be responsible for all facets of his hypothesis.

Gary said, "I still don't believe it."

"You don't have to. I'm not saying this is the way it is. It's just a possibility. I don't see why this is coming upon you by surprise. Even the police have considered it."

"How do you know that?" I asked. I was thinking of Alexandra.

"When Bonnie was being questioned, one of the cops asked her if she knew anyone, male *or* female, who might want one of these girls dead. That means they're at least thinking about it."

"Maybe it's possible," Gary said, "but it's not a woman. I'm sure of it."

"And how can you be sure?" Roger said. He was anxious to give Gary a bad time, now that he had Gary agitated and backing up.

"The girls were naked. He undressed them. Or made them undress." Gary said this so delicately that it seemed out of character for him.

Roger leaned forward. "You know, Gary, some women like to look at, and even touch, naked women. These women are often called lesbians, an ancient term meaning homosexual women from the isle of Lesbos. I know it's strange, but it's also true."

"Goddammit, Weiss. I'm not stupid. Cut it out. I was just trying to discuss this subject with you. If you're going to be a prick—forget it. Let me out. I've got to take a leak."

As Gary got out of the booth and walked in his peculiar bowlegged way to the Men's Room, I looked over at Roger to see if he was enjoying his victory. He was. He drained his glass of beer and poured himself another as if he had worked hard to earn it. "That guy," he said, "is something else."

"How can you argue with him? Don't you feel as though you're taking advantage of the less fortunate?"

"Nah. He enjoys it. So do I. What's the matter with it?"

"Nothing. Unless you really piss him off. Then he's going to deck you."

"You mean he'll try. I've got reach on him."

Gary came back and sat next to me in the booth. He poured a glass of beer and said, "You might be right, but I'll bet you a hundred bucks it's a guy. How about it? A hundred on it?"

"I'm not going to bet. I'm just telling you what I know. Not a trace of semen has been found. So maybe it's a woman."

"That sounds like a police report," I said. "Where are you getting your information?"

"From John Rausch. He lives next door to a cop."

"I still say it's a guy," Gary said stubbornly. He was beginning to get drunk and he was talking louder. "I'll put a hundred bucks on it. And when they catch him I hope they string him up by those swollen nuts and pound sand up his ass until the rope breaks."

"In other words," Roger said, "you don't believe in capital punishment for this criminal?"

"Go fuck yourself, Weiss."

I became more and more uncomfortable with their arguing, and I finally had to say something. When I was a child, I would lie in bed at night, listen to my parents arguing, and when their voices rose to where I could no longer stand it, I would yell out for them and pretend I was so sick that I felt like vomiting. The pretense was only partial; the sound of their fighting made my stomach feel as though I had swallowed something cold and metallic. "I don't mean to change the subject," I said, "but has anyone received a contract yet?"

Roger said, "Contracts don't come out until the end of the month. But nice try."

And although Roger saw through me, it still worked.

"That reminds me," Gary said, "do you know these murders are costing me money?"

"How, pray tell?" Roger asked.

"They canceled track for the year, and I was going to be one of the coaches. I would've been paid, and I would've gotten some professional growth points. I'm getting screwed."

"I don't know how it's possible, but for some reason I just don't feel sorry for you."

"I didn't think you would be. But that would've meant a few hundred bucks." Gary started to leave, but when an older woman came in and walked to the bar, he sat back down. He bent over the bar and motioned for us to come closer. "Do you know who that old lady is?" he whispered.

Neither Roger nor I knew her.

"That's Mrs. Hudnall. She's a klepto. She's lifting things from stores all the time. But no one's supposed to do anything about it. Her husband goes around to all the stores at the end of the week and pays for anything she's taken. When my wife worked at Sears the manager told all the sales people to keep track of anything she took. As a matter of fact, some of the people who worked there used her as an excuse to lift things themselves. Watch her and see if she tries to take anything."

There was nothing at the bar for her to take but pickled eggs or peanuts, and she made no move toward them. She was a pleasant, stout woman in her sixties, and she wore an expensive (it seemed to me) wool suit and a hat, and she smiled mindlessly and constantly, not as though anything amused her, but as if she always smiled no matter what the circumstances.

"What does her husband do?" I asked Gary.

"He's a vice-president at First National Bank."

After she bought a pint of cheap blackberry brandy, she left, and when it became apparent that she was not going to steal anything, Gary and Roger left as well. I stayed to finish what little beer was left in the pitcher. And I became sentimental. And depressed. Nothing seemed sadder and smaller to me than the old woman in the hat who had become a community joke because she couldn't keep from stealing. And nothing seemed as quietly lovely as her husband paying off her crimes without her knowledge. Even if he did do it to protect his own reputation. But mixed in with my tender feelings toward the Hudnalls was Roger's suggestion that it may be a woman's hands that are choking young girls. That confusion of the maudlin and the morbid, along with the beer, combined to give me a headache and a wish not to consider further today the world we live in.

11 April 1973, Wednesday

I overslept this morning. I was in a hurry to get dressed so I grabbed the clothes that were closest at hand—a light blue shirt and a pair of brown slacks. I intended to throw my corduroy jacket over these items as I throw it over everything else I wear. Then it occurred to me that my shirt and trousers did not match. And I never give any thought to what does and does not match. I've tried over the years to buy conservative clothes in quiet, basic colors, so I can wear whatever is most convenient. And so I do not have to concern myself with "matching." I pay no attention to such things. Until today. I had already left my apartment when I decided I had better go back to change either my shirt or my pants. This is why.

At school there is a young man, a senior I think, whom I see every day at noon by the candy machines outside the old gym. He is always alone, and he is always eating candy bars. Hershey bars, to be specific. But it is his appearance that causes me to remember him. He is tall and pale, and he wears always, no matter what the weather, a navy-blue windbreaker. I have often seen him outside carrying an umbrella. He has long, black, kinky hair that has been cut and forcibly combed so that it falls so symmetrically it looks like a molded plastic wig. It reminds me of the hair style of an ancient pharaoh. He tugs and yanks at his hair constantly and runs his long, bony fingers through it. Perhaps I imagine it, but his hands seem to tremble slightly. He wears loose-fitting, brightly colored sports shirts and black, shiny, cuffed polished cotton slacks. No one wears clothes like his any longer. His appearance is so intense, so quivering, so odd, so neurotic, that I know he is a disturbed young man. And, as I would ask of anyone disturbed, I wonder if he is troubled enough to be capable of murder. In short, I suspect him of being the killer, and I suspect him because of his unusual appearance.

Now then, if I am considering people as possible killers because of the way they look, are not others doing the same? Might they not scrutinize my appearance as well? And make judgments accordingly? Therefore I groom myself carefully (but not too carefully—I don't want to appear obsessive about this). And this morning I returned to my apartment and put on gray pants.

12 April 1973, Thursday

Warm again today. This evening I had papers to grade, but I didn't have the energy to work on them. We have had one day too many of spring heat, and everything seems to have turned to dust. The first few days of warmth everyone seems vitalized by it, eager to start playing golf or tennis, or to work on the lawn or garden, to resume any of the summer's activities. But it's lasted too long now, and we all remember that we aren't prepared for the new season. The storm windows need to be taken down, winter clothes folded and put away, the oil changed in the car. Tonight, I sat in front of the television set, the windows open and no cool air coming in, and I waited for the sky to darken and the temperature to begin to drop. At about seven thirty someone knocked on the door. When I opened it, Alexandra was there, holding out a large, ceramic coffee mug.

"Good evening," she said, with a mock bow. "May I borrow a cup of coffee? I'm out, and I'm too lazy to go to the store."

It's difficult to say how the sight of Alexandra standing in my doorway affected me. Perhaps it was something like this. If it were July, and I was walking down a city street, the sun so hot above me that the black asphalt beneath my feet was as soft as foam, if under these conditions, I should suddenly see my breath cloud in front of me as it would on the iciest of January mornings, then that sight of my breath in summer would not surprise and delight as much as the sight of Alexandra.

"Of course," I said, and I stepped back, hoping that she would not stand in the doorway but would come in without invitation. She did. I took her cup and stepped toward the kitchen. My kitchen and living room are one room, and standing by the front door one can either lean to the right and be in the living room or to the left and be in the kitchen. The kitchen begins officially where the carpet ends.

"Sit down," I said, trying not to sound as excited as I felt. "I'll make some fresh coffee."

She went into the living room, and I heard the springs of my old sofa creak as she sat down.

"Do you like it strong or weak?" I yelled out to her. I had a moment of panic as I reached for the coffee and considered the possibility that I might not have enough. When I saw that the can was half full, I began to feel that everything was going my way, as if I had been chosen without my knowledge on this day to have everything I say find favor, to have each gesture a movement of grace and composure.

"Actually," she said softly, so softly that she startled me because she was standing right behind me, leaning against the refrigerator, "if you have any wine, I'd rather borrow a cup of that instead of coffee." Further proof, I thought.

"I've got some Chablis. How would that be? It's cheap but it's cold."

"That would be perfect. Just pour it into my cup. That's good enough."

"All the oenologists of the world would be horrified. But at two-eighty-five a gallon—what the hell." Perhaps it was because she was in my home—because Alexandra came to me—but I felt comfortable and at ease with her. What few things I had said, I spoke spontaneously, and I did not, as

I so often do, consider the consequences, before and after, of my every utterance.

As I got the wine out of the refrigerator, Alexandra stepped back against the kitchen wall, her hands worked tightly into the pockets of her faded jeans. She wore a frayed, light blue man's work shirt, the top two buttons undone. Her long neck had lines running around it, not the deep creases and wrinkles of old age, but what looked like the lined skin that is dried by exposure to the sun. In the V made by her open shirt, I could see the gentle curve of her collarbone, her freckled chest, and because she was so thin, I could see the shadow of where her ribs attached themselves to her breastbone. That sight of her throat, chest, and her wrists rising thinly from her pockets combined to make her seem frail, as if her bones were like those of a bird, as breakable as toothpicks. I had always thought of Alexandra as a thin woman, but stylishly, fashionably thin, not someone who could be close to the weakness that comes from loss of weight. Standing there, all blue angles against the pale yellow wall, she reminded me of a child who has been sick and in bed for a long time and who was only now taking the first shaky, uncertain steps of recovery. These perceptions may have come to me because I had never before, as far as I could remember, seen her when she was not wearing the dressier clothes that she wore at school. I handed her her wine, and as I stood close to her in the harsh kitchen light, I noticed other signs of strain. Dark crescents showed under her eyes. When she smiled, her face tightened and, like china, seemed as though it could crack or break. I don't want to exaggerate her appearance. She did not look as though she were about to collapse, as though she were going to shatter at any second. She did not, in fact, even look unattractive. Not to me. She could not. She is truly a lovely woman, and her beauty is unmistakable and durable. It does not depend upon cosmetics or eating the right foods or getting eight hours of sleep every night. It has settled itself easily and permanently about her. When Alexandra is an old woman, and because of her dry skin she will age quickly, everyone will know that she is a woman who has always been beautiful. There is also something about her, something having to do with personal style, that suggested to me that if she was going to break down in any way, it would not be into hysteria but into trembling. And that I was much less afraid of. That I could handle.

"Let's go into the living room," I said. After my observations about her appearance, I felt as though I were guiding to rest a woman in the last months of pregnancy.

I sat on the couch, and I thought for a moment she would too, but she sat cross-legged on the floor, her back against the couch.

"Are you comfortable?"

"Sure, I'm a lifelong floor-sitter. You should try it. It's good for you."

"I'd better not. Every time I sit on the floor my legs go to sleep." It occurred to me that she may have been offering me an invitation to come closer, and I was filled with the pain of missed opportunity. Suddenly I no longer felt as infallible as I had only moments before, and now I had to grope for something to say. "Is this apartment just like yours? The floor plan, I mean."

She looked around the room. "My carpet is a different color, and so is the kitchen and the appliances. All of mine are a sort of terrible avocado shade. But I've got the same imitation wood paneling and the same built-in bookcase that's too small to do any good."

We spent some time complaining about our apartments, about the frost that formed on the windows in the winter, the air-conditioning breakdowns in summer, the year-round plumbing failures, the provincialism of the neighbors, all of the large and small dissatisfactions that had accumulated in the time we had spent living in these apartments (though they are certainly among Wanekia's finest).

I began to feel at ease again. In the months I had spent in admiration of Alexandra, in my desire to have her as close to me as she was then, I never had been able to overcome my slight fear of her, my sense of awe and intimidation. I know she is a woman of experience and sophistication. She has, no doubt, been with many men, and I imagine them to have been successful, older (but not *old*) men, men whose lapels (of their pin-striped suits) are always the correct width, whose short cuffs always protrude the proper length. Men who never shine their own shoes. Their shoes of soft, Italian leather. Alexandra has probably been to Europe, eaten foreign dishes that I cannot pronounce, and drunk liqueurs from fine crystal. And although I do not think of myself as sexually inexperienced, socially inept, cloistered, or naive in the manners of the world, I have always felt boyishly inadequate in Alexandra's presence, that if I had anything to offer or attract someone like her, it would be an oafish, rural sort of charm. Yet as she sat on my floor, sipping my wine (from a coffee cup, at that), and as we began to talk easily, much of my fear dissolved. She did not thrust out her little finger as she drank, she did not sparkle her conversation with French words and phrases, she did not smoke imported cigarettes in dark wrappers (Marlboros rather), she did not laugh at me unless I invited it. She swore, she stretched herself in various positions of relaxation; in short, she seemed human in every way, and therefore she inspired in me a new terror, albeit a smallish one.

As we were talking about the number of students we'd like to fail but wouldn't, Alexandra suddenly sat up straight, put down her cup, and said, "My God, I just thought of something."

"What is it?"

"I'm sitting here, drinking your wine, taking up your evening, and I wasn't even invited. You've probably got something to do." She began to get up. Her humility, her thinking that there might be something that I would rather do than be with her, further endeared her to me.

"Sit down," I said firmly. "I wasn't doing a thing when you came in except watching an old movie. I've got papers to read, but I probably won't do them until Monday. Besides, we've been neighbors too long not to have gotten together until now." That last remark took courage for me to say, but she did not seem to single it out as I did.

"In that case, I don't feel so bad barging in on you. What were you watching? I love old movies."

"*Dark Victory* with Bette Davis."

"—And George Brent. That's a great movie. Can we watch it?"

"Of course." I turned on the TV and adjusted the picture. Bette Davis was shouting at Humphrey Bogart. "Bogart's in it."

"It's a terrible role for him. He plays a stable hand or something. Ronald Reagan is in this too. He's the guy who doesn't get Bette Davis."

"Good for Bette."

We watched what was left of the movie in silence. Bette Davis and George Brent married and moved to the country so he could continue his research. Although she had only months to live, they were deliriously happy. Whenever Alexandra's glass emptied, I refilled it, and she never protested. When Bette Davis was about to die, she lay on the bed as if she were waiting to receive a lover. The movie ended with her death, and Alexandra crawled across the room and turned off the TV.

"The first three or four times I saw that movie," she said, "I bawled like a baby at the ending. I must be getting tough."

"It's pretty soapy. They pull out all the stops. That final shot of Bette Davis makes it all seem glorious."

"A victory over the dark," Alexandra said, as she fluttered her eyelashes and placed her hands over her heart.

"Do you think it's like that? That it can be? Whitman talks about death as if it should be embraced."

"I don't know." She put her head down and ran her finger around the rim of her cup. I should have noticed that something was wrong and shut up.

But I went on. "I'm sure it wasn't anything like that for those three girls. For them it hasn't been anything glamorous or tragic in any poetic sense. Or like anything in the movies.

For them it's been ugly. I guess what's happening here makes everything else seem awfully unrealistic." What I said came out sounding like a speech, like something rehearsed and saved for any possible excuse to drop it awkwardly and haltingly into a conversation. I even stammered as I spoke. But it was a calculated thing to say. I wanted to impress Alexandra, and perhaps I thought something like that might show her how sensitive I was, how I felt compassion and outrage for what had happened to those girls. There were other things in my mind as well. I thought that by talking about the murders Alexandra might become frightened, too frightened to run, after dark, the hundred-yard distance from my apartment to hers. If bringing up the murders didn't work in quite that specific way, I thought there might also be a chance that bringing up murder and death might lead us into subjects that were weightier than apartment dwelling and class scheduling, possibly into such subjects as love, or better still, sexual relationships. These hopes and plans may have been far-fetched and idle, but nevertheless I wanted to bring them up because of the chance that they might drive Alexandra into my bed.

She kept her head down for a long time. When she finally did look up, she was very serious. "I have to ask a favor of you, Peter," she said softly.

"What is it?"

"I want to ask you please not to talk about that—about the murders. Not tonight. Please. Let's just have some wine and pretend that nothing like that is happening where we live. Would that be okay?"

"Of course it's all right," I said. "I'm sorry." In truth, I was more than just sorry. I felt like an insensitive fool, a clod, and I was sure that whatever chance I had with Alexandra I had thrown away by not being careful what I talked about.

"Oh, God, don't be sorry. It's not your fault. You didn't know I wanted to play this little pretend-game. I mean, why shouldn't we talk about it? It's what everyone always talks about." She grabbed the wine bottle and poured herself a full glass. Although I could tell she was angry, her anger did not seem to be directed at me; rather it seemed the sort of fury that occurs when you bang your knee on something in a dark room—the curses come out, but they have no target.

She lit a cigarette and ran her fingers through her hair. "Shit," she said. "It's my birthday." It came out sounding like a confession, and she seemed exasperated that she had been forced to tell it.

"What?"

"It's my birthday! My birthday. I'm twenty-nine years old today. I wasn't going to tell you, but I guess there's no reason not to. Not now."

"I don't know what to say. How about 'many happy returns'?"

"That's not necessary. But it's another reason I came over. I didn't want to spend my birthday alone. I don't know why—it's no different from any other day. Maybe I'm not so tough after all."

"Nobody should have to spend his birthday alone. I never have."

"Another reason I came over is that I knew you wouldn't ask me any questions, and I am so incredibly tired of answering questions about myself. You never ask questions, Peter. Why is it? Don't you care?"

I could tell that she was getting drunk and coming closer to that edge of irrationality that comes with being drunk. I felt now that I needed to speak carefully to her, that I had to keep her from whatever point of breakage or explosion that she may have been moving toward.

"Sure, I care. But I don't want to pry."

"And I appreciate that, Peter. I really do."

It seemed appropriate to change the subject. "April twelfth. What sign are you?"

She rolled her head to one side, smiled at me, and said, "I'm an Aries. But you don't believe in any of that, do you?"

"No."

"I didn't think so. You don't have to make conversation. That's not necessary. We don't have to talk about anything."

She shifted so her head was against the base of the couch, and she let her head fall back on one of the cushions. Her hair fanned out, and when I looked down at it in a certain way, the curls and waves of it reminded me of dark water. She closed her eyes and put her wine on the floor. She rested her hands on her lap so her parallel forearms touched. I hoped she wouldn't get sick, and I watched her closely for any signs of that.

For a long time she did not move. When she did it was only to stretch out stiffly her long legs. And then she was still again. Her breathing became softly audible and very regular. I was sure she was going to sleep, and I edged closer to her so I could look closely at her eyes. I wanted to see if the eyelids were bulging from the dreaming movement of her eyes. Yes, she slept and she dreamed. I could see her eyes jerking back and forth as if, in sleep, she read pages of print.

I wondered what she dreamed of, and I wondered if I figured in her dreams. Perhaps the texture of my couch at the back of her neck caused her to dream of leaning against a pine tree. The room was beginning to cool, and as the night air crossed the room to her she may have had a vision of us together on a wintry day crossing a lane of frozen wheel ruts. If I quietly got up and got a blanket to cover her, without her waking, would I enter her dream as someone who could offer her protection? But I did not get up. I did not want her to wake. And I knew that she probably did not dream of me, and there was no reason why she should. I was the smallest sliver in her life, nothing at all compared to her past, most of her present, and, in all likelihood, all of her future.

I might have been too harsh on myself. At that moment, looking down at Alexandra, her lips slightly parted, the lines on her face that signified tension probably beginning to erase themselves, I did not want only to take her to bed. That warm, electric, tightly wound core of feeling that I had for her was not located only below the waist, although that feeling was still strongly with me. But I liked her being there; I liked hearing those small puffs of breath that came from her; I liked the smell of her, that slight odor that I could detect when I wanted to but that never imposed itself when I did not desire it. And I reached out and touched her hair, touched it close enough to her face so that when I moved my hand it would graze her cheek. I lightly stroked her face and hair, and she did not wake up. Gradually, I let my hand fall down to her neck, and I traced my fingers down her throat so lightly and softly and slowly that I thought I could feel the pulse that beat there. Still she did not move, and I let my hand go down into the open V of her shirt. As my hand moved downward I felt first the tension of bones, of her ribs and breastbone, and then all hardness vanished as I came to the softness of her breasts. I stopped my hand there, at the top of one breast, and I spread my hand out flat and pressed down gently and evenly and firmly. There, there I could feel her heart beating. And with her heart and breast both beneath my hand, her life suddenly leaped into many dimensions, and she became at once sexual and human, and the woman I wanted lying beneath me in my bed was the same woman whose voice tonight in my home I had welcomed with more relief than I realized. I became confused as I tried, with thought, to pick at these revelations, but they folded themselves into my brain and would not be exposed further and would not be coaxed forth.

Suddenly, Alexandra put her hand over mine. I was startled, both because she had not moved for so long that I must have begun to think that I had a kind of immunity and because I was sure she would jerk my hand away, accuse me of all manner of dishonorable behavior, and walk out of my apartment. But she did not. Rather, she pressed her hand against mine and held it in its place. Her eyes were still closed.

We remained like that, motionless, for a long time. Then, still holding my hand tightly, Alexandra got up and led me into the bedroom.

The room was dark. I had left a window open, a breeze

had come up and blew the white curtains into the room so they billowed and waved like the tattered sails of a ship. Alexandra undressed quickly and without modesty. She did not lie down right away but sat on the edge of the bed, her right hand hooked at the back of her neck as if she were working out a stiffness. When I lay down, she turned quickly to me and wrapped her arms tightly around me, so tightly that I became frightened for an instant; there seemed almost to be something desperate in her action. She turned her face from me, deliberately I thought, as though she wanted to watch the door.

Our lovemaking was, I suppose it may be said, usual. It was neither hurried and urgent nor slow and leisurely. Our position was the one most commonly used. Indeed, if we had been observed in a laboratory by those people who observe such activities, our placement on the charts and graphs would have been, no doubt, disgustingly close to whatever norms, averages, and medians are available. Only once did either of us speak. I began to trace, in exploration, down Alexandra's side, a line with my lips, down toward the sharp edge of her hip. As my lips skimmed along her skin, she would arch her body, and as she stretched, her skin tightened, her flesh seemed to disappear, and bones popped out to my touch. When my face was near her hip, she put her hand on my cheek and said, "Do you want me to go down on you?"

She surprised me when she spoke, but it was not what she said but her voice. It was not low and husky, but clear, and though it was not loud, it seemed the speech that one would use speaking across a room to a stranger.

"No," I said, moving upward toward her face, "that's all right."

"Just tell me what you want," she said, and nothing could have discouraged me more than her eagerness to please me.

She startled me at one other time. When I was lying on top of her, and she had her hands upon my back, she suddenly moved her arms and stretched them out across the bed. Spread-eagled beneath me, her attitude reminded me of the position of someone tied down to be tortured—a victim of the rack or of someone stretched out across a desert anthill. Or perhaps I thought of a Victorian wife who, once a week, bore her husband's attention and weight by gripping the bedpost until he rolled off her.

But if our union was something less than mystical, neither was it disappointing, at least for my part. And I did not care to ask Alexandra how it was for her. I was content to accept her continued presence at my side as a gesture of a certain sort of satisfaction. At least there was no evidence of disapproval. The room began to feel cold when we moved apart, and I reached down and pulled a blanket over us and I fell asleep.

I woke to the sound of water, and the sound made it impossible to separate immediately waking and sleeping. I had been dreaming that I was standing on a city sidewalk, a sidewalk so sharply sloped that the city must have been San Francisco. I stood by the curb, and in the gutter was a slow trickle of clear water. Suddenly the trickle became a torrent, and I looked up to see a wall of water rushing toward me. I came awake with a start, but I still heard water roaring. Then, as my senses returned to me like things jerked back on a string, I was able to settle fully in the world of wakefulness. Alexandra was not in bed. The only light in the room came from the corner of the room, from beneath the bathroom door. The slit of light was yellow, and it seemed to invade the room like a cheap, unwelcome presence. The noise of water also came from the bathroom. By now, I identified the sound as water filling the bathtub. I got up, pulled on my shorts, and went to the bathroom.

When I opened the door, the room's bright light and its reflection off tile and white surfaces was like a flashbulb going off in my face. Through my blinks I saw Alexandra lying in the bathtub, the level of water almost to the top of the tub. Most of her body was obscured by the bubbles that floated on the water's surface.

"Did I wake you?" she said.

"No, I usually take a bath in the middle of the night

myself." I sat down on the toilet and crossed my arms and tried to keep myself warm. "Did I have bubble bath around here someplace?"

"No. I got some over at my place. Along with some clothes to wear tomorrow. But I've got to leave early."

"Slow down." I rubbed my eyes. I had a headache that seemed to be caused by an ice cube that was inside my forehead. The pain also seemed to be connected to the lights in the room, as though if I turned them out the ache would go away. "I don't get it. Why do you have to leave? We still work at the same school, don't we?"

"I don't think it would look very good if anyone saw us coming out of your apartment together. Not at eight o'clock in the morning."

"Jesus. You don't care what anyone around here says, do you? Or what they think?"

"You know I don't. But I care about my job, and I want to keep it. At least until I'm ready to give it up."

"Carry some eggs with you. Pretend you're borrowing eggs."

"Don't be silly. I'll leave just before it gets light. And why don't you go back to bed. You look terrible."

"I feel even worse. But I'm not tired. How about you? Are you going back to bed . . . coming back to bed?"

"No, I'm up for good now. Besides, I slept a few hours."

"Is that enough? A few hours?"

With one hand she gathered the bubbles into a mound on her stomach, and then blew them away. If I hadn't been so cold and my headache so severe, the sight of her would have excited me. Lying in the water, she seemed fleshier, more luxuriant, and less thin and drawn, almost as if the water restored her in some way. But, Christ, I felt terrible. For a moment I considered the possibility that perhaps I had awakened with a cold or the flu or something, but I knew they did not come on that quickly. I didn't think I had drunk enough wine to cause a hangover.

She stopped playing with the bubbles and looked up at me. "I slept more tonight than I have in days."

"What's the matter?"

"Are you serious?" Her voice rose and she smiled as if she were about to laugh, but I knew she would not. "I'm afraid! I'm afraid that someone's going to break into my apartment and strangle me in my sleep. I'm so terrified that I won't turn out all the lights. And I never let the front door out of my sight. If I lived on the first floor I'd watch all the windows too. It's so goddamn bad I won't even shut the door when I go to the bathroom."

I wanted to say something to reassure her. "I don't think you're in any real danger. The way the pattern has been going it doesn't really pose a threat to you."

She looked down at the water and laughed. "Do you think I don't know that? And don't you suppose I know that carrying a brick around my apartment wouldn't protect me if someone did attack me? But I do it anyway. When I take a bath I take my damn brick with me, and when I go to bed, I keep it on my night stand."

"Have you thought of sleeping pills? You've got to sleep."

"Peter, thank you for your concern, but I've been taking sleeping pills off and on since I was in high school. And they just don't do the job anymore.

"But there's more. It's worse than just carrying a brick around. The other day I was in the hardware store, and I started looking at the guns. I even had the salesman show me how to operate this small Browning automatic. I was determined to get it. I still don't know why I didn't."

"If it would make you sleep better, maybe you should get one. You can really wreck yourself if you don't get any sleep."

"I'm terrified of guns. My hands shake when I hold one. Literally. And the ultimate irony is that one of the reasons I left my husband was because he was a gun freak. He used them for hunting, but I always thought he took up hunting so he'd have an excuse for owning guns."

"I didn't know you were married." It was a lie, but I thought by pretending ignorance, by making believe that I, unlike others, had taken no interest in finding out about her past, she might confide in me, thinking that any knowledge in my possession would be harmless.

"For four years, and we hated each other for three and a half of those years. He accused me constantly of being unfaithful and said he'd kill me if he ever got any proof on me. Now I know how crazy he was. I was scared of him most of the time, and when I wasn't scared I was mad. He wanted to spend his time hunting or fishing or playing poker or riding dirt bikes or snowmobiles of just drinking with the boys. Anything but be with me. I guess I should have been grateful."

"What did he do? For a living, I mean."

"He was a minor-league baseball player when we got married. And he stayed in the minors. He was good enough to play big-league ball; it was only a matter of time until he made it to the majors, but he hurt his knee and he tried to come back before it was completely healed."

"What position did he play?"

"Outfield—but he wasn't a very good fielder. That was one of the things he was supposed to work on in the minors. He was a hitter, a long-ball hitter. He was so big and strong, he was a home-run threat every time he came up to the plate. God, I said that just like a sportscaster, didn't I?"

"Curt Gowdy couldn't have said it better."

"It's funny, but for all his threats, he never hit me. I think he was afraid of what he could do with his strength.

"When he couldn't play baseball anymore, he got a job selling insurance in his hometown. I was the wife of the hometown hero. The wife who never left the house. Jesus, I don't know when I was supposed to have cheated on him. Maybe he thought other men came to me. Shit, we didn't even have a milkman. Then one day I couldn't take it any longer, so I loaded everything I could—everything I felt I had a right to take—into the Mustang and took off. I'm sure everyone felt sorry for him because I ran out on him."

I had heard enough of him, and I began to feel jealous of this man whom Alexandra hated. As she talked, there seemed to be something that pulled at her, something about him, about that time in her life that drew her, willingly or unwillingly, toward itself. And drew her, therefore, away from me.

Maybe she read my feelings, because she said, "Peter, have you ever wondered what athletes are like in bed?"

"To tell you the truth—no."

She went on as if she hadn't heard me. "Of course you have. Everyone in the world wants to know. And I'll tell you. They're lousy. The worst. Alan was faster in bed than he was going to first. And since he was left-handed, he got down the line awfully fast."

I laughed, but I didn't care to hear more. I suppose I am like other men in that I am uncomfortable hearing women rating sexual performances, especially women I have slept with. The conclusion is inescapable: if other men are ranked, certainly you are not going to escape comparison. Besides, implicit in what she said was the message that there had been others (who took longer to round the bases?), and though I knew that about her and could live with the knowledge, neither did I care to have my nose rubbed in it.

"I shouldn't generalize," she said. "Obviously all athletes aren't like baseball players, and all baseball players aren't like my husband. But I do know of a football player who wasn't much different."

The conversation seemed more and more confessional, and I thought it was time to change the subject. "Bench," I said, "is that your married name?"

"No. I started using my maiden name right away. Even before the divorce was final. My husband's name was Nelson. Not as good a baseball name as Bench, is it?"

"But easier to live up to. Where did you go after you left your husband?"

"Back to school. Not right away. When I packed the car that day I just knew I was leaving."

"Like in Ibsen?"

"Like in Ibsen. I knew I couldn't go home to my parents. They're not the kind to take in a daughter who'd walked out on her husband. They wouldn't have been on my side even if I had walked in with fresh whip marks. They would have just *known* I must have done something to deserve it. I went to live with my brother in Minneapolis. Then I got a job, an apartment, and soon I was just sort of floating. I took some classes at the University of Minnesota, and pretty soon I got a degree. Almost by accident. Then, since I had it, I decided to do something with it. And there's not much a French major can do but teach, so—here I am."

"Why here? Why Wanekia?"

"There aren't that many jobs. I took the first one I could find."

"University of Minnesota, huh? I'm from the University of Wisconsin. Just think, one-fifth of the Big Ten is represented here in my bathroom."

"How did you get here, Peter? Wanekia's not even in the same state."

There was no way I could make clear to her what I was not even able to understand fully. But I knew at that moment that nothing I had been telling myself since the time I decided to come here had been wholly the truth. But if I was unable to work it out satisfactorily in my own mind, I was certainly unwilling to speak to Alexandra of it—not at that time; too much seemed at stake.

"I don't know," I said. "I was sick of graduate school. Somebody offered me a job, and I took it. I didn't even know I wanted one until I was asked. Simple as that." That much of an answer even satisfied me for a moment.

Alexandra ran more hot water. "It occurs to me, Peter, that I've been doing all the talking, and I've been here for hours. You tell me—aren't *you* ever afraid?"

What a question it was! If I closed my eyes at that moment, all that I feared in the world would begin, even without my bidding, to parade through my consciousness; if I let my tongue rattle without control, the chant of my fears would recite itself like a litany. How close to the surface it all was! Strangers, friends, relatives, lovers, colleagues, enemies, all that breathed, blinked, spoke, and walked on two legs was capable of bringing forth in me trembling, nausea, paralysis, cold sweat, and always, shame, dismay, and disgust with myself. Everything living in the world could bring out in me the most profound fear, and could do it so effortlessly; all that needed to be done was to know the reason why. However, I am often able to cover this knowledge of my nature from myself. I can tell myself the lie that I have come to this place because I want to be cured, that I want to overcome my fear, and I want to do so by coming to this small city of unknown people, people who will not shrink backward when I decide to reach out. Of course, the truth is that any coming here is necessarily a removal. Any time, that is, but now, now when the worst of any society's diseases—these brutal murders—is epidemic in this community of thirteen thousand. And Alexandra speaks of irony! What I could tell her of its nature! And a part of me wanted to tell her of these self-discoveries, to tell until more revelations came to me in the speaking, to talk to her until the bath water turned so cold that her nipples shriveled, until her lips, fingers, and toes turned blue, and her teeth chattered when she tried to speak. But within me a voice just as strong said, keep quiet, don't expose yourself now, there's no point to it, it requires too much.

Besides, when she asked me about being afraid, I knew what she meant. She referred to death, to dying. No, I was not afraid of that. It is only the survivors that cause me concern.

"No," I said, rubbing my eyes, "I'm not. I told my mother the same thing a few days ago—it's young girls who are in danger—not me."

"It must be wonderful to be so rational about it. But you don't have any nightmares? Anything like that?"

"Nope. Nothing."

"Let me tell you something. Before I came here, when I was living in Minneapolis, I had all the usual urban fears—rapists, muggers, killers, and I had two locks on my door. But a new fear started to hover over me. No matter where I was, I was sure something was going to happen—something terrible. If I was downtown, I thought the buildings were going to collapse, or windows would fall out on me, or cars would jump the curb. When I was in shopping centers I thought there was a maniac somewhere who was going to start shooting wildly into the crowd. During the summer, every dark cloud looked as if a tornado were going to drop out of it any second. It got so bad there were times I wouldn't leave the house. I knew I was just being paranoid, but I couldn't help it. When I found out I was coming here, I knew I'd hate it, but I thought there was one good thing: I wouldn't have to be afraid. How do you like that? That's really what I thought."

"Irony," I said, "it's everywhere. The sign of the times."

She picked up the thin bar of soap and lathered her arms, rinsing each in turn as soon as she had washed it. "I also want to say," she said as she sat up and brought her knees toward her chest, "that I feel better tonight. I don't remember what I dreamed about, but I didn't have any nightmares. Even having no dreams is a distinct improvement."

"Is this your way of saying 'Thank you'?"

"I guess so." She seemed slightly alarmed at what I said, as if she weren't able to read accurately something in my tone of voice or in the expression on my face.

"You can leave the money on the bed or on the dresser. I'll find it." I left the bathroom.

I waited on the bed. My headache became worse as I examined my motives for what I had said. Occasionally I speak according to mood—my mouth opens, the words come out—and it is only upon reflection that the significance of what I have said, the "secret meaning" if you will, is fully revealed to me. I wanted, simultaneously, to examine and ignore my shift in temperament and attitude. Earlier I felt tender and now I felt brusque, gratitude gave way to resentment, passion and excitement shifted toward disgust and guilt, cynicism and sarcasm overcame good humor and courtesy. Am I aware, ahead of time, of these changes that come over me? Occasionally. Do I have control over them? Seldom. The best I can hope for is to undo the damage once it has been done.

After about five minutes, Alexandra came out of the bathroom. She was wearing my old, white, terrycloth bathrobe that

I kept on a hook on the bathroom door. She was brushing her hair, and for the first time, it occurred to me that she was conscious of her beauty and that vanity, as much as nature, had a hand in the maintenance of that beauty. And it also occurred to me that such a thought would only come to me in my present mood.

She sat down, on the side of the bed opposite where I lay and close to the foot of the bed. "What's bothering you, Peter? Is it something we should talk about?" She was forthright, and it was a quality I had suspected her of having, and at any other time I would have admired her for having it.

"It's nothing. I just have a headache."

"Isn't that what the tired wife is supposed to say? I promise I won't attack you. Come on, tell me what's on your mind."

It was very curious. Our roles seemed to be reversed. Earlier she had been helpless, childlike, and now petulance seemed to glow around me like an aura, and she was the parent, the teacher, the protector, the confessor.

"You're not going to like it," I said.

"Give it to me. I can take it." She lounged across the bed and leaned on one elbow. Her robe fell open, and her exposed flesh seemed to signify her unwariness, her willingness to confront openly whatever it was I was going to say. But I was also suspicious enough to think that she may have allowed her robe to fall open as a ploy.

"All right." I pretended to look at her eyes but let my gaze rest upon her forehead. "You keep saying how coming here tonight has kept you from being afraid, has let you sleep. And is that why you went to bed with me—to pay for the few hours of comfort you got out of the evening? It's almost as if you were saying, 'It doesn't have anything to do with you, it's nothing personal, I just needed a warm body.' I don't like feeling as if I'm being used, and you haven't said anything about me."

"Jesus Christ, Peter," she said, more astonished than angry. "Do you really believe that?"

"I'm not sure. But there's a lot of evidence to support that interpretation."

"And you'd like me to persuade you otherwise?"

"That would be nice. If you could."

"I did come here, you know. I could have gone to lots of other men's homes."

"You could have, but I'm closest."

She sat up and pulled her robe around her as if she were suddenly embarrassed. "Let me try this out on you," she said, speaking slowly. "I came here tonight almost by accident. Because I was frightened, because it was my birthday, because I didn't want to be alone. It came to me, rather suddenly and unexpectedly, that I could relieve the situation by coming here. If you hadn't been here or if you hadn't invited me in, I would have gone home. You weren't my first choice—you were my *only* choice. And I went to bed with you because I felt like it, because I wanted to. That's the only reason I'd ever have before I went to bed with a man." She paused, looked down at the bed, and then looked up at me. "And if that doesn't convince you that I came here and slept with you out of some feeling for you, you might consider this as evidence: the fact that after what you just said, I'm still sitting here, and I didn't slap you, tell you to get fucked, and walk out of here."

She spoke so surely, so unhesitatingly, that I felt I was defeated and without a point to argue from. And I knew at that moment, almost as well as I know it now, that my quarrel with Alexandra was not truly about the cause that I put forth; it was not about my displeasure over feeling "used." In fact, if Alexandra chose to despise me personally but use me sexually, I would not find it the happiest of situations, but it would nevertheless be one I could tolerate, if not actually welcome. And if I could ever offer her any feelings of comfort, I was happy to do so. No, I was angry for what she had caused to happen within me—she had forced me to examine myself, even if only briefly, and as a result of that examination, self-revelations had come to the fore like air bubbles upon a water's still surface. If I had not revealed myself fully through that process, it had been a close call. The desire to talk about myself, my fears, had all washed away. I wanted no more of self. If the conversation threatened to approach any inner part of me, I was ready to shriek "No!" and insist we talk about weather, architecture, her—anything. It should not have been remarkable that I felt anger and resentment toward her. Her talk, my own thoughts, the sight of her in water, all of these combined to open, like a wind, a door within me. This door does not close easily. Surely she had led me toward more than the bedroom—one more example of control on her side. She could not know of any of these things, and she would not. A headache and a feeling of being taken advantage of seemed to serve as valid reasons for displeasure. The headache, at least, was real enough.

She stared steadily at me. It was my turn to speak. If she had strengthened because of her hours with me, it was now working against me.

"I'm convinced," I said, trying at once to sound both conciliatory and unapologetic. "I'm sorry. It was a lousy thing to say."

"It was a lousy thing to *think*."

"All right. I said I was sorry."

"And now I should believe *you*—right?"

"I wish you would."

"Okay, let's quit. I can't do this anymore. Not tonight. Not this morning. I'm going to go home. It's going to be light soon."

And she dressed, as without modesty as she had undressed, and left. Just as she was going out the door, I asked her if I should call her, if she wanted to do something Friday night. She said she was going to Minneapolis for the weekend with Bonnie Jacobsen and Jean Nordstrom. I did not, do not, know how to interpret that.

I decided not to go back to bed but to use the hours before school to write in this journal.

What is there to think of in the early morning? On this day, in this town, we may wonder if today someone might be killed. These thoughts, morbid, dark, and inappropriate to the dawn as they might be, are readily available as an alternative to the possibility of confrontation with the self. We may look forward or we may look backward.

It was getting light. It was as dark as ever outside, but the blackness was beginning to acquire texture and degree. The birds began to sing with an insistence.

13 April 1973, Friday

*T*he whole day has gone by, and I didn't notice until now that this is Friday the thirteenth. The discoveries that accompany keeping a journal! I also didn't notice if people were more uneasy today than usual. I am not superstitious, but had I been aware of the date I would have gone through the day as cautiously as I would walk through a field where there might be snakes. But nothing happened. All the females who stepped fearfully from their doors this morning returned safely.

I was tired all day. And the illness I worried about in the middle of the night is now with me in full force. My throat is raw, my nose runny, my head feels so filled with fluid that I think I would slosh if I moved quickly, my temperature is slowly rising, and the inevitable coughing attack will probably not come until I am asleep. I plan to dose myself with brandy and go to bed early.

Two student contingents visited me today. The first was a group of four girls—Terri Moeller and Donna Purcell from my one o'clock English class and two girls from I did not know where. Terri and Donna are both pretty and popular and, as basketball cheerleaders must be, continually effervescent. They did all the talking. They were visiting me because they were collecting for a memorial fund for "Debbie Spencer and the other girls." I suspect Debbie Spencer was the most popular of the three victims and the one closest to these girls' hearts because they never did mention the names of the other murdered girls.

"A memorial fund sounds like a good idea," I said, reaching for my wallet. "What are you going to do with the money?"

"We're not exactly sure yet," Terri said. "But we're pretty sure we're going to donate the money for a new trophy case or else try to set up a kind of scholarship fund or something like that. We want to have something so that people remember the girls and remember them in the right way."

I resisted the impulse to ask them what the right way was just as I held back the impulse to suggest to them that they might want to wait on the memorial until they could be certain that murders were no longer being committed.

Donna said, "Debbie's parents gave us all the money that people sent to them. A lot of people gave them money instead of just spending it on flowers. Her mom said she hoped that the money could be used for something that had to do with education."

I put five dollars in the small green construction-paper-covered box. The box had no writing on it. The two quiet girls whom I did not know muttered thanks and Donna and Terri thanked me profusely.

I thought of how strange it was that these girls could be so calm and cheerful. They were not collecting for muscular dystrophy or the heart fund or cancer research or kidney disease or diabetes. But their sense of mission was strong. I remember how, as children, we walked up and down the residential districts of our hometown collecting for the March of Dimes and for polio victims. No matter how cold it was when we walked, no matter how long the route, we did not complain. When might come another time in our lives when we could know absolutely that we were doing something good and right? I know I, for one, kept fixed in my mind the image of Johnny Buckner, a student at our elementary school who, because of the metal braces on his legs, creaked as he walked painfully through school with his stiff-legged gait. I imagined that every dime that was dropped into my collection jar would help Johnny and the children like him. Not once did I consider that the money might help me in any way. The girls who visited me today seemed to be infused with the same spirit, but something was mangled, confused, twisted. What good could they be sure they were accomplishing? Could they think the money collected might stop a disease? Might give anyone immunity? It was pathetic, absurd, and perhaps to them, selfless and noble.

The other group that came around (and also wanted something from me) was composed of five males, all of whom would have been members of the track team had track not been canceled with all other extracurricular activities. They wanted to know if I would sign a petition to allow track to be reinstated as an official after-school activity. I knew four of them: Kent and Jerry Kugler, brothers who made themselves passable middle- and long-distance runners by chasing each other around their father's farm; Chuck Rittel, a senior who was a starting forward for three years on the basketball team; and George Hall, a popular, tall, muscular, handsome boy (who looks as if he could be twenty-five) who made All-State Honorable Mention as a middle linebacker. George was a student of mine last year and if proof was ever needed to put the lie to stereotypes, he was the exception to the stupid-athlete notion. He was quiet in class, but he was a sensitive and careful, if plodding, reader of literature, and the essays he wrote were imaginative and so embellished that they were florid. I think I may have saved one. The boy whom I did not know had the awkward, pimply look of a student manager.

They had plenty of reasons for wanting track to resume. They missed sports, the release, the competition, the identification it gave them. They weren't able to articulate their cause very well, but I knew, I thought, what they were feeling.

"Besides," Chuck said, "George has got a good chance to

break the state record in the javelin. He can't do it if we don't have a track team."

I looked at George. He was blushing. I considered his long, muscular arms, his broad shoulders, and his hands—they were so thick, bony, and large that they did not seem extensions of his arms but things that existed by themselves. He had the physical equipment for record-setting. Colleges were recruiting him already for football, and I suppose if he held a record in track he could be assured a free ride at practically any university in the country.

"Is that true, George," I asked, "are you going to set a record?"

"I don't know," he said shyly. "Probably not."

"Don't be modest."

Chuck said, "He's not if we don't have a team."

I looked over the petition, and once I saw who had signed already and I knew it was safe, I signed myself.

I doubted that their petition would accomplish any more than the girls' collection, but what the hell, certainly no harm was going to come of their trying, and none of them were asking for anything which they did not deserve. Maybe the only way George Hall is going to get to college is on an athletic scholarship.

In the teachers' lounge this afternoon, Mal Coxe was offering, to everyone who came in, a note he had taken, intercepted, from a girl in his typing class. The note was in two different styles of handwriting. The first half of the note was obviously written by a male; the second by a female. It read:

I can't pick you up till 8 tonight. I hope that's not to late. I think we'll go right out to that spot. You know what we'll do don't you.

The half written by the girl read:

8 is okay with me. I know what we're going to do & I can hardly wait. My heart beats faster thinking about it and I breath faster too. The last time it hurt but when

I think about it I don't think about anything painful but how wonderful it was. You could put your hand somewhere and feel what happens to me when I think

Mal obviously took it from her before she could finish writing. As I read the note, Mal read over my shoulder.

"My God," he said. "Look at that language. Do you know how old she is? She's a sophomore. That makes her fifteen years old. Her boy friend's the same age. They're just kids. Their parents ought to lock them up."

John Turner said, "If it's any consolation, Mal, I'll bet they're not going out tonight. You've nipped that in the bud."

Gary Clubb, one of the first to read the note and now taking it from me for another reading, said, "Mal, you're just jealous 'cause someone's getting into this young stuff and all you can do is stare at it. What's this girl look like anyway? What's her name?"

"Her name is Melanie Dosch," Mal said soberly. "She's a pretty girl but her complexion is horrible. Sometimes I wonder if any of them ever wash their face."

"Don't worry," Gary said. "That's going to clear up *real quick.*"

Mal took the note from Gary. "Maybe I'll show this to Mr. Proctor. He might have some idea about what steps should be taken."

So many things about the incident distressed me. Mal Coxe is a fat, vain, prissy, self-righteous man who constantly deplores the current generation of students. He is sure the murderer is a student, and though he is not alone in that belief, he believes it because of his hatred of a whole social class—students—all of whom he regards as his enemies. He does not like Roger or me or any of the other younger teachers because we are, to him, closer to the generation of students than to him. And he may be right in that; I don't know. Had I not disliked him already, I would have hated him for taking the note and showing it to readers. I was disappointed in myself for reading it. I kept thinking about the note itself as well. There was something odd about what each of them had written. The part written by the boy was almost, in the last sentence, like a threat or a warning, not a promise of any sort of romantic lovemaking. Her half of the note was less disturbing, but the mention of the pain was still bothersome. I have no feelings one way or the other about the morality of teenage sex. (I suppose indifference is the same as being for it.) But all I hoped for at the moment was that this couple planned to do nothing sinister or evil. I hoped all they had in mind was to drive into the country, twist, wad, and push their clothes out of the way, avoid the hazards and the discomfort of the gear shift and steering wheel, and screw their adolescent brains out. I would prefer that they at least think they love each other but that I would not insist upon. With all the possibilities of human behavior, that seemed one of the best activities to wish for.

Instead of going out for a beer after school with the rest of the Friday-afternoon group, I came home and called Alexandra. After five rings she did not answer, and I hung up. She must have gone to Minneapolis after all.

I wish I could have seen her tonight. When I sit alone, the range of subjects available even to think about is small and unappealing. I can never watch TV when it's my only option. For weeks, I have not been able to concentrate well enough to read anything but newspapers and magazines. (Does murder affect one's reading habits? It does, although I am not certain how or why.) I'm going to begin on the brandy. Didn't I spend last Friday in the same company?

14 April 1973, Saturday

I thought often today of Diane Kastler, a girl who has not been in school since the second murder. As far as I know, she is the only student who has stayed out of school for an extended time. It was her mother who notified the school, indirectly, that her daughter would cease attending. She told the police to tell the school that her daughter would not return "until something is done about the situation." Mrs. Kastler, a widow, is very active in community politics, and she is a brash, outspoken woman. Her message was meant, no doubt, to chastise both school and police. Diane is a senior and is scheduled to graduate this spring. But she has not officially withdrawn, and I remember that school authorities were in a quandary trying to decide whether or not she should be allowed to graduate if she did not return to school this semester. No policy was formed; rather it was decided that each case would be judged on an individual basis.

But I did not think of Diane today because of the absurdities involved in the issue of her graduation. I thought of her shut up within her home, and I wondered if she spends much of her time in front of the window, if friends visit her, if she ever goes out when she is not in her mother's company. And I wondered if many other citizens of Wanekia are, like Diane, prisoners in their own homes. Have husbands forbidden their wives to leave the house unaccompanied? Are fathers chauffeuring daughters on the least occasion? Do elderly women drink water rather than walk to the market for milk? Do secretaries and salesgirls suffer nicotine fits before they will go out alone for cigarettes? Do parents prohibit their children from dating unless an older brother or sister goes along? How many faces are pressed against the glass of how many windows? I exaggerate the situation, but I am certain that others, besides Diane Kastler, are staying in. Thinking of it reminded me again of what Alexandra said about how she became so frightened in Minneapolis that she often could not force herself to go out.

But mainly I thought of Diane Kastler, and others like her, because an old feeling returned to me today and I stayed in for most of the day and would not have gone out at all if it had not been for Roger. Since I was a child, I have had a tendency, an idiosyncrasy, a quirk, that operates almost like a law of personal behavior. It is this: at certain intervals of my life, I begin to "stay in"; a feeling comes over me, a mood, and I lose all desire to venture out of whatever dwelling I occupy at the time. I become rooted, and the longer I stay in, the more difficult it becomes to go back out. It is as though I settle into a state of inertia. There were days my parents had to force me to go to school. And I did not particularly dislike school. Indeed, my desire to "stay in" has never seemed to be a response to any crisis or pressure from the outer world. If that were the reason, surely it would have happened before today; it would have happened when it was necessary that I go out—when I had to discuss with students the symbolism of "The Bride Comes to Yellow Sky" while their minds were focused on the possible murderer among them. But this syndrome must arise from a wish to escape the world, because when I think of my "staying in," two images of the world dominate. I imagine myself standing before a window, and everything outside the window is blotted out by blowing snow or by fog. No matter whether it is winter or summer, the images are the same and so is the effect: the wind increases and the blowing snow swirls and slants more heavily or the fog thickens and everything—grass, trees, cars, buildings, men walking their dogs—everything further than the reach of my arm drops from view. When this feeling began today, it was the first time in years. It has not happened, at least not significantly, since I was a senior in college. Then I stayed away from classes, and everything else that was not in my apartment, for two weeks. The consequences were not severe. Those professors who noticed my absence willingly assumed I was ill. I finally went out for food and that broke the spell. And it may not seem that my staying in today, particularly when I had no reason to go out and had, in addition, a cold as an excuse to remain indoors, was as serious as being in for two weeks, but I do believe that when Roger came over this evening he disrupted something greater than my privacy. It seems unlikely now, but maybe I would have, like Diane Kastler, given my life over to staying in. Citizens here have, after all, better justification for such an action than Alexandra's Minneapolis paranoia or a creeping state of inertia.

Roger came over about five thirty. When I answered the door, he was standing in the hallway, glancing furtively about. He was wearing his bulky green Army fatigue jacket and held a grocery bag in his arms.

"Let me in," he said. "There's plenty of people who'd like to lay their hands on what I'm carrying."

He came in, went to the kitchen, and began to deposit the contents of the bag on the table. He put down two six-packs of Budweiser, a bag of potato chips, a jar of peanuts, a Sara Lee coffeecake, and two limes.

"Limes?" I said.

Roger held up an index finger, signaling me to be patient. He unzipped his jacket, and from a pocket in the lining, brought out a fifth of tequila. "You can, I assume, furnish salt?"

"I can probably scrape up a little. What's all this for?"

"This is not all. One moment." He reached into another pocket and pulled out a small Sucrets tin. He opened the tin the way butlers open humidors of fine cigars. Inside were seven or eight tightly rolled joints. He went into the living room, threw himself onto the couch, and said, "Let's order a pizza."

"You still haven't told me, what's the occasion?"

"I don't know about you, but I got paid yesterday. I had to spend it on something, and it was either this or fly to Rio de Janeiro."

"Beware of Greeks," I muttered. "What are we going to do with all this—in case the Russian Army calls and can't make it over tonight?"

"This is the way I figure it," Roger said, sitting up straight. "If we pace ourselves just right, if we're careful, if we're moderate—that's where you can help, Peter—we can probably get ripped three or four times before morning and still live to tell about it."

"What if I would rather not?"

"Who gives a shit? This is all for you, man. This is therapy. You're going to get loose."

"Whether I want to or not?"

"Exactly. Now, shall we get started?"

My feelings were, at that time, ambivalent. On one hand, I was perturbed that Roger was imposing himself on me, taking away my right to be alone, that he was not considering my wishes or whether or not I had plans. And I suppose I resented the fact that he was not Alexandra. I was probably thinking that if someone had to knock at my door, why couldn't it be she? On the other hand, I was grateful that he had shaken me from the mood I was falling into, grateful even if his knock at the door did have an initial effect on me similar to a sleeper being awakened. Also, he *did* mean well. No matter how pushy he may have seemed, Roger did believe he was doing me a favor.

"Look," I said, "I've got a cold and a sore throat. I don't feel like smoking anything."

"No problem. Just tilt your head to one side, sprinkle

dope in your ear, and pour in some Crisco oil. In seconds it'll permeate your brain. The effect is terrific. And you don't have to draw any of that nasty smoke into your lungs or fuck with brownies."

"I think I'll pass."

"Suit yourself. Try some beer and tequila. Guaranteed to drive the evil spirits out of your body. When you wake up tomorrow, your cold will be gone."

"*If* I wake up."

"Shit, there's bound to be risks. No one said it was going to be easy. Now how about that pizza?"

"Call it in."

Roger called Maxine's and ordered a large pizza. Since we could not agree on what we did or did not want on it, he told them to make it a house special. That way, he said, we could pick off what we didn't want. He told them to deliver.

While we waited and drank beer, Roger asked me what I did the night before.

"Nothing," I said. "Stayed home. Went to bed early. I told you, I'm sick."

"I forgot. How long has it been since you went to St. Cloud?"

"I don't know. Weeks, I suppose."

"That's over then, huh?"

"I guess so. I think it just died a natural death."

"It's just as well. That's too far to go just to get fucked. If your sex drive got out of control, it could cost you a fortune in gas bills."

I could have told him then about Alexandra, and for a moment I considered it. If I chose to be serious as I told him, I knew I could trust him to be *reasonably* serious about it. He'd give me as little shit as possible (and still preserve his reputation), but he would ask questions, and I didn't feel like answering questions, particularly those that concerned my feelings.

"Staying home doesn't bother me," I said. "I don't mind it."

"Of course you don't mind. That's not the point. But it's bad for you. It's unhealthy. Tell me, do you watch TV?"

"You know I do."

"All right. That's what I'm trying to tell you. TV will fuck up your head for sure. It's only a matter of time."

"I've been watching TV for twenty years."

"Exactly! And look at yourself!"

I walked into that one. The line of talk made me uneasy. I was troubled by, for one thing, the thought of a public debate that has been waged in this country for a number of years. The debate is about television, chiefly about whether or not the excessive violence on television is in any way responsible for the violence in our society. Many people, of course, believe there is a correlation. (People, in fact, in this city. Weeks ago, after the first murder, the Alfred Hitchcock film *Psycho* was scheduled to be shown on the Saturday-night Late Show. The station scheduled to show the movie pulled it off at the last minute, and they announced on the air that "due to recent events in this community, WNKA has decided that showing this film would be inappropriate at this time and will show the film at a later date." In its place they ran *Drumbeat* with Alan Ladd. Roger said at that time that it was a good thing they canceled since he knew what a powerful effect the movie would have. A girl he knew, he said, hadn't taken a shower for eight years—ever since she saw the movie.) I do not know if there is any truth to the theory, but I do not like the insinuation, playful as it might be, that I am the way I am because of the television I have watched. Let that be true of murderers, rapists, child molesters. Let the psychotics, the perverts of this country be formed by hours of watching "Gunsmoke," "Have Gun Will Travel," "Dragnet," "The Untouchables." I want no part of any influence stronger than the "Ed Sullivan Show" or "Leave It to Beaver." Ultimately, of course, I did own a TV, and I did watch it; the fact was inescapable.

The pizza finally came, and, because we had carefully primed our appetites with a couple of joints (I coated my throat, to avoid irritation, with a few shots of tequila), we consumed the pizza wordlessly and swiftly. Like spoiled children, neither of us ate any of the bare crust. After we finished eating, Roger said. "Do you feel like having some company?"

"I don't, but I let you in anyway."

"What a quick-quipper you are. No, I thought I'd call Bonnie Jacobsen and see if she wants to come over. You're probably going to turn on the TV any minute now."

I started to say, No, there's no point in calling her; she's in Minneapolis with Alexandra and Jean Nordstrom. But if I said that, I would have to say how I came to possess such information. "Go ahead," I said, waving him to the telephone.

Roger called, and to my surprise, Bonnie obviously answered. "Hello," he said, "this is Roger. How'd you like to come over to Peter's? You see, we are two hopelessly confused young men, and we need someone to talk over our troubles with." The fact that Bonnie is a guidance counselor continually amuses and delights Roger. "If you can't help us with our problems, you can fuck up your head with us. What do you say?" In the pause, she must have said yes. Roger said, "Terrific. I'll pick you up immediately."

He turned to me and said, "Why don't you make some coffee. We'll give Bonnie a chance to catch up. And while I'm gone—don't touch that dial."

While Roger was gone, all I could think of was Alexandra and of the lie she had probably told me. If she were not going to Minneapolis, or if she were going in the company of someone else, why would she not say so? Was another man somehow involved? Did she think I would be jealous? Hurt? And if I would be, why would she care? She did not seem to be the type who would practice deception. Perhaps she might have gone to the trouble at some time in her life, but not now; now she did not seem to care to have any part of anything dishonest. My impression of her was that she would prefer to suffer the consequences of any action rather than become entangled in any deceit. That morning we did not part on the most amicable terms; it did not seem likely that she would be terribly concerned about sparing my feelings. Something else. I—and I suppose every other citizen of the town—have reached a sensitized state in which I have become acutely aware, and suspicious, of any irregularity of behavior. Does your employer now chew his cuticles and he previously only bit his nails? Does your son take all his meals in his room? Does your husband come home with his shoes muddied from walking strange alleys? Is that the clink of empty gin bottles underneath the seat of Cousin Albert's DeSoto? For every odd or unusual action there is a pair of eyes to notice it. (And since no one's life is any longer as natural or as usual as it was before the murders began, there is much to notice.) It was in this suspicious, dark-minded way that I recognized the discrepancy between what Alexandra told me were her plans for the weekend and what appeared to be truth. And I did not like that frame of mind; it made me feel as though I had knowledge of a dirty secret, and I wanted to divest myself of it. I decided to ask Bonnie what had happened to Alexandra this weekend.

Roger returned, with Bonnie, in less than twenty minutes. Bonnie went to the kitchen table, looked down, and said, "God, where do I begin?"

Roger opened the Sucrets box. He said, "May I make a suggestion? Try a couple of these and a few shots of the favorite beverage of our friends south of the border. And call me in the morning."

"I don't like to smoke and drink at the same time. Do you have a soft drink or something?"

I got a bottle of Coke out of the refrigerator. She said she didn't need a glass or ice, that she'd drink it out of the bottle.

She sat on the living-room floor in a sort of halfhearted lotus position. Cross-legged, her Coke and ashtray and Roger's Sucrets tin in front of her, she looked as though she were settling down to very serious business indeed. She was wearing jeans, a bulky, fraying gray sweater, and she still had on the red-and-black-plaid wool shirt-jacket that she wore when she came in. Bonnie Jacobsen is an exuberant, short, toothy, pretty woman. She is slightly overweight, but she is uniformly overweight, and she seems athletic and carries her weight well. Her short brown hair is always falling over her face, and she is continually pushing her hair away from her wire-rimmed glasses and out of her line of vision. Like Jane from St. Cloud, she looks tan all year round. She has always struck me as immature, but I am never certain whether she actually is or if she seems that way because she affects as youthful an attitude as possible to help her gain rapport with the students she counsels. And she *is* relatively young; she is, I think, only twenty-two or twenty-three. Like Roger, she is at ease with students, and they in turn have genuine affection for her. They regard her as a comrade, an advocate, someone whom they can trust. This is her second year with the Wanekia school system. She, like Roger, like Alexandra, like myself, and like two or three others, is part of the recent educational "hiring boom." That boom has occurred here because of the area's population increase in the last five years. The population rose because of an increase in industry. There is a large sugar-beet processing plant here that has had a business surge recently. And about five miles outside Wanekia is a farm-implement factory that greatly increased its production and its profits when the company began the manufacture of snowmobiles. The hiring that these companies have done, along with the area's slow, but steady, natural growth, has accounted for the increase in students in the schools and the necessity for more teachers.

Bonnie Jacobsen is also something of a phony, always adopting some new, unusual fashion of speech, dress, life style, or taste. The fact that she refers to pop as "soft drinks" illustrates an eccentricity of speech that she has adopted. She, no doubt, grew up using the term "pop" (she is from the same dialect region that I am from), but at some time in her life, for God knows what reason, she decided to say "soft drink." But she is so obvious in her affectations, and so artless and awkward and childish about them, that this quality of hers becomes harmless and inoffensive.

We sat on the floor and talked. Bonnie smoked one joint and shared another with Roger. I sipped a beer slowly. The room was dark except for the dim, shadowy light given off by my old metal-shaded library lamp. Roger flipped through the records and played Crosby, Stills, Nash, and Young— "Four Way Street." And he played it too loud. I had to remind him I had neighbors.

Roger looked around the room as if he were in a place he had never been in before. "You know, this little congregation of the three of us is, I'll wager, probably the closest thing to a party this town has seen in months. Shit, that's pathetic."

"*Au contraire,*" Bonnie said. Her pronunciation of French was not as good as Alexandra's. "Florence Gresh has had two parties since the murders started. Excuse me—she doesn't call them parties. One 'dinner party' and one 'little get-together.' She has them because"—Bonnie imitated Florence Gresh's southern accent—" 'it is *so* important that we keep our spirits up and try to keep our lives from being *to*tally disrupted.' I wish she'd take that Scarlett O'Hara number and stick it."

Florence Gresh teaches sophomore English. As a hobby. She certainly doesn't need the money. Her husband is a very successful real estate man. She's in her fifties, she's lived in Minnesota for at least thirty years, and she's managed to hold onto her thick Alabama accent. She always makes it plain that though she teaches, it is *not* for the money. She says she would get *so* bored sitting around the house all day. This short, wiry, white-haired woman is one of Wanekia's feeble excuses for a socialite.

Roger said, "She's had parties, huh? And why haven't I been invited?"

"Because, dear boy," Bonnie said, "you are obviously not her kind of people."

Roger turned quickly to me. "How about you? Have you been invited?"

"Nope."

"And you?" he said to Bonnie.

"Sure. I even went to her 'get-together.' It was shitty. People standing all around the Gresh home holding their drinks and eating these incredibly tiny canapés. Be thankful you haven't been invited. And if you ever are, don't go. But I don't think that will happen. Not to people of your inferior breeding."

I was invited to the Gresh's once, the fall of my first year here. It was a large party, and even their spacious home was crowded. I knew no one; I wandered around for about an hour and then left. And I have no desire to return.

Bonnie told us about the increase she's had in the number of girls coming to her for counseling. But they don't come with problems that are more or less murder-related. They don't complain of being broken down by fear or tension. Their approaches are far more oblique. They want to know how, upon graduation, they can manage to leave town and still make their way. Should they get jobs? Should they simply move to another city? Last year, Bonnie said, a few girls came to her and said that they wanted to get married and settle in Wanekia. Now they want to know how soon they can get out of town.

Bonnie also told us about a girl who has been to see her. This girl, a shy blond sophomore who wears braces, is afraid of boys. The development, apparently, is recent. (However, as Bonnie said, there must be other "factors.") This girl becomes agitated any time she is in the presence of boys. Her pulse quickens, she experiences shortness of breath, she begins to perspire. (All normal adolescent behavior, Roger insisted.) This girl has these symptoms even in large groups. When she finds herself alone with a boy, or boys, she becomes so panic-stricken that she feels as though she will faint; she becomes disoriented, and it is difficult for her to hear. Bonnie said that, with the exception of the hearing impairment, these are typically neurotic reactions of a person who is phobic.

When Bonnie told us about this girl and about others, I thought it was remarkable that there were not more (and more serious) instances of young girls being stricken, and breaking down, from the stress and anxiety of living here. And I thought how ridiculous and difficult it is for me— and for everyone else—to pretend to teach them English, history, typing, or anything else. It's surprising that they do not laugh out loud at us.

After what I considered a sufficient length of time, after I thought I could ask without being obvious, I said to Bonnie: "I thought you were going to Minneapolis this weekend. What happened?"

"Yeah," she said, "I was going to go with Jean and Alex, but I changed my mind at the last minute."

It was the first time I had heard Alexandra called "Alex." I wondered if anyone besides Bonnie called her that. "What changed your mind?"

"I'm trying to save some money. And if I went with those two, I know I'd end up spending a lot. They really throw it around. I went with them once before, and I had a hard time keeping up with them."

"What could you possibly want to save your money for?" Roger asked.

"This is going to be my next to last year here. I'm going back to grad school."

"Where?" I said.

"I'm going to try to get into the University of Michigan. I'm going to apply there and to the University of Colorado and the University of Illinois and to Northwestern. I could live with any of them, but Michigan's my first choice. If I'm accepted there, I'll go even if I didn't get any money."

I was afraid I would give myself away with the next question, but I asked it anyway. "Did Jean and Alexandra still go?"

"Sure. They wouldn't stay just because I couldn't go. Besides, I think I get in their way. I'm not very good at that fancy-restaurant-and-cocktails-and-exclusive-shops thing." This was quite an admission for Bonnie. "A big thing for them is going out to lunch to this special little café they know about. I'd like to get away for a while, but that's not my trip."

I was relieved. Alexandra may have been perched on a bar stool in Minneapolis trying to pick up a man—it would not be difficult for her—and although the thought of that was not comforting, it was easier to think of her in that way than it was to imagine her lying to me.

Roger was quiet for a long time. He toyed with the cigarette butts in the ashtray and nodded his head gently in time to the music. The silence was uncharacteristic, and it ceased abruptly.

"Hey," he said, sitting up and speaking to both of us, "do you know about Bobby Wald?"

Bonnie and I both said we did.

"Well, here's my theory," he said. "I think Bobby Wald has been released from the state mental hospital, has returned to Wanekia, and he's the goddamn murderer. What do you think?"

Bonnie fell slowly backward so she was lying on the floor. "Oh, my God!" She put her hands over her face in astonishment.

"That's good," I said. "That's terrific. I think you've outdone yourself."

"I'm serious."

"Did I say I thought you weren't? I never doubted it."

"What's more, I know where the Wald house is. And I'll bet you Bobby is in there right now. Hiding out. Yeah. That's it. He's hiding out in the fucking house. Right at this moment."

"Roger," Bonnie said, placing her hand on his shoulder, "this is the real thing. The big time. This isn't a Suspense Theater script."

Roger reached up and patted her hand. "Art imitates Life. Haven't you ever heard of that, love?"

Bonnie looked over at me as if to say, you try—I can't do a thing with him. It was at that time, I believe, that I decided that Roger and Bonnie had been sleeping together.

Roger tapped on the ashtray as if to command our attention. "And I think we should go out there." He paused and put his chin down as if he were belching silently. "And investigate. That's what we should do."

"Now? Tonight?" Bonnie asked.

"There's no time like it."

"Just a minute," I said. "Do you honestly believe that Bobby Wald could even be alive, much less released, without anyone knowing it? In this town? And to add to the ridiculousness of your goddamn theory, do you think he's living in his old house after—what—forty years? Do you think any of that could be true?"

He stroked his beard and said, "Nah. It's not likely."

"That's more like it," Bonnie said.

Roger jumped to his feet. "So what's the harm in going out there? I happen to know that the Wald house has been vacant for almost three years. And that it's been rented since Mrs. Wald died ten years ago. So what do you say? We'll just drive out there and look around."

I asked him where the house was.

"Just a few miles out of town. It's on that road that goes out to the airport and the city dump."

Bonnie and I looked at each other again. It may have been my imagination, but that time I thought there was something in her expression that was asking me for help. It was obvious by that time that Roger was determined to go out there, and it was likely that he would go either with us or without us. I felt a little as though I were conspiring with Bonnie, as if I were working with the daughter of a drunkard, helping her get her father out of the bar and back home to his family. But Roger was neither drunk nor stoned. He had, however, had enough to drink and smoke to make him intractable. Perhaps because I did not say anything, perhaps because she simply made up her mind at that moment, Bonnie stood up too and said, "All right, I'm game. Let's go."

They both stared down at me. I did not want to go. I felt lousy. I had not even planned to leave my apartment that evening, and I certainly had no particular desire to accompany Roger (and Bonnie) on this expedition. But I said yes, and I'm still not certain why. I may have wanted to prevent what thoughts they may have had of me if I refused, thoughts of cowardice, of simple poor sportsmanship, of petulance. Perhaps I wanted to shatter completely that "staying in" trance that started to come over me earlier. Maybe there was something inside me that was attracted to the small adventure of the idea. But it would have been deep within me, because on the surface I was reluctant.

"Just the three of us?" I asked, standing up.

"I think it would be best," Roger said solemnly. "I don't think we should call the FBI in on this caper, not just yet."

"You know what I mean, asshole. Any other friends you care to share this with?"

"No," he said, putting his arms around Bonnie's and my shoulders. "This is basically a sound unit. Besides this is an operation for three good persons. Or a whole army. So let's get the fuck going."

"Grab a warm jacket," Bonnie said to me. "It's cold tonight. And drizzly."

I grabbed an old leather Navy flight jacket that once belonged to an uncle of mine. The jacket is so old that the fur collar is matted, the cuffs are unraveling, and there are flaps torn into the leather all over the jacket. I intend to wear that jacket until it disintegrates.

As we were going out the door, I asked Roger, "Do you mind if we take your car? I'm almost out of gas." I *was* low on gas, but that was not the reason I did not want to drive. If we were not in my car, I would merely be going along on the excursion; I would not be leading it. That was a distinction I wanted to preserve.

"Sure," Roger said. "It'll be tight, but it's all right with me."

It was crowded. The back seat of Roger's Volkswagen was filled with his art supplies. There were large canvases back there, squares of masonite, two or three large brown, hand-thrown pots, two metal cases that looked like tackle boxes and that must have been filled with paints, assorted rags, rolls of cloth, and odd pieces of wood. There was a strong smell of paint and turpentine. "My studio," Roger said.

We all sat in the front. Bonnie was in the middle, but because Roger needed room to shift, she was squeezed into the seat with me. I was against the door, but at that, she was partially in my lap.

"God," she said, "I feel like I'm back in high school."

"You are. Remember?" Roger said.

We drove southwest through town, across the bridge over the Wrong River (renamed after an early explorer's inability to tell east from west), past Bud's Standard, by the rows of colored light bulbs and pennants of Bjerke's Chevrolet—New and Used Cars, and after four more street lights, we were, quite suddenly, outside the city limits. Roger began to speed up as soon as he was officially on the highway. Mingled with the high, tinny whine of the engine was the zip and hiss of the tires on the wet pavement. None of us spoke. Roger reached into his coat pocket and pulled out a beer. He popped it open deftly with one hand, took a long pull, and handed it over to me. Roger's heater was throwing out enough heat to keep my feet and legs warm, and Bonnie's closeness warmed my left side, but my right side was freezing. I didn't want anything cold to drink, but I drank down about half the beer anyway. I was having more and more doubts about what we were doing.

After about three or four miles, Roger turned off the highway onto a gravel road. He slowed down, but still the car threw up stones that clattered against the metal underside of the car. Once, it felt like a large rock hit right underneath my left foot. I was afraid for a moment that something beneath the car might have been damaged.

The road was very dark, and the rain had not dampened the road much. When I looked behind us, it looked as though we were being followed by a red cloud. The dust behind us was colored by the taillights. The headlights lit the brown dirt road, the yellow weeds in the ditch, and then, further ahead, the lights seemed simply to drop away. I knew there were trees along this road, but I could not see them; rather, it was as if I could feel their presence.

Roger slowed down. "I think it's right along here someplace," he said, and leaned over to look out at the right side of the road.

I could tell then, still mostly by feel, and also by the sound and how it was no longer muffled, that there were open fields on each side of us. Barbed-wire fence lined the road.

I saw ahead a break in the fence and the weeds—a driveway on the right.

"This is it," Roger said, and turned so sharply I could feel the wheels slide on the loose gravel.

Once there had been a wire and wooden gate across the driveway, but it was now open, hanging limply by its broken hinges in some brush. We could drive right through the yard and to the house, about twenty-five to thirty yards in front of us.

But Roger drove no further, and we remained parked in the driveway. Bonnie pressed herself against me, but there was nothing personal in her action. She was frightened, and her movement toward me was reflexive. In spite of that, I enjoyed the soft, warm pressure.

"Let's get out," Roger said.

"If you don't mind, I think I'll wait in the car," Bonnie said. She folded her arms in front of her as if she were trying to keep warm.

Roger left the car running and flicked the headlights on to bright. We got out and walked to the front of the car.

A cold wind was blowing. It pulled and waved the weeds and the brush and rattled the bare branches of the trees. But it tore nothing loose; anything out there that could be blown away was gone long ago.

As I stood there, looking toward the house, it became apparent how foolish Roger's theory was. No one lived in that peeling, rotting, white, wooden two-story house, and it was obvious that no one had lived there since the last official tenants three years ago. It was not the hideout of a murderer; it was an old, rundown, abandoned farmhouse whose interior had, no doubt, been taken over by rats and pigeons.

We walked forward slowly; we were not moving cautiously but disinterestedly. It was plain what the yard had been used for. Lying about were scattered piles of beer cans and broken bottles. There were charred circles of ground where the partygoers had built bonfires, and there were still some loose stacks of firewood that had been gathered for the fires. My guess was that no parties had been held there since last summer.

As we came closer to the house, we could see that all the windows had been broken. They must have been shattered in some rock-throwing exercise because the wood and paint around the window frames was chipped and splintered. The house's side door was closed but looked as though it would come open with the slightest pressure. The screen door was lying on the ground. Roger and I stood by a cellar trap door that had no lock. We were standing directly in the path of the car's headlights and our silhouettes were thrown onto the side of the house.

"Do you want to go in?" I asked.

Roger kicked at the crumbling cement foundation around the cellar door. "Not particularly," he said. "How about you?"

"I can live without it."

"Yeah. Not much point to it, I guess."

I was not afraid, and neither was Roger. I did not expect to see any kill-crazed maniacs running at us from out of the trees. But neither Roger nor I cared to compound the ludicrousness of the moment by remaining there much longer. Even if we had not realistically expected to find anything, neither could we have realized how empty, how pedestrian, the trip out there would be.

Roger looked at me. Behind him, I could see the faint, dark outline of a line of trees that must have been planted by the Walds years ago as a windbreak. His face, heavily shadowed in that light, was as solemn as I had ever seen it, and he looked older at that moment.

"Let's split," he said. "I'm freezing my ass."

We walked back toward the car, squinting to avoid being blinded by the headlights. I kicked down the driveway a partially burned beer can that had enough of its red-and-white label left so I could tell it was a Budweiser can. The entire scene reminded me of all the occasions when I was in high school, and friends and I used to gather at just such country locations to drink and raise hell. But on all those occasions, drinking the beer or liquor we had stolen or browbeaten and bribed a drunk into buying for us or that we had pilfered from our parents' cupboards or that had been bought by someone's older brother, I had never felt as strongly that I was doing something wrong. Out there tonight I was in a place where I had no business being. Roger must have been feeling something like that too, because he was quiet as he walked with his head down and his hands jammed into his pockets.

When we got back in the car, Bonnie said, "Nothing here, huh?"

"Nothing," Roger said. "I've had some stupid goddamn ideas before, but this has got to be right up at the top of the list."

He backed the car out so violently I was afraid for a moment he was going to lose control of it. He jammed the gears into first while we were still rolling backward, popped the clutch, spun the wheels, and we took off.

The trip back to town was as silent as the drive out to Walds'. There was no traffic until we got back on the highway. I could have said something to Roger but didn't. It was the perfect opportunity to gain revenge for the multitude of times he had ridden me for actions or ideas of mine that were far less foolish than this. But I felt sorry for him. I had never seen him as abashed . . . Bonnie did not say anything either.

By the time we got back to my apartment, it was raining steadily. It was colder than before, the wind was gusting, and as we ran from the car to the building, it felt as though we were pelted by bits of ice.

Inside, Roger said, in his best Irish brogue, "Petey me boy, break out your brandy and heat up some coffee. I'm so frozen I could piss icicles."

He had overcome his shame over having carted us into the country on such a miserable night.

I asked Bonnie if there was anything I could get her.

"I am chilled to the *bone*," she said. "Do you have an afghan or something I could wrap up in?"

Bonnie's request broke Roger up. "An afghan! Sure, he's got one. Hell, he's got two, but the butler is walking them right now."

Though her asking for an afghan was another example of her affectation, I felt sorry for her. "Just a minute. I'll see what I can find."

I went into the bedroom. From my closet shelf I brought down an old wool Hudson's Bay blanket, a gift from my grandfather. He presented it to me when I planned on spending one month of my sixteenth summer at the cabin of a friend in Canada. It was, he said, "to keep me warm on those cold Canadian nights." I left it at home and relied on my sleeping bag for warmth. Later, when I found out how expensive the blanket was and how much thought had gone into the gift, I felt guilty. I've kept the blanket with me ever since.

That feeling of Bonnie and I conspiring together, of she and I being on one "side" and Roger being on the other, was even stronger as I stood in the dark bedroom. It was Roger who wanted to go out to the Wald house, not Bonnie and I. She and I had been the sober ones during the evening. And both of us, but Bonnie in particular, had been the object of his jokes. So, I began to fantasize that somehow, out of our being "teamed" together, out of our physical closeness in Roger's Volkswagen, we were going to be alone together in my apartment that night. I began to think that, in the car, her pressure at my side was not impersonal, that it was not prompted only by fear and cold, that she was telling me something. I turned on a light and looked around the bedroom, trying to see if, lying in a corner, there were pairs of dirty underwear or anything else that might prove embarrassing, so convinced was I that Bonnie was going to be in that bed. In my mind, I compared her with Alexandra, and though she was inevitably a distant second to Alexandra, there were features that consoled me. She was fleshier; her breasts fuller, her hips without any cutting edge of bone. I imagined that what I saw in her as an athletic quality would somehow in bed transform itself into sexual inventiveness and abandon. The contrast between Alexandra and Bonnie, for some reason, revealed itself to me in terms of moisture, and in my mind, Alexandra was associated with the dryness of bone and ash; Bonnie all wetness, the wetness of a clear, thick oil. With neither of these images was there anything pejorative *or* positive; they were simply there, and even while I held onto them, I was not especially convinced of their accuracy. I was not certain how the logistics of the rest of the evening would work out—how Roger would leave and Bonnie remain, how her soft thighs would finally part— but these considerations were incidental.

And as soon as I walked out of the bedroom, the blanket held in front of me to conceal the erection that was a product of my fantasy, I realized how ridiculous it is to confuse any singular activity of thought, any intricate plans of the mind, with the solidity of reality. Roger and Bonnie were in the kitchen. Bonnie's back was against the wall, close to the door, and Roger was pressed up against her. Her hands cupped his buttocks so tightly it looked as if she were trying to lift him. His arms went around her neck, and his chin rested on the top of her head. They were so close together, so motionless, it looked as if they were one unit, as if they had frozen in that position, had been brought in and leaned stiffly against the wall to thaw.

What is the passage from Joyce? "I saw myself as a creature driven and derided by vanity." It is, I think, from "Araby," but the important thing is that it described perfectly the way I felt. Like Roger and his notion about the occupant of the Wald house, I was duped by my own thoughts. At least Roger recognized on one level the unlikelihood of his theory. Of course, as long as I held the blanket in front of me, I was not going to be publicly found out.

I used a stage throat-clearing. "Ahem. Would you like me to go get another pizza?"

Not even startled by my appearance, Roger turned and

looked sleepily at me. "Nah. Just go wait in the hall. I'll tell you when you can come in."

"And I can assume this blanket is no longer necessary?" It was, by that time, no longer necessary for me.

Bonnie said, "Thanks, Peter. You didn't have to go to all that trouble for me." She took the blanket from me, and I could see she was blushing. If she had been sweating heavily, she would, I'm sure, still have insisted she wanted the blanket.

We sat on the living-room floor again, Roger and I drinking brandy and coffee. Bonnie wanted nothing more to drink. Wise, in light of the beer and tequila that had already been consumed. Roger and I sat cross-legged across from each other. Bonnie lay curled beside Roger, the blanket covering her legs. Roger put his hand on her head and stroked her hair unconsciously. When he glanced down he pointed suddenly at her neck.

"Look at that!" he shouted.

"What? What is it?" Bonnie clapped her hand over her neck and sat up.

"Right there—moles. Three of them. A sure sign that you have been having congress with devils."

"God. You scared the shit out of me. I was sure a tarantula was on my neck. At least."

"They used to believe that. In the fifteenth century. Moles and warts on a woman meant she had been getting it on with demons."

"Well, if they had anything catchy, you've got it too."

From behind her, Roger reached around Bonnie and clapped his hands over her breasts. I winced. In all my years of feeling breasts, I have never, never squeezed any as tightly, as roughly, as Roger did. I guess I always bought the belief that that sort of thing could cause breast cancer.

"I'm not scared," Roger said. "I get a penicillin shot every month. I believe in preventive medicine." He squeezed harder and pulled her back against him. I was sure she was hurt; if not physically, then certainly she was embarrassed by his actions.

But I was wrong. She leaned into him, tilted her head back against his chest, and wrapped her arms over his, keeping them on her breasts. I felt, at that moment, as if I were building a career on mistaken judgments.

I said, "Are you *sure* you don't want me to go get another pizza?"

"Really," Roger said, "it's not necessary." Then, in his best Groucho Marx imitation, "but maybe you'd like to watch TV for a while while Bonnie and I catch forty winks?"

"Go ahead. But I don't think anything's on. Would it be all right if I read instead?"

"Of course. And would it be all right if I turned the stereo up ever so slightly?"

"Sure. Then I won't have to cough all the time."

They rose, and as they went into the bedroom, Bonnie whispered, "Rog, we could've gone over to my place."

"What the hell," he said, "we're here."

As soon as the bedroom door closed, the inevitable happened. I had to piss. And the only way to the bathroom was through the bedroom. I stood, resisted the temptation to listen at the bedroom door, put on my jacket, and went outside.

It was no longer raining, but it was cold. When I looked up at the sky, I could see darker patches here and there, places where the clouds were breaking up and the night sky showed through. I crossed the parking lot, and behind the large yellow garbage cans, at a spot where I could see the windows of my apartment (the only lighted windows in the building), I pissed and watched the steam rise from the cold, wet pavement. And I wasn't going to go out, I thought. Jesus Christ, they bring it to you. "An outcast from life's feast." What a fine night for Joyce!

I took my time going back in. Once I was inside, I began to put away the food and the bottles, to throw away the garbage, and to clear off the table. I was too tired, too cold, too embarrassed to be titillated by any thoughts of what was going on in the bedroom. In the silence between the cuts on the record, I halfheartedly listened for any moans or creaking of bedsprings, but I heard nothing. I paged through a *Time* magazine and waited. I was very tired.

When I was down to reading the "Economy & Business" section, Roger came out. Alone. He closed the door softly but tightly. He was wearing jeans, his flannel shirt—unbuttoned and untucked—and white socks. When he saw me, he made a mock bow, and said, "Ta-da."

"You wore your socks?" I pointed to his feet.

"My feet were cold," he said sheepishly.

"Very poor taste. And very dangerous. Apparently you don't know that leaving your socks on is an almost certain guarantee of impregnation. I almost knocked up a girl that way once. Fortunately, she was aware of the danger and got my socks off me in time." What the hell, I thought, I'm chattering so *he* won't be uncomfortable.

"I'll be more careful." He opened the refrigerator and looked in. "What's for eats?"

"Not much. *Now* do you want me to go for a pizza?" I began to sound, even to myself, spoiled and bitchy, and I did not like the sound.

"Have you got any peanut butter?"

"In the cupboard over the sink."

Roger made two sandwiches, opened a Coke, and sat down at the table. "She's going to sleep for a while. If it's okay."

"Sure."

Roger let out a long sigh, but let it out slowly so that it whistled past his lips. "Some night, huh?"

"Some night." My exasperation, my fatigue, must have begun to show in my voice.

"What's the matter? Did we screw up your plans for the evening?"

"No. I told you, I wasn't going to go out."

"Shit. Don't be a martyr. Even when you *do* go out, you don't go out."

"Hey, not all of us look so good in lampshades. We're not all cut out to be Mr. Good-Time."

"And what the hell is that supposed to mean?" He was

not smiling, and at the base of his neck, at the upper part of his chest, I could see angry, red splotches. He put down his sandwich carefully as though he were getting ready in case he needed his hands free.

It was all perfectly comic. Here we were, like boys in a schoolyard taking turns pushing each other. But though I could see the absurdity of the scene, I was not about to back down. I was irritated, angry, but I was no longer tired. The tension was waking me, exciting me, and I felt that any attempt to cool the situation would push me back into that dim, woolly, heavy fog of sleepiness. And I became very objective. Well, I thought very matter-of-factly, I had better get in the first punch. There was, believe it or not, nothing particularly malicious about that thought. It was simply a matter of strategy, and once I decided what I was going to do, I felt a kind of eager anticipation.

"It means," I said slowly, looking down at the gold-flecked pattern of the table top, "that you refuse to take anything seriously, and you have nothing but contempt for those who do. You fuck around constantly. You judge everyone by your own dizzy, screwed-up life. It can get tiresome. I get sick of it. Others probably do too." Oh, I was cool, I was so cool. And I was ready.

"Jesus. Jesus H. Christ," Roger said, shaking his head the way he does to slow himself down when he has too much to say. "What do you want? You want me to go crazy? You want me to go around looking like I'm going to a goddamn funeral? What the fuck do you want? What am I supposed to do? How am I supposed to act? Tell me, goddammit!"

He held his hands up, and it was plain he had no intention of balling them into fists. Rather, he was pleading; he was still angry, but at the same time, he was close to tears.

My God, I thought, I was about to hit him. One hand was still clenched. I looked at him, at his contorted face, and I felt as if I were all fangs, hair, and horns. "I don't know," I said. "I don't know what you're supposed to do."

"No *shit* you don't. Nobody in this town does." He was shouting, but I could tell it was working as a release for him.

Just then, Bonnie came out of the bedroom. She had pulled a sheet off the bed and had wrapped it around herself. One shoulder and one arm were exposed. The flesh of her upper arm widened from her elbow up to her shoulder, and her shoulder was round and plump. Squinting in the light, she said blurrily, "What's going on? Are you guys fighting or something?"

When she came into the kitchen, her bare feet slapped on the tile floor. As she came closer, I could see the red indentations made by her glasses on the sides of her nose. She looked frightened, like a child awakened by a thunderstorm.

Everything came down at once. It became suddenly as late as it was, the kitchen light hit upon the bottles, the cans, the crumpled cellophane—and all the garbage that I had stacked in the corner now seemed to dominate the room.

Roger got up and put an arm around Bonnie, more courtly than I had ever seen him. "That was just me shooting my mouth off," he said. "I didn't mean to wake you up. Why don't you go back to bed?"

Bonnie stared down at her feet as if the sight of them surprised her. "I better get home. It's really late."

"Okay. You get dressed. I'll be ready in a minute."

When Bonnie padded back into the bedroom, Roger paced back and forth, running his fingers through his hair. He stopped, leaned on the back of a chair, then suddenly hit himself twice in the forehead with the heels of his hands. "SHIT!" he yelled, then quieted down right away. "I don't know what the fuck's the matter with me. I come over here, drag you out into the country on some half-assed scheme, I drink your booze. Then I jump into the sack with Bonnie, cream your sheets, while you wait for me to finish my number. Then I gotta go and fucking insult you! Sometimes I don't believe myself."

"And eat my peanut butter. Don't forget the peanut butter."

He laughed politely and walked over to my chair. He clapped his hand roughly on my shoulder. "I'm sorry, man. Jesus Christ, I am sorry."

I was embarrassed and ashamed of myself. "Forget it. There's nothing to be sorry about. Just get me some more peanut butter. Skippy. It's got to be Skippy."

Roger slumped back into his chair and looked around the kitchen as if he were seeing it for the first time, as if he had forgotten to note his surroundings. "Wow," he said. "It's really late. I guess we came damn close to my goal, huh?"

The bedroom door opened and Bonnie's arm and Roger's boots came out. She dropped them, and they landed next to each other, right side up, waiting for someone to step into them.

I asked Roger if he wanted his Coke.

"No. Go ahead, help yourself." He was very eager to please.

I drank it to keep myself awake. I felt as though I had been taking speed for days and its effects were deserting me.

"You know what I said about going crazy?" Roger spoke slowly, lacing his boots methodically.

"Yeah."

"That was no shit. I mean, I was serious. It happened to me before. The real thing. Hallucinations. Voices. The works."

"And do you vish to speak of zis to ze doctor?" I pretended to take notes, and of course, inside I did.

"When I was at Illinois I was into a lot of political shit. This was the late sixties. Everything *was* political then, right?"

"Just about."

"It got so the world—or the way I saw the world—split itself into good guys and bad guys. 'If you're not with us, you're against us.' Just like that. Black and white. Very neat. How about you, Peter? What were you doing?"

His question startled me; it was almost an accusation. "Not much. Went to a couple rallies. Read some stuff. My heart was in the right place."

"See, that wasn't good enough. That would've made you one of them. And when the time came—" He slit his throat with his finger, "Sorry."

"You were only doing your duty."

"Right. That's the way we saw it. Anyway, I was one of the leaders of the good guys. And I took my job *very* seriously. I stopped doing acid, grass, booze—anything recreational. I took a lot of speed because you had to be right on fucking top of everything. The bad guys never rested. I was probably paranoid all this time, but it was hard to know for sure. I mean, there really *were* cops in the student union reading upside-down newspapers. Just last year, a friend of mine in Boston was visited by the FBI. They were looking for a mutual friend of ours because they found explosives in his apartment years ago. This guy in Boston said he flushed a lot of good shit down when he saw the Feds at the door. But just think, after all these years, they're still after his ass. They still *care*. So there were bad guys around. Maybe they weren't sleeping under my bed like I thought, but they were around. I bet they know where I am now. They're still keeping track."

"But you're not just talking about a little paranoia, are you?"

"You bet your ass I'm not. See, I was doing so much—organizing and making speeches and writing letters. Everything. I was into everything. And I began to feel like I couldn't handle it, like parts of me were breaking off and going in a hundred different directions. Literally. It was like there was this central command post and I'd say to part of me, 'Go brace this professor,' and to another part, 'Make a speech to this women's group.'"

Bonnie came out of the bedroom. Roger looked up at her and said, "I'm telling Pete about when I went bananas. We'll go in a minute, okay?"

"Sure. I'm not in that much of a hurry." She hiked herself up to sit on the kitchen counter, and let her legs dangle back and forth the way a child does keeping a private rhythm.

Roger went on. "Anyway, I was getting worn pretty thin. I wanted help, but I couldn't say to anyone else, 'Can you take over some of this shit—it's too goddamn much for me.' I couldn't do that because it was a real ego trip for me to be in charge. But I kept saying to myself, I need help. I need help. It was like I was praying, but there wasn't anything I believed in to pray to. Here's the weird part. I got help. One day, these voices came to me." He must have noticed my expression when he said that. "That's right, folks," he assured me. "Voices. They started telling me what to do, what to say, how to handle everything. It was like I could relax because the voices would take care of things. It worked great. I was goddamn dazzling. I didn't really know what was happening while it was happening because I lay back and let the voices take over. All this time, I knew there was something not exactly normal about the voices but I didn't give a shit. It felt so good. I knew I couldn't fuck up because the voices were directing me. I was cruising. I had the golden touch. I figured maybe I was a goddamn genius or something. Then things started to go wrong. I didn't even know it. But people came up to me and said things like, 'Were you serious?' or 'Are you trying to screw up the cause?' At this one student-faculty symposium on revolution, a young history prof—a real asshole—he was from the University of Chicago and was trying to make himself the resident conservative—really started backing me into a corner, kept asking me questions. He asked me what we were going to do with all those innocent people who neither actively opposed nor supported the revolution, the people who just happen to be in the way. I guess I snapped then. But in a very quiet sort of way. I said we'd have to kill them. Then I went on, very calmly, to say *how* we'd kill them. We'd kill them with rat poison, with shotguns, with machetes. When I got to the part about machetes, a couple of my friends got me out of there. Of course, I didn't know a goddamn thing about what had happened. I just said what the voices told me to say. Then I thought the voices were, I don't know, from the devil or the enemy or something, and that they had just set me up so they could get me in their power and fuck me over. Shit, man, I was in a bad way. I could no longer function."

"What happened?"

"This chick got me to see a shrink. He gave me some drugs. Thorazine, maybe, I don't remember. Some other things. I got better. Not *well*, but better. I was able to finish the semester, if you can imagine that."

"Back from the edge, huh?"

"Back to the living. During the summer, I went back to Chicago and stayed with my parents. I hardly ever left the house. I limped back to school in the fall, sort of hung on for a year, and graduated. Then I split. I drove around for the summer, bumming off friends all over the country. I just kept doing that. I took things *very* easy. Shit, I don't remember how I ended up here. I know it had something to do with needing money. I sort of think of myself as a scrap of paper blown up against a fence."

"The 'Fence of Life'?"

"Okay. I'm tired. Anyway, when I talk about 'crazy' you can be damn sure I know whereof I speak. When the murders hit full stride, I got worried. I was listening all the time—I still do—checking to make sure I don't hear any fucking voices. But I'm careful. I don't let steam build up. I don't let things get screwed out of perspective."

"I wish you would have told me about this sooner."

"It's hard to work it in. Besides, I'm not exactly proud of it. I mean, I'm not ashamed, but it's not something I want to brag about."

"Yeah, I know what you mean." But, I thought, you were able to tell Bonnie. I was not jealous, but it bothered me. Where was I, what kind of a shit was I, that my best friend never felt he could tell me about this?

Bonnie hopped down from her perch on the cupboard. "We better get going. It's really late."

While they put their jackets on, I remained sitting at the kitchen table. I could see them out from there, and besides, I did not have the energy to get up.

Bonnie walked over to me to say good-bye. For a moment, I thought she was going to bend down and kiss me. "Good night, Peter. Thanks for everything. Next time we'll mess up my apartment, okay?"

"Okay."

"Get some rest, old boy," Roger said. "You look like hell."

The feeling was very strange. I felt as though they were saying good-bye to someone they did not expect to see for a long time, if ever. Good-bye, terminally ill friend! Good-bye, brother across the sea! Good-bye!

I crossed the room and looked out the window. I heard the car roar out of the parking lot, and I could hear Roger going through the gears—second, third, fourth—growing fainter as he drove away. If I were outside, I thought, and if there were no other cars on the street—which was likely at that hour—I could probably hear them all the way to Bonnie's.

When they left, it was raining again. The clearing had not lasted. In the puddles along the edge of the asphalt parking lot—black and glistening from the rain—in those small pools I could see the rings made by the falling rain. And in the light from the street lamps, I could see the rain coming down so heavily it was like looking through cellophane. It could still snow. The middle of April is not too late for snow. At this time of year, in this part of Minnesota, it can be in the eighties one day and snow the next. At another time, I will pursue the theory of the effect of unpredictable weather on the unstable personality. At another time.

They had not made the bed. The spread and the blankets were at the foot of the bed, and the sheets were twisted and rumpled. It was my first impulse to change the sheets. Then I thought, no, I will lie there and I will smell them, and if they left any dampness, I will feel that. I wanted that.

It is customary, I know, to summarize the events of the day, to state their significance, to analyze them; this is particularly common among those who are, by nature, introspective. But I do not do that. I am only the reporter.

15 April 1973, Sunday

*C*lear today but cold. It felt more like fall than spring. I slept late, as late as I could. Each time I woke up during the morning, I pushed myself back into sleep as if I were holding my own head under water. I slept so long that when I could sleep no longer, I was in a state of torpor and I lay in bed, unable to summon the will or the energy to get up. After an hour of staring at the ceiling, of trying to find a pattern in the stippled plaster, I finally got out of bed.

I hate Sundays. Aside from the aversion that I've always felt for the day—that it signifies the end of the weekend and the all-too-soon return to whatever one returns to, work, school (both in my case), I dislike it because I feel such a sense of isolation on this day in this community. Stores are closed, there is no school or work, and since I do not attend church, I have no access to other people. The local newspaper is not printed on Sunday; there are no local news broadcasts on TV. I leave the radio on and put up with it on Sunday, because I am afraid something is going to happen, and I'm not going to know about it. It's this feeling of being cut off that bothers me about the day. Of course, not *everything* is closed. A city statute requires that a drugstore

121

remains open to dispense medication; the local druggists alternate Sundays. There is also a small, overpriced grocery that is open every day. It's not as bleak as I make out.

And Alexandra returned today. She called me at about five o'clock. Her voice over the telephone was faint, as if she held the receiver too far away. I was surprised when she called.

"Hello," she said. "Do you know who this is?"

"Of course I do."

"I just got back. Are you still angry? Do you feel like coming over for a drink?"

"I'm not mad. I thought you were mad."

"Let's not start fighting about it. Do you want to come over? I've got a surprise for you."

"Pour the drinks. I'll be less than five minutes."

It was the first time I had been in Alexandra's apartment, and its appearance startled me. It unnerved me, first of all, to be in an apartment that was exactly like mine only backward, like looking in a mirror. I had expected it to be tastefully, maybe even lavishly decorated, like something from a designer magazine. Lots of plants, knickknacks, sort of stylish clutter. By contrast, it was Spartan, practically barren. In the living room, there was an old wooden trunk on which rested a tiny Panasonic TV. On the floor next to the trunk was a portable stereo. Records were stacked next to that. One chair, wooden, straight-backed with a cane seat. Pillows and cushions on the floor across from the TV. Four or five un-framed prints tacked on the walls. Along the windowsill some tiny cactus plants were lined up. Books were stuffed vertically, horizontally, and diagonally into the bookcase. In the kitchen was a small, round cloth-draped table and one chair. The bedroom door was open. The single bed—mattress and box springs on the floor—was covered by a patchwork quilt. There was a small pine four-drawer dresser. She's ready to move, I thought. She's ready to get the hell out on a moment's notice.

We sat on the floor and leaned against the cushions. Inside of, I'd guess, twenty minutes, and before either of us finished our drinks, we made love. Nothing urgent. No button-popping or cloth-tearing. No desperate grasping at each other. No hurried fumbling. All as smooth and quiet as warm water. Clothes neatly draped across a chair. It was sort of pleasantly inevitable, as though we both knew it was going to happen and got right to it. I do not say "got it over with," although that double-preposition closing may be the way that one of the participants chose to characterize our coupling.

I did try one thing. As Alexandra lay beneath me, I placed the heel of my hand on her breast, and remembering what Roger had done the night before when he so violently clasped Bonnie from behind, I began to press down, rotating my hand, testing, waiting to see how hard I could press before I caused her pain and she stopped (or she cried out) or until I was stopped by my own inhibitions or peculiar sense of propriety or bedroom etiquette or whatever you choose to call it. The experiment ended when she shifted beneath me, rolling her shoulder to the side. I do not know if her movement was deliberate. I doubt that I will try again.

As we lay on the floor, Alexandra said, "Something funny happened to me in Minneapolis. When I was registering at the hotel, a man standing next to me said, 'Hey, you're from Wanekia!' It scared me at first. Before I knew he read it off the registration card. And then it pissed me off, but he looked harmless enough. He was young and kind of pudgy and very double-knit—a salesman. He told us he worked for Liggett and Myers, the tobacco company. Anyway, I thought maybe he was from here, and that's why he was so excited, because he was meeting someone from his hometown. So I was nice, even though it gave me an eerie feeling that a stranger knew things about me. It was sort of like finding out a peeping tom has been watching you. I told him that I taught in Wanekia, that both Jean and I did. And he said, 'Wow! Tell me about the murders! You gotta' know who's doing it, right? In a town that small. They just can't prove it, right?' He said he got caught in a blizzard here once and had to spend the night. We told him that we didn't know who the killer was, that nobody did, and we tried to get away from him. He wanted to buy us dinner just so we'd talk to him about the murder. I felt strange all the time I was in Minneapolis. I kept expecting people to rush up to me and say, 'You're from Wanekia! Tell us all about it!' It was a terrible feeling."

"Can't handle the pressures of being famous?"

"Is that what it is? God, it's awful. I felt as if I *looked* different. As if I were a freak of some kind."

"As if you were wearing a red letter 'A'?"

"What?"

"Forget it."

I had difficulty believing that she could be so unnerved by the stares of strangers. She must know that she is the invariable object of attention in any gathering. I put that down as the polite, if slightly dishonest modesty of the lovely.

And on the subject of fame and freakishness, I believed both were true of us all—that we are all made famous by living in this community at this time, and that we are made freaks by the same circumstances. And unlike Alexandra, who feels herself shaken by being such a celebrity, I cherish the dubious prestige. It is enhanced by the fact that I am more than simply a Wanekia resident; I teach in the high school where it all happened. I expect to carry this renown with me all my life through. At dull parties when I am one of the duller participants, I expect to work into the conversation that I, in the spring of 1973, taught English in a school where girls were murdered. Around kitchen tables, bars, and campfires, to grandchildren, old friends, and used-car salesmen, I expect to tell of how women locked their doors, men looked over their shoulders, and children played murderer instead of cowboys and Indians. I expect to tell all of it, and if people don't ask, I will volunteer the information. I am ashamed of feeling this way, and I know that it makes of me a monster of sorts, but in these pages, I will not deny that it is so. If I were in a Minneapolis hotel lobby and met a tobacco salesman, the only way I could be at ease with him would be if I could talk to him about the subject I have only recently come to know so much about. It is dark, twisted, and shameful. Perhaps I should deny it even in these pages.

Alexandra did not—does not, will not—know of these thoughts.

She sat up and said, "I almost forgot. I told you I have a surprise, didn't I?"

"Well, I don't want to seem push—"

"Wait right here. I'll get it for you."

She walked naked from the room with that characteristic lack of self-consciousness that was becoming familiar to me. The curtains were closed, but I somehow felt that she would not have behaved differently if they were open. When she returned, she was wearing a white terrycloth robe (which was in much better condition than the one of mine she appropriated the other night), and she was carrying a red clothing box. *"Pour vous,"* she said and tossed the box to me.

"Speak English." I opened the box. Inside was a cardigan sweater, very light tan.

"Try it on." She sat on the edge of the chair, smiling down at me like a parent on Christmas morning.

"Like this?" I was wearing nothing but my shorts.

"Just to see how it fits."

I pulled the sweater on and buttoned it. "A perfect fit. Or it will be when I get some clothes on. Thank you. It's very soft." I was, as always, uncomfortable receiving gifts.

"It's part cashmere. I thought that color would go with almost anything. Maybe you can wear that sometimes instead of your corduroy jacket. Are you sure it's all right? If it's not, if you don't like the way it fits or the color, I can take it back."

"No. It's great. Perfect. Did I say you shouldn't have? You shouldn't have." I was afraid to take it off. It was obvious that she took great pleasure in gift-giving.

Once the formalities of giving and receiving were over, Alexandra said, "I hate to shoo you out, Peter, but I've got lessons and papers to prepare for tomorrow. And I've got to write up a short exam. I'm sorry, but I've got to get it all done tonight." Obviously, the primary business of my visit was to receive the present.

I couldn't have dressed faster if she had told me her mother and father were coming through the door. "Sure," I said, "I understand. I've got a helluva lot of work to do myself." But I did not understand. I was hurt and angry. I had hoped we might go out to dinner, that we could spend the rest of the day together. But I left quietly.

As I was walking back to my apartment, I smelled food being grilled outdoors. That smell—that special combination of the organic and the artificial, the mingling of lighter fluid and meat—annoyed me. I looked around and sniffed the air to see if I could detect where the smell was coming from. But I saw no clouds of smoke, no gatherings of shirtsleeves and lawn chairs, and I heard no one coughing from the inhalation of smoke. I was in bad temper because Alexandra had kicked me out, so I guess I was capable of being irritated by any activity. And in an attempt to justify my annoyance, I settled on something like this: I blamed these people, whoever they were, for having their cookout, probably their first of the season. I thought it was audacious and callous and that it signified a lack of propriety. Young girls were being murdered—how dare they pass their time in celebration with beer and barbecue? It was stupid, I know, to feel this way. If I had been walking along and been in a better mood, if I had been concentrating on Alexandra, on those parts of her that stayed with me, stayed at the edges as something finer than memory, less solid than touch—if I had been holding onto these thoughts, then my attitude would have been different. I would have smelled the grease dripping onto the white-hot charcoal and thought, how brave of them! In the midst of suffering—in the face of murder—these people continue to live their lives, to enjoy the fine spring weather, to persevere.

Better, I suppose, to let people cook their meals without the interference of interpretation.

16 April 1973, Monday

*D*uring sixth period this afternoon, I had nothing to do. I sat at the desk in a third-floor classroom, and I stared out the row of windows, looking out each window singly, seeing what kind of composition each frame created. Someone knocked, timidly, on the open door.

When I turned around, I saw a plump, older woman, probably in her fifties, standing in the doorway. She was dressed gaily, brightly. Her slacks were peach-colored, and her loud, floral-patterned silky blouse had enough colors in it to match anything. But her expression was not at all bright. Her round pie-face was, it appeared, sharpened by worry. She came forward—one step only—very hesitantly. "Excuse me," she said. Her voice was soft and high.

"Yes," I said, "what can I do for you?" She was old enough to be my mother, but, by God, she was in my territory.

"I'm sorry to bother you." She moved a few steps closer. She was bent over slightly, and it made her seem as though she were in a continual state of expectation. She gripped tightly a slip of paper and glanced at it from time to time as if it contained her reason for being there. "Do you happen to know Barbara Gerber?"

"Is she a student?"

"Yes. She's a junior."

"I'm afraid I don't. Are you trying to find her?"

"She's my daughter." I was surprised. She seemed too old, too slow, to have a daughter in high school. "I came to pick her up. I always pick her up since . . . I pick her up every day." I did not detect it at first, because her voice was so high and she spoke so softly, but her speech had some of the thickness and heaviness of an eastern European accent. That is not uncommon around here.

"Yes?" I was as pleasant as I could be, for the woman was becoming more and more agitated, and I still did not understand why she was here.

"I came to pick her up and she wasn't there. I've been waiting outside, and she never came out. I didn't know what I should do."

I knew then why she was becoming unhinged. "Have you tried the office? They could help you locate her. Maybe you just missed her." I was still somewhat puzzled. And obviously, the idea of going to the office had not come to her because she seemed surprised when I mentioned it.

She looked down at the slip of paper again. "I've got her schedule right here. I made her write it down for me." She held the paper out to me, as if it were proof of something, as if I could be convinced of something by reading it. "See, it says right here, seventh period, American Government, Room 312. That's why I came here. I waited outside in the car, and I waited in the hall. I thought maybe she had to stay after school. That's why I came up here."

I knew then what the difficulty was. It was two fifteen. The seventh-period class did not start until two thirty and would not be dismissed until three twenty. This woman was what—over an hour early? Was that possible? I looked at her wrist. She wore a watch and it told the correct time.

I told her, as gently as I could, what her mistake was, that her daughter would not be in this room for fifteen minutes and that she would be in school for over an hour. She simply stared at me for a moment, dumbfounded, unbelieving. She looked at her watch, she looked at the clock on the wall, and blushing then in full and final comprehension, she said, "I'm so sorry. I shouldn't have bothered you. I'll just wait outside." She backed out of the room, stammering apologies all the way.

How could it have happened? What had propelled her from her house with the illusion that it was time to pick up her daughter? Maybe a clock at home was fast, but still, as she sat nervously waiting in the car, she must have glanced at her watch constantly when her daughter did not appear. And did she not notice that other students were not leaving the school? As she walked through the school to my room, to Room 312, didn't she see the classrooms filled with students? What had happened to this woman? Was she so eaten by worry, by fear of what might happen to her daughter, by her desire to protect her child, that she could not tell time, that she could not see what was plainly before her, that she could no longer build a logical construct? My God, I felt worry for the woman, but she frightened me also. She scared the hell out of me.

17 April 1973, Tuesday

A rumor is going through town today, and it moves, with its speed, like a train passing at night; at every point of contact, sparks fly forth. The word is that someone has been captured. At school, in the teachers' lounge, I heard it was a transient, arrested at the bus depot and identified as the murderer by having in his possession items that belonged to the victims. I also heard, in the hall, two girls whisper a name. I did not catch the name, but from their looks and from the fact that the name was preceded by "mister," I'm guessing that they heard a teacher was arrested. That, I'm sure, was not so. That much I would have known. At the drugstore at noon to buy some aspirin, I overheard the pharmacists, and from what I could gather, they seemed to think that the arrest was of someone reasonably well known.

But in spite of the prevalence of the rumor, the general reaction seems to be, "I don't believe it." This attitude is not a shocked and relieved disbelief that the nightmare may finally be over; rather, people literally do not believe that it is so. (Of course, they continue to spread the rumor, always beginning, "I heard . . .") The unwillingness to believe may be from the lack of any official announcement. After having this go on for so long, citizens may rightly expect the end to come with fanfare, with sirens sounding the all-clear and people hesitantly stepping from their homes and blinking in the sunlight. They may expect their lives to change suddenly, to regain their appetites, to sleep soundly again. And if they believe these things, they are foolish.

I myself do not believe an arrest has been made, and I'm not sure why. I guess it simply does not *feel* like a practical rumor. Perhaps it is because the story shifts and has too much the character of a small-town rumor and has no sanction of authority. In some vain attempt at corroboration, I drove by the courthouse and jail on my way home after school. I don't know what I expected to see, perhaps a recognizable pair of hands wrapped around the bars at one of the high cell windows. I saw nothing, but others seemed to have the same idea. Traffic was unusually heavy around the courthouse, and it is not normally a busy street. And I watched, wherever I went, to see if anyone was not in his usual place, to see if the school-crossing guard was a substitute, if the radio announcer's voice was an unfamiliar one, if any of the carry-out boys at the grocery was absent.

I suppose I could have made a crusade of it and traveled around town, checking on those individuals who are, both by public consensus and by my private suspicions, prominent suspects. I could have gone to see if Leo Kuntz was behind the counter of his hardware store. Leo is a notorious voyeur, and he has been arrested, but never charged, for window-peeping. Many people find Leo threatening, but I think he is harmless. Also harmless, in my view, is Stewart Humes. Humes owns and operates a music store, and he is suspect because he is one of the town's few *obvious* homosexuals. He also wears a toupee which is even more obvious than his sexuality. But aside from setting a bad example by washing his car once a week, he too is harmless. I could have made it a point to notice if Herman, the school's aging, menacing, Germanic janitor was at work today. Herman believes that he runs the high school and that students and faculty alike exist only to make his work difficult for him.

But though Herman is sour, sullen, taciturn, hateful, and has the slumped posture and wall-eyed look that characterize those who have something to hide, I don't believe he is murderous. But lately his presence in the halls, never a calming and cheering influence, is particularly ominous. Or I could have checked to see if Broomie was sweeping the streets today. I could have called the state mental hospital and asked if Bobby Wald was still a resident. I could have gone to Sheller's Implement and asked if the owner, Del, was on the premises. (Del is my personal suspect. In the town's view, he is successful, outspoken, self-reliant, fun-loving, and rambunctious, something of a town darling. In my opinion, he is a greedy and grasping, crude, philandering bully. There is no reason he should be a suspect; I simply dislike him so much that it would give me a perverse pleasure to see him, or someone like him, arrested. I prefer his type as a suspect to those in town who are mentally infirm, harmlessly perverse, or whose sexual preferences do not conform to community standards. But I suppose we're getting into matters of taste.) I could go on like this at length, listing the names of all those who could have been arrested, all those who are suspected by me, by someone, someplace. After all this time, who has not been looked at questioningly even by friends, neighbors, or lovers?

Something else occurred to me when I was wondering if everyone were in his place today. (This begins to sound, I know, like grade-school roll call.) I wondered if others were checking to see if someone was not at his desk, behind his counter, in his truck, at his register, or at his appointed station. And when I thought of this, I came directly to my apartment, lest anyone be curious why I was not at home at the usual time. I did not want anyone thinking, even temporarily, that I might have been arrested.

Shortly after I got home (and opened my curtains and turned on the television and made myself generally conspicuous before the windows), the telephone rang. It was Mrs. Dohr, an elderly widow who lives in my building. Mrs. Dohr, who was the eminent Judge Dohr's second (and scandalous) wife, is always seen carrying a cane and an apricot-colored toy poodle (the only pet allowed in this apartment complex). I lived here for six months before I knew anything about Mrs. Dohr; Roger told me everything about her that I now know. The only words I have ever exchanged with her have been an occasional hello when we bump into each other in the parking lot, in the laundry room, or by the garbage cans. I wouldn't have thought she even knew my name.

"Mr. Leesh?" Her voice was low and confidential and she spoke rapidly. "This is Mrs. Dohr and I live on the first floor, and I just noticed that your car was in the lot, and I thought I'd give you a call. I need some information, and perhaps you can help me."

"I will if I can." I found myself becoming, as I usually do in any contact with older people, extraordinarily polite. Soon I would be playing the little boy.

"I've had my radio on all day, and they haven't said a word about it, but I heard some women at the Coffee Cup Café say that someone has been arrested. My paper hasn't come yet, but I thought you might know something since you teach at the high school."

"I don't know, Mrs. Dohr. I heard the rumor too, but I don't know if it's true. I wouldn't have any way of knowing."

"You'd think if it was so it would be on the radio and TV, wouldn't it? There isn't any reason they'd want it to be a secret, is there?" My politeness seemed to feed her aggression. Her voice began to rise as if she no longer cared who heard this conversation.

"I can't think of any. Unless they don't want to get people's hopes up." I hadn't even considered that possibility myself, not until I said it out loud.

"I don't think so. My husband was a judge, and I know something about how the minds of the police and the judiciary work." Now she spoke so loudly that she seemed to be talking long distance, trying to shout her words across miles of wire. "If they arrested somebody, they'd say so. Hell, they'd brag about it."

She was boasting herself, but I believed she knew what she was talking about. "You're probably right, Mrs. Dohr."

"You bet I'm right," she snapped. "If there isn't anything about it on the six o'clock news or in the paper, I'm going to write it off as a bad joke."

"That's best, I think."

"So. Thank you anyway, Mr. Leesh. We'll have to get together sometime and discuss this whole sordid business."

There was no conviction in her invitation, and I was grateful for that. We said good-bye.

The *Wanekia Herald* came, and I searched it carefully. Among the pages of farm news, city and county finances, weddings, engagements, and funerals, there was no mention of any arrests, and there was nothing on the evening news.

Following Mrs. Dohr's lead, I cautiously dismissed it as a false alarm.

And with that dismissal of the rumor came a feeling of relief. So help me, it is true. Although I did not believe the rumor, perhaps a part of me considered the possibility that someone had been arrested, that the murderer was in jail and would remain there so long that no one would any longer be able to remember the number of victims.

It's strange, I have always believed, with a childlike faith, that the killer would sooner or later be found out, captured, tried, convicted, and imprisoned for life. But while I have believed that, I have simultaneously and contradictorily believed that the murders would continue. Indefinitely. Infinitely. Although they have been a fact of our lives only for weeks, they have become as much a part of them as the sun rising, the spring grass growing. Like a baby left on the doorstep, we have adopted murder into our lives, accepted it, adjusted to it, fit our lives around it. How easy it has become!

And no one is worse than I am. If it had been announced on the news that the killer had been caught, would I have greeted that report with the same relief that I felt over the absence of such an announcement?

I want the murders to go on.

When I write that sentence, those seven words, even my fingers do not wish to be a part of it. They become cramped, stiff, uncooperative, as if they have been uncovered in extreme cold.

I want the murders to go on.

It must be true.

Each day, I want to rise and drive to work with the possibility that a young girl has been strangled in the building where I teach the art and craft of written communication, the reading of literature. I want women to be driven into my arms out of their fear. I want the security of an automatic topic of conversation. I want parents and old women to call me for inside information. I want all the excitement, the danger, the prestige, the intrigue—everything that makes this atmosphere so charged that it is not hard to imagine the smell of ozone.

And I see clearly now these desires within me. They are as apparent as laboratory spores—bacteria that seem to grow before our eyes.

Is this why I put these words to paper? To discover this about myself? Is this what it is for?

I had planned on calling Roger or Alexandra this evening to learn what variations of the rumor they might have heard. But I have decided not to call them. I am afraid that the quality of my voice may reveal what I know now about myself. I am afraid that an attempt to speak may be met by a base growl. I am afraid of my own voice.

A few years ago, on a summer day, I was riding with Peggy Dahl in the red Camaro convertible her father had given her for having maintained a 3.0 average throughout her sophomore year in college. In spite of the fact that we did not particularly like each other or have much in common, marriage to Peggy seemed imminent. We had gone together habitually for two years, we slept together, and marriage seemed an inevitability, something we were moving inexorably toward, like a boat drifting on a current. But all that is another story. On the day I remember, we were fighting. I do not recall what it was about but that is not surprising; we fought constantly, and when we were not fighting openly, we seethed inwardly. Anyway, on that day we were riding through a residential district, and Peggy, as she always did when she was angry, was driving too fast (which gave me something else to be mad about). As we drove, I noticed children playing on the lawns and sidewalks. I was so angry at Peggy over whatever we were fighting about, and so frustrated and perturbed over her refusal to slow down and drive sensibly, that I entertained a fantasy calculated to humble her. All right, bitch, I thought, let's have one of these children run out into the street, and at the speed you're traveling, you'll never be able to stop in time and the child will fly through the air like a balloon with the air released and you'll feel like the shit you are and I will have been right all along. . . . We came to a stop sign, and as we were stopped, I looked over to my right and saw a three- or four-year-old boy standing on the grass by the curb. There was nothing particularly endearing about the sight of him. He was dirty, runny-nosed, dressed only in shorts, and his face was smeared red, presumably from a popsicle. But he was alive, and he was there, and I realized that perhaps he was the one I was wishing into the street, that he was the sacrifice to my quarrel with Peggy, that he was the one chosen to vindicate me. The sight of him revealed to me how heinous that fantasy had been, and how awful I must have been to entertain it. But it *was* a fantasy, I rationalized. I did not truly want any children harmed. I didn't.

(The eventual disintegration of the relationship between Peggy and me probably had nothing to do with that day. Still, in my mind, I mark that day as one of discovery, as the day I recognized what we—what I—was capable of as long as we remained together, how destructive she and I could be in each other's company. We did begin to move apart. Gradually, and probably to the delight of both of us.)

The dark discovery I have made today has had the same diminishing effect on me, on my estimation of myself, as the "shock of recognition" of that summer's day.

I am in my twenty-sixth year. It is not unreasonable to expect, as statisticians and insurance-company actuaries tell us, that I may live another fifty years. And I would like to hold my life with some tenderness and with some regard. And I would like to be able to believe that there is some jeweled magnificence of spirit that the race is capable of and that I am a part of that race. But in the face of such self-knowledge as I came to today, I do not know how that is possible. I know—we all know—that the aberrant, the demented, the psychotic walk among us, but apparently I support their needs by feeding off them.

And what in my past has caused this state of mind? What has gone into my making to cause me to want the perpetuation of murder? Is violence some irresistible lure for me? Am I attracted to it like an insect drawn to the brightness of a street light?

I am a passive individual. I am unnerved by the threat of the mildest conflict, and the closest I have come to a personal act of violence as an adult occurred when I became involved in a shoving match during a college intramural basketball game. As a boy, I had what I believe would prove to be an average number of fights, and like the pushing of that basketball game, they came through explosions of temper. I had no great love for bloodying noses, skinning my knuckles on other boys' teeth, or trying to bend limbs with hammerlocks and half-nelsons. And I did not like having these inflicted upon me. They were, however, a necessity of childhood; on occasion, push *did* come to shove. (And in writing about and remembering those skirmishes does my pulse quicken?)

But I have not, have *not* believed that my redemption lies in aggression.

Perhaps violence has some attraction for me because of that normal, average boyhood? I may be what I am by the youthful gunfights and ambushes that I engaged in, those battles in which the enemy fell as bloodlessly as when shot by Roy Rogers and John Wayne.

My father used to take me hunting. I remember so well that smell of the oil that came from the shotguns that lay on the floor of the back seat. I remember the bumpy ride across the rutted, harrowed fields, the scrape of stubble along the bottom of the car, the dusty warmth of the October sun, the ooze of the marshes and sloughs. And I remember how I hated the sight of the dead birds, how a dull glaze settled over every part of the bird that had once shined or glistened—the half-opened eyes of grouse and partridge, the green heads of mallards, all the rusty colors of pheasant. I remember how their mouths set barely open, as if, in death, they held something gently in their beaks. But until the guns were fired, and the feathers flew from the birds like the blown heads of dandelions, and they fell as surely as stones, until then everything was fine, delicious anticipation. We walked through the fields of corn stalks or we sat in the marsh weeds and rushes, and we waited for the honking or quacking or the sudden whir and clatter of something breaking into flight. And the shotguns boomed as if they were firing themselves. Then, standing over the kill, half deaf to the silence around us, the excitement was over, the sadness or the sickness or the disgust arranged itself on me like a coat.

Is this what I am attracted to here? The promise of the explosion, the anticipation of death?

I am not at ease with confession.

Psychology was never my field. And this is murder, murder by the laying on of hands, murder bound up in something sexual. I should leave John Wayne and my father and this country and shotguns out of it. What I mean to say, I suppose, is that I am unable to solve this riddle of my own life, that I am too stupid, lazy, or cowardly to try further. Living here has made a celebrity of me and has rippled the calm, dull surface of my life. For now, I will leave it at that. It is bad enough.

Tonight, when I lie in my bed, unable to sleep because I

do not grieve over a murderer loose in this town, tonight I will close my eyes tightly and try to see the faces of young girls. These faces will belong to the girls whom I see in the building where I work, on the streets where I live. Like a boy and his adolescent fantasies, I will imagine them as vividly as I can. Behind my closed eyes, I will see their awkward smiles, their clumsily rouged cheeks, their eyelashes as fine as feathers, the light down above their upper lips. I will see their crooked teeth braced together with silver and wire, their foreheads and chins pitted with acne. I will see the structure of those young faces still finding their final shape. I will see their eyes, those clear eyes that can be so calm you think nothing could possibly move behind them and can so suddenly twitch into fear. And I will ask myself if I wish to be responsible for the meanest of those young lives by wishing the murders to continue.

18 April 1973, Wednesday

I do not wish to write today. If I did not have the force of sixteen previous entries pushing me, I would not pick up the pen.

Gusty winds all day. The sky would be filled with clouds, the sun would be blocked, and the air would be cold. At one time all the clouds seemed to be pointed toward the northwest, as if something below that horizon were sucking them downward. Then, the wind would scatter the clouds, pushing them away as quickly as if they were stage scenery controlled by ropes and pulleys. And with the sun out, the temperature seemed to jump at least ten degrees. On days such as this I love to watch, from indoors, the motion of high grass and the tops of trees. That shimmering movement looks as if everything is under water.

But these are descriptions of the weather.

With the exception of students, I spoke to no one today. And I spoke little in the classroom. I busied them with an in-class writing assignment.

All day I have had trouble catching my breath. It feels as though I have something sharp, like a fishbone, caught in my throat, but it is further down, into my chest, close to the heart. And I feel pressure on my chest. I have read in psychology texts that these are the physical symptoms that frequently overcome an individual who has an inability to shed tears. I don't know what to think, I haven't eaten fish in over a week.

If we continue to use the fire metaphor for the rumor of the arrest of a suspect, today it may be said that the wind has shifted, the fire burned back on itself, and is now extinguished because of lack of fuel. Maybe people are still considering the rumor as a possibility, I don't know. But I heard no conversation that could have been about that, and I saw no gleams in any eyes that could have been attributed to that rumor being alive. In short, nothing was in the air today; after this long, one can sense when something is about.

Late this afternoon, the wind blew in a solid block of clouds that show no sign of blowing out again. Probably colder weather coming in from Canada or the Dakotas. It looks now as if it's going to rain.

This is enough. There are limits. One should say only so much about the texture of the sky, in spite of the relief it might offer.

19 April 1973, Thursday

*B*rown hair," Roger said.

"What?" We were sitting alone in the Art Room after school. Roger was cleaning up some of the mess left by his classes during the day. Notice I say some of the mess. He likes the room to look, as he says, as if people really worked in there. It does. Worked, played, ate, slept, threw up, played handball, made pizza.

"Brown hair. All of the girls have had brown hair. Long brown hair. You haven't noticed?"

"I haven't. I mean, should I? What's to notice? Most of the girls in this school have long brown hair." I was being truthful; it did not seem to me a significant discovery.

"Right. And it's probably just coincidence. Or the law of averages, or whatever governs this kind of thing. But maybe we've got a goddamn brown-hair freak on our hands. Who knows?"

It was the first time I had talked to Roger since he and Bonnie were at my apartment, and I was grateful for the topic of conversation. (Haven't I said it can make matters easy?) I was afraid we were going to have to go back over some of the intimacies of that night.

"A brown-hair fetishist? That's one for the psychology journals. Or *Police Gazette*."

"Scoff if you will." He pointed one finger in the air, as if he were an orator trying to indicate emphasis. "But what common feature among our victims has inspired a new fad here at Wanekia High?"

"Okay. Enlighten me."

"Blond hair. Now *that* you must have noticed. At least four girls, formerly brunettes, have bleached their hair."

"No, I hadn't noticed that either."

"Jesus. For an observant person there sure is a helluva lot you don't see. What do you do to keep from taking in the world around you?"

"I spend a lot of time in the bathroom."

"That's bad. Causes hemorrhoids. Or blindness. Either way, not a good idea."

"Yeah. Enough about my welfare, tell me about this blondness that's going around." I was very skeptical, but I was becoming interested.

"Two of the girls in my last class, Sharon Gallup and Joyce Tyre, have become blonds in the last week or so. In fact, now that I think about it, they've cut their hair too. Both of them had long brown hair. Now they've got it short and blond. Actually, it upsets my sense of color to call it 'blond.' It's more like piss-yellow. I think they must have used food coloring. And Sharon looked *so* good before. Do you know her?"

"I think I had her last year."

"How was it?"

Roger is as capable of crudity as Gary Clubb, and I had just fallen into what is one of the commonest teaching pun-traps. You'd think after this length of time, that I would know enough to avoid the forms of the verb "to have" as shorthand for "teaching a student in a class."

"It wasn't bad. But it was distracting with the other twenty-nine students in the room."

"See, that's what I mean, Pete, you've got to overcome

your goddamn inhibitions. Stop being such a private person."

"I'm trying."

"Christ, yellow hair. It makes me sick just to think about it. Have you seen that body she has? Indecent. And an outrageous set of tits."

"If you go for excess."

"I do, I do."

Roger and I have somewhat different attitudes toward female students. Although he knows as well as I do that students are as untouchable as certain castes in India, as Gila monsters, as Elliot Ness's agents, he simply cannot resign himself to the fact. Placing young females before him is, in his own words, like putting a reformed alcoholic to work in a liquor store. On the occasions when he has been called upon to chaperone dances, he looks upon the assignment as a peculiarly concocted form of torture. It is one thing, he says, to look at these girls in their desks; to watch them dance is agony. As I said, my feeling about female students is different. I *notice* what they look like, but their appearance, their presence does not affect me in quite the same way. My attitude is not exactly paternal, not exactly protective, but these factors are probably involved. I am, finally, I suppose you could say, disinterested. Besides, Roger exaggerates their pulchritude. This is a small town; the number of real beauties is small (and dwindling all the time). There is a large body of sort of second-rank attractive girls. They are nothing exceptional, but if you were driving all night and pulled into a truck-stop café at three A.M. in western Nebraska, and one of these girls was your waitress, you would find her pleasantly attractive.

Another thing. I always find Roger's remarks about his girl students in somewhat questionable taste (and in recklessly poor judgment should the wrong person overhear—Mal Coxe, the typing teacher, for instance), but at this time, with what is happening now, it becomes especially dangerous, unsettling, and disturbing beyond simple bounds of propriety.

"Let's return to your brown-hair theory if we may," I said.

"It's not really a theory, and it's not very elaborate. Nothing fancy at all, in fact. Just based on a little observation and some common sense. I guess the girls around here think there's some chance that the common denominator among the dead girls has been their long brown hair. And they're trying to remove themselves from any potential-victim list by bleaching their hair. Either that or they're after that California-living-in-the-sun look."

"That's more plausible. You don't believe it, do you? Does anyone?"

"That these girls have been killed because of their hair color? I don't, and these girls probably don't either. But hell, why take a chance? Better safe than, and all that."

"I guess maybe I noticed that all the girls were brunettes, now that you mention it, but I didn't attach any special significance to it. I still don't, but . . ."

"My dear Watson," Roger said in his best British accent, which was terrible, "how many times have I told you to overlook nothing? The tiniest of clues may lead to the culprit."

"Spare me, please."

"Besides, this is as believable as that crazy goddamn rumor that was going around a few days ago. That one about someone being arrested. Some people will eat anything." Roger stacked crude, misshapen bowls, pots, and vases onto a high shelf. He handled them so roughly that it seemed he knew about some special property they had, that they could not be broken if one handled them in a peculiarly rough way. When he was done, he turned to me and wiped his hands on his long gray apron, the apron that was so spotted, smudged, and streaked with paints, glazes, and clay that I expected to see his hands dirtier than when they went on. "Do you want to go get a beer?"

"I thought you'd never ask," I said. "What the hell do you think I was waiting around for?"

As we were going down the steps to the back door and the parking lot, we were stopped by someone shouting,

"Wait! Wait!" The shouts were accompanied by the clunky tapping of a woman running in high heels. We stopped by the heavy glass door and waited, looking backward.

Coming down the steps, panting, one hand over her heart was Thelma Engerman.

"I'm so glad I caught you," she said. I automatically put the word "boys" on the end of her sentence.

"Is there something wrong?" Roger asked. He had a startled, worried look in his eyes, and he was tense, as if he were ready to act.

"Oh, my God, no," Thelma said, blushing. "I'm sorry. I didn't think. I'm always doing something like that. I just wanted to talk to you." Again, I added "boys."

I was envious and chagrined at that moment. Like Roger, I thought—was afraid—that something had happened, but I doubt that I would have been able to marshal my muscles into any positive action. If Thelma had yelled "Help! A girl is being strangled!" two things likely would have happened to me: I would have been paralyzed, rooted to the spot in fear, panic, and confusion; or I would have split neatly in two, half of me wanting to run out the door, get into my car, and drive as far away as possible, and half of me wanting to go help. But Roger's attitude at that instant had no trace of hesitancy or uncertainty. There was no question about it, he had it all over me, and he, and I imagine almost everyone else, would certainly score much higher than I in the keeping-a-cool-head-and-springing-into-action crisis test. I don't mean to make a joke of it. I was not proud of myself. Another illusion that I entertained about myself, that I was capable of heroism, of split-second instinctive rescues or cool-headed emergency treatment, went flying out the window like a canary escaped from the cage. No, children in the paths of runaway trucks, drowning swimmers, accident victims needing someone to apply pressure to spurting arteries, or young girls screaming and struggling in the grip of a murderer could not depend on me for help. It was not pleasant to admit, but it was very unlikely that I would ever be cited for bravery. Roger, on the other hand, rose in my estimation. He had never seemed the type, but maybe he was of the kind who fell on grenades, who got written up in *Boys' Life* as a brave, quick-thinking "Scout in Action."

Roger relaxed visibly. "Well, you sure as hell got our attention. What's on your mind?"

"Really," Thelma said, "I didn't mean to alarm you, and I apologize. What I wanted, actually, was to extend an invitation. I'm having some people over this Saturday night, just to talk things over, maybe have some wine. Would you two like to come?"

Roger said, "Talk things over? What's it going to be—a meeting or a party?"

"Oh, goodness, it's not going to be a meeting. I didn't mean to make it sound like that. It's just that 'party' sounds so—so frivolous. Noisemakers and hats and streamers . . . It won't be anything like that."

Thelma is the assistant principal; if this school possesses any of the attributes of a quality educational institution, it is because of her. Proctor handles most of the "business" of dealing with the school board, juggling finances, speaking at PTA meetings, and lately, acting as a liaison between the high school and the police and the press. He maintains a high profile; Thelma handles almost all relationships between administrators and faculty and students. In short, she does all the work. She also teaches, wherever and whenever any understaffing occurs, and she has taught everything from math to home economics. She is undoubtedly underpaid, but she receives some thanks in the form of admiration and respect from students and colleagues. And of course when she retires, they will name something after her—an addition to the high school, an auditorium, or an elementary school. I have never heard anyone speak ill of her. *Everyone* likes Thelma Engerman.

And why should they not? She is, besides being a hard worker, fair-minded, kind, gentle, friendly, generous, cheerful, honest, understanding, and a score of other adjectives.

And as a bonus, as a sort of overkill on the part of the gods, she is pleasant-looking as well. She is, I'd guess, between forty-five and fifty, tall, rosy-cheeked, and there is a perpetual smile on her wide, open face. She has good legs, a narrow waist, large breasts, broad shoulders, and big hands. She is able to suggest that she is prim, and at the same time sensual—a kind of chaste voluptuousness. I've never seen her wear anything but very proper skirts and blouses. One would say that she is unmarried, or single anyway. The way the story goes, she was married to an alcoholic, a man who mistreated her horribly. This was all many years ago, at least twenty. He finally left her (for another woman, so one story goes), and he never returned. Someone once said that he was killed in an auto accident, but apparently there is some question about that. No one ever says anything about a divorce to make their separation permanent and official. I would be far from the best authority on this, but I suppose there has not been a man in her life since her husband left. They had no children, which I always thought was unfortunate; Thelma seems maternal, and that's why, since I am younger than she, I always feel that she wants to address me as "boy" or "sonny." Or maybe she's been teaching for so long and is so dedicated to her profession that everyone is turning into "boys" and "girls" for her.

Roger looked at me, apparently waiting for me to acknowledge the invitation. If I could not be braver than he, I could at least be more polite. "I'd like to come," I said, trying to make it clear that I was only speaking for myself. "What time? Can I bring anything? Anyone?"

"You can bring a date if you wish, but it's certainly not necessary. It's up to you. And I'll furnish the wine and light refreshments. Why don't you come about eight?" She looked at Roger and smiled harder, waiting for his response.

"A party sounds terrific, Thelma. Just what this town needs." I could not tell if he was being sarcastic, though I think not. "I'll be there."

"Wonderful. I'm so glad you'll both be there. I so rarely

see either of you around school, so you're the last ones to be invited. If I didn't catch you today, I was going to call you tonight. I don't like to wait until the last minute on these things, because people make other plans." Thelma is a marvelous person, but she does have a tendency to run on a bit. "So I'll see you Saturday night if I don't see you sooner." She began to walk away, still talking. "And I'm so sorry if I startled you." Boys.

Roger poked me in the side. "How about that? A party! And what was I saying just the other night? All *right!*"

"And with free drinks yet."

We drove out to the south edge of town, to the bar in the Star-Lite Motel. Both the motel and the bar are of reasonably high quality—for a town of this size (the closest the community comes to fine accommodations and an elegant eating and drinking establishment—if the President were to come to Wanekia, he would be housed and fed at the Star-Lite), but the location is definitely not a plus. It is on the strip of highway dominated by fast-food franchises. Next door is the Colonel Sanders' Kentucky Fried Chicken restaurant, and the greasy smell of the deep-fat fryers permeates the air constantly. As a result, any trip to the Star-Lite is marred because you either become ravenous for fried chicken or become nauseated by the smell. I decided I'd buy a small bucket of chicken on my way home.

The bar was dark, the tables small. The seating was awkward; each table was kept as far as possible from the center of the tiny room. The effect of this was the feeling that your table was out of place, that your back was toward the direction you should be facing. To add to this muddle were the three or four alcoves that made it seem as if someone had once tried, unsuccessfully and repeatedly, to tunnel out of the place. At one end of the room, on a six-inch platform, was a piano. Appearing there nightly was DeDe Frisco, singing all your old favorites and all the songs that were going to be your new favorites.

As we sat down, I made a mental survey and tried to

figure out if Wanekia had any bars I had not yet visited. I could only think of two: a so-called "Indian" bar on the east end of Main, and a crossroads bar right outside town at the intersection of Highway 83 and County Trunk A, out by the snowmobile factory and patronized mostly by farm workers and the factory employees. I think I'll check the Yellow Pages to see if I'm missing any. Here, each table had a small candle in a net-covered glass. The barmaid lit the candle when she brought our drinks. In keeping with the high-class surroundings, we decided to have hard liquor instead of beer, and I ordered a Scotch and soda, Roger a gin and tonic.

"Do you want to hear another theory?" Roger asked, after our drinks were set down.

"Sure. Go ahead and make me feel like an even bigger idiot."

"Okay. This particular hypothesis is popular with a group that shares a certain political philosophy. A minority philosophy in most of the country, but here, in the heart of the heartland, surrounded by all this corn and wheat and self-reliance, it's stronger. A more dominant political persuasion."

"Could you be a little more elliptical? All this forthrightness is hard to handle."

"Shit, I was just getting warmed up."

"Get to the point."

"My," Roger said, flopping his wrist and lisping like someone's cheap idea of a homosexual, "aren't we touchy today."

I was. I hadn't begun the day so irritable and snappish, but two things had brought on this mood. First, I wished I had noticed for myself the "brown-hair factor" (as it was coming to be known in my mind) and the subsequent switches to blond. At one time (in these pages? I can't remember and am too lazy to leaf backward), I prided myself on my gifts of observation, my skills at putting things together from clues that were overlooked by others. What have I noticed since the similarity of names? Nothing. God (and everyone else) knows what has escaped my notice.

When I was in junior high school, an older man in his sixties

lived down the street from my parents. He wore western clothing, boots, shirts with pearl snaps, and a narrow-brimmed
Stetson. He had been a rancher and livestock dealer at one
time. He was a big man, barrel-chested, and a beer gut hung
over his fancy belt buckles. Anyway, for as long as I could
remember, he would stop at our house, unannounced, on a
Sunday afternoon, for coffee and talk about the weather,
crops, or politics with my father. He would stay for about
an hour, and when he left, he'd always say, "I gotta go. I
can hear the old lady yelling for me." His name was Lee
Schuster, but my sister, my friends, and I called him "Lee,"
at his request. Perhaps I missed Lee's visits for quite a time
or perhaps I took him so for granted that I did not notice
him any more than I noticed furniture or the front lawn.
When I saw him one afternoon he was changed; he was
gray and gaunt, stooped over, his barrel chest was sunken,
and the flesh of his belly was slack. I asked my sister,
"What's with Lee? Is he on a diet or something?" She looked
at me incredulously and impatiently. "Are you serious?"
she said. "He's got cancer. He's dying. He's got six more
weeks. Where have you been? God, how can anyone be so
dumb?" The news withered me. I liked Lee, and of course,
I wanted him to live, but what stunned me more than anything else was the fact that he (someone I knew) had been
dying—and I had *not noticed.* Later, when I was in high
school, and a friend committed suicide, it seemed that everyone expected it, that his act surprised no one. No one except
me. (Although their grief was more demonstrable than mine.
That did not escape my notice.) So what *do* I notice? Am I
the worst person possible to be keeping this record?

"Sorry," I said. "Go ahead. Lay it on me."

"All right. Now as I was saying, this theory is popular
with our right-wing politicos, you know, Dr. Trent and Betty
Berdor—the John Birch faction. They think the murders have
been committed not by a crazed individual but by a gang."

"Oh, Jesus."

"That's right. They think a gang of students is responsible.
And how do these gangs of perverted, murdering young

ruffians develop? They get started because the schools are not doing their job."

"Huh? You want to run that by me again?"

"Hell, you know what it is. It's the same old shit. Schools have become too permissive, they no longer provide discipline, they don't teach the old tried-and-true values, blah-blah—that line. These people see four kids smoking outside school, and they think it's a sure sign of the imminent fall of America."

"But still, why a gang?"

"Well, aside from the fact that they think this generation is going to hell in a handcart, you know, 'all that pot and long hair and fuckin' right out in the open' "—this last he said in his best Southern-redneck twang—"they have some practical reasons as well. They figure one person couldn't overpower a girl completely, not without her screaming and putting up a fight that would make a helluva lot of noise and bring some help."

"That at least has some merit. But I'm not convinced." Nor did I want to be. The thought of a lone, deranged, psychotic killer is horrible enough. The idea of an entire gang of murderers, a cult of killers, is too chilling to contemplate even momentarily. The memory of the Manson family—that terror that spread inland like an invasion force—is still too fresh.

"No, Jesus, neither am I. If for no other reason, no members of a gang could keep that kind of secret. But shit, those folks want it to be true because it would reinforce their prejudices."

"Haven't you been telling me to rule out nothing? To keep an open mind?"

"Sure. But make sure your motives are pure. You don't want someone to be guilty just to prove you're right about the murderer—murderers—do you? It's not revenge we're after. Right?"

The conversation had an odd tone to it, and at first I could not identify what that strange quality was. Then I knew. Roger was doling out the morality lesson; *he* was lecturing *me* on matters of conscience. I was supposed to be—and almost always was—the stiff-necked arbiter of decorum and right living. It was all right for him to advise, badger, bait, and cajole me about my rigidity, my failure to expunge from my behavior those elements that Roger would see as repressed, codified, Victorian, conservative. But it was up to me to be the guardian of the "correct," the tasteful, the moral. And now he was educating me on the decency of motive, the purity of heart. And how little he knew of how well warranted his teaching was, how deserving I was of instruction.

The door opened, and Ed Bender, the Wanekia Warriors' football coach, entered and sat down at the bar. I was, frankly, surprised. It was all right for Roger and me, disreputable low-life that we were, to spend our after-teaching hours in the cups, but it was not all right for Coach Bender. He belonged at home, mowing his lawn, trimming his shrubbery, playing catch with his sons, diagraming plays for the upcoming football season (assuming there will be a season).

As discreetly as I could, I mentioned to Roger how the sight of Ed, alone at the bar with his bourbon and water, shocked me. I wondered if he were meeting someone.

Roger laughed out loud, and I signaled him to keep quiet. "Are you shitting me?" he said, still too loud for my comfort.

"No, why?"

"He's a lush." I winced when he said it, sure that Ed could hear us. He was whispering, but Roger's whisper is louder than many regular speaking voices. "There's a lot of places where you might be surprised to see him but not here. He's got it bad. I teach in the same room, right after his World History class, at ten o'clock every morning. When I sit at the desk, the fumes are still so strong you could light them. At ten in the fucking morning. Incredible."

"Wow, yeah, that's having it bad. I had no idea."

Roger reached over and pinched my cheek. "That's right,

baby. You never do. You know what's driving him to drink?''

"He hasn't had a winning season in six years, but I don't suppose that's it, is it?''

"Were it that simple. Do you know his wife?''

"I know who she is.''

"She's never made a pass at you?''

"No.''

"Are you sure?''

"I'd know if she had.''

"I'm not so sure. But you do possess that quality that she finds so irresistible—you wear pants. Get the picture?''

"Right. It's the old lonely-coach's-wife routine. He's too busy patting his players on the ass to spend any time at home keeping his wife happy. Come on. This is like a movie I saw once. More than once. More than one movie, in fact.''

"So don't believe it. I don't give a shit. Come on, let's go say hello to good old Ed.'' Roger began to walk over to the bar. I was afraid of what he might say, of how he might embarrass me, but I followed him because I thought it might not be as bad if I were there.

Roger slid onto the stool next to Ed, and I stood next to Roger. "Hey, Ed,'' Roger said, slapping a hand on his shoulder. "How's it going?''

Ed turned slowly, not in the least startled by Roger's sudden appearance at his side. "Well, what do you say. Sit down and have a drink.'' He waved a heavy, thick hand at the row of empty stools beyond Roger.

"Thanks,'' Roger said, "but we've had our ration.''

"I'm just having a quick one on the way home.'' He was not apologizing or excusing himself. He was simply stating a fact. "That school is so goddamn depressing lately it gets to you. Hard to leave it behind at the end of the day.'' Ed's voice is, simultaneously, soft, deep, and loud.

"You said it,'' I agreed. I jumped in quickly as if to make my own excuse for him, to say I don't blame you, it's been a hard day, we're all entitled to a drink now and then. I like Ed. I didn't want him to think I knew his secret, if indeed it was much of a secret any longer. And I didn't give a damn if his teams always had losing seasons. He seemed to care about his players, he never went in for locker-room histrionics, and he relied more on strategy than emotional upheaval for his team's successes, what few they had. Besides, Ed liked to teach as much as he liked to coach—even if he was as unproductive in the classroom as on the athletic field.

"Has George Hall picked a school yet?" I asked. I thought Ed might feel comfortable with the safe subject of football.

"Hell, no. And it's probably too late by now. He should have signed a letter of intent long ago and made his application and all the rest of that good stuff. He hasn't done a damn thing. And he could have his pick of schools."

"Is he leaning toward a particular school?"

"Yep. Mankato. He wants to be close to home. I told him, I said, George, the U. of M. is close to home. But he said that was too big. But lately he's been making sounds like he doesn't even want to go to school, like he's not even planning on it anymore. That would be a waste. I tell you, he is a strange boy. I'm fond of him, but I sure as hell can't figure him out."

"Ed," Roger said, "are you going to Thelma's party this weekend?"

Again I winced. Such a question was, to me, unthinkably risky. What if Ed weren't invited? He would now know that he had been overlooked, and inevitably, he would be hurt. What could be gained by such an insensitive question? I would never ask such a thing.

And what would I lose by not asking such a question? Only a chance at a shared experience, an acknowledged commonality. Ed said to Roger, "I wouldn't miss it. Maybe it will be good for folks to get together. We'll see you there."

We walked out into the sunlight and into the smell of the fried chicken. The smell was so thick and so strong that it seemed to congeal around us. I had no appetite. The bubbles of the soda were forcing their way out of me in quick, hic-coughing belches, and the Scotch and the sunlight combined to give me the headaching feeling that was like inhaling turpentine fumes.

As I drove home, I kept thinking, I should be doing *something*. I should be investigating these murders, probing them, anything. And I should notice something. I should notice something more than the distance that falls between me and the rest of the human race.

20 April 1973, Friday

Alexandra and I went to a movie tonight. That's not exactly accurate. I saw Alexandra at lunch today, and over the meatless spaghetti, limp carrots, and warm milk, I asked her if she'd like to go to a movie. She accepted but with reservation. She couldn't be ready in time for the seven o'clock feature (since the murders, neither of the town's two theaters—owned by the same man—remains open for a nine o'clock second show), she had something she had to take care of, but she said she would meet me at the theater.

"That's all right," I said. "I'll wait for you. I don't mind coming in late."

"God, don't be ridiculous. There's no sense in us both missing part of it. I'll meet you there. What I have to do shouldn't take long."

"Maybe we should try another night. There's nothing that says we've got to go tonight."

"Now, I *want* to go. I mean it. I think it would be nice. I haven't been to a movie in months."

Neither had I, so I sat in the darkened theater—on the left side, toward the back, just where we had arranged to meet in advance—and waited. I have never, in all of my twenty-six years, gone to a movie alone. I'm not exactly certain why. I guess it goes back to my adolescence when solitary moviegoing was, to my friends and me, an activity only for the unpopular, the lonely, the pathetic. Anyway, I have always thought automatically of going to the movie as something—like dancing, tennis, baseball, or lovemaking—that is to be engaged in by two or more. And tonight, I didn't want anyone to think that I was there alone. I carefully draped my jacket over the seat next to me, trying to make it plain that that space was "saved," only temporarily unoccupied.

Alexandra came in about twenty minutes into the main feature. She sat down heavily in the seat next to me, put her feet on the back of the seat ahead of her, leaned over to me, and breathlessly, gaily, whispered, "Sorry I'm late. What'd I miss?"

I hate to summarize the plots of novels or the story lines of films. I have a fairly high regard for detail, so I hate to leave anything out, yet I know the person who wants the summary is interested in only the bare bones of the narrative.

"How those guys got there," I said.

"And where are they?"

"In a boat. On an ocean. Actually, you haven't missed much."

"Can we stay for the part I missed?"

"There isn't going to be any, remember?"

"That's right. I forgot. Damn it."

If having missed part of the film bothered Alexandra, she did not show it. She talked constantly, joking about what was going on up on the screen, giving new, ridiculous readings to every serious line the actors spoke. When she was not laughing at the movie, she was making fun of a couple sitting two rows in front of us. They had their arms around each other, and they wriggled and squirmed in their seats in such a way that considerably more had to be happening than what we could see from where we were.

"Do you want to do that?" Alexandra whispered, referring to the writhing couple.

"Nah. That guy looks pretty big. He'd probably kill me."

Alexandra elbowed me in the ribs. "Boo! Have you no shame? No pride?"

"Sorry, but I've been waiting all my life for a chance to use that line. I couldn't help myself."

"Let's do *something*," she said softly. "I've got an idea. I read this in a novel. We get a box of popcorn, and we open the bottom. Then you unzip your pants, and we put the box of popcorn on your lap. And I pretend I'm eating popcorn, and . . ."

"Wait a minute. Do you pretend you're eating popcorn from your hand or right out of the box? And is this *buttered* popcorn?"

"Pick, pick. Don't you just want to try something?"

"Maybe later. And I want to speak to you about your reading habits. What's the name of this novel—*Hot and Buttery?*"

"It was a good book, really." Then Alexandra pointed to an older couple sitting a few seats over in the row ahead of us. They were staring sternly at us. We shut up, slumped down, and watched the movie.

Or pretended to watch. Alexandra continued to act up. She pulled my arm over to her side and pressed it against her breast. She pushed her knee against mine. She moved her hand up and down the inside of my thigh. And she continued to giggle quietly at what were supposed to be dramatic, suspenseful moments of the film. But all this playfulness, this girlish exuberance seemed to be displaced. Her good spirits, I felt, had nothing to do with being in the darkened theater. It was not exactly like laughter at a funeral, but I thought nevertheless that I was in the presence of a similarly inappropriate response.

And I didn't care. In fact, I loved it. The two of us, nuzzling, stroking, squeezing, and petting each other, created a picture that was so adolescent, so sleazily, torpidly romantic that I wished someone (besides the annoyed older couple) would see us, someone who would see us and say, "My God, look at them. They can't keep their hands off each other—carrying on like animals in heat."

It ended as quickly, as reasonlessly, as it began. Alexandra changed quite abruptly. She slumped over her side of her chair, away from me, pulled her hands back through her hair and held them there, and withdrew into herself as surely as if she had been wrapped in a blanket. She stared at the screen. The change in her was so complete that I thought the smell of her was different. She had, when she sat down, given off the faint, sweet-smelling aroma of the mixture of perfume and wine. Now the smell, it seemed, had turned sour, into some peculiar combination of sulfur and brass. It was not a real scent that came to me but an essence, something more of the mind than of the senses.

I leaned over to her. "Are you all right? Is something wrong?"

"It's okay," she said. "I'll be all right in a minute."

Another five or ten minutes passed, and obviously she was still not all right. She became pale, so pale that the colors from the movie seemed to reflect against her pallor, giving her a ghostly, flickering look. Then, she sat up abruptly and began to rise from her seat.

"Peter, I've got to get some air. It's so stuffy in here."

"Are you okay? Can I come with you?"

She put her hand on my shoulder and gently pressed me into my seat. "No, I'll be okay. I'll be back in a few minutes. Just watch the movie. You can tell me what I've missed."

I couldn't concentrate on the film. She left so quickly that I thought perhaps she was sick to her stomach, that she had to get out before she threw up. While she was gone, I kept looking backward, hoping to see her shadowy form coming down the aisle. For a moment, I fantasized that she was not going to return. I imagined that she was out in the lobby, phoning another man and asking him to rescue her from an evening of misery. Shortly, he would drive up, screeching his brakes in front of the theater, and Alexandra would run out, jump into the car and slide next to him, and together they would drive away. Shit, I thought, I'm going to leave this theater as alone as I came.

She returned when I was not looking, and she glided quickly and noiselessly to her seat. She must not have been sick to her stomach, I figured, since she smelled of tobacco and had obviously gone out for a cigarette. She seemed better, but she did not touch me.

"Are you okay?" I asked.

"Yes. I just couldn't breathe. I'm all right now."

But obviously she was not. Soon she began to fidget, shifting nervously back and forth like a child trapped in a church pew on Sunday morning. Then she stopped watching the movie and stared at the floor. I wanted to ask her what was wrong and to insist upon an answer. But I could not. I was afraid she would tell me and that somehow I would be involved in her response, that *I* was what was wrong. I did not even look directly at her but stole furtive glances at her when I thought she would not notice. Gradually she stopped squirming. She stretched out her legs as far as the narrow row of theater seats would allow, she rested her arms and hands limply on the arm rests, and she tilted her head back. The attitude was one of relaxation, but it was false—the pinned butterfly, frozen and open-winged. She was making an attempt to compose herself. Occasionally, I could hear her take a deep breath and let it out slowly.

Finally she looked at me and said, "Peter, I'm sorry, but I've got to get out. I really can't take it any longer."

Rather than ask questions, rather than have her tell me to stay, that she didn't want me to miss the movie, I simply took her hand, grabbed my jacket, and led her from the theater. There was, I'd guess, between fifteen minutes and a half hour left of the film.

When I entered the theater, there was some daylight left, and the sky, to my recollection, had been clear. Now it was dark, and while we were inside, there had been a rain shower. The pavement was dry where we stood beneath the theater marquee, but everywhere else the sidewalks and the streets were wet and glistening and reflected the flashing traffic lights, the rows of neon from the theater and the other stores and businesses. The cars driving by swished through the water still standing in the street. For some reason, the scene cheered me, and standing there, I had the tiniest seizure of elation. The emotion was not one of unqualified good spirits, for along the edges of this feeling was an inexplicable tinge of sorrow and loss.

"Must have been a cloudburst," I said to Alexandra.

She leaned back against the building and lit a cigarette. She was relaxed now. Whatever had been bothering her seemed to dissipate in the fresh, cool, damp evening air.

"Oh, Peter," she said, "I can always count on you to talk about the weather."

"What does that mean?" I was curious, but I felt too good to allow myself to be angered by the remark.

"Nothing. Forget it. I'm sorry I fucked up the movie for you. I'm okay now. Do you want to go back in? I'm going to stay out here, but you can go watch the end if you want to."

"No, that's all right. It was really a dog anyway." I didn't tell her that walking out of a movie before its conclusion was another first for me. "But I wish you'd tell me what was wrong."

"I'll tell you over at my place. I've got a couple bottles of decent wine. What do you say, big boy?"

"I had a friend in high school who said his greatest fantasy was to have a girl call him 'big boy.' And mean it. There were some additional lurid elements involved in this fantasy, but what set it apart was the 'big boy' bit."

"This isn't another one of those 'I-have-this-friend-who' stories, is it?"

"No. Nothing like that. I've always thought 'big boy' was a designation best left to hamburgers. And football players. And porno movie stars."

After agreeing to meet at Alexandra's, we set out in opposite directions—she to the Red Owl parking lot and I to a space in front of the Elks Club. As I was driving to Alexandra's, I had this feeling that I was back in those high school days when, after working furiously all night long at the dance to pick up a certain girl, I struck out because she had her own car or because she came with the girls. I followed Alexandra closely—the private eye determined not to lose his prey. I didn't care who knew I was tailing her.

Alexandra's apartment seemed more barren than ever, but as I looked around, I couldn't see that anything had been subtracted since I had been there last. She brought out two glasses and a bottle of red wine. I sat backward on the single chair, and she sat on the floor. It was an interesting seating arrangement. As long as someone took the chair, it was certain to be a submissive-dominant arrangement. Someone talked down, someone looked up—to speak, to be patted, to be scratched behind the ears. If I remember correctly, the last time I was there it was my turn on the floor.

"Are you going to Thelma's tomorrow night?" Alexandra asked.

"Yeah. I was going to ask you about that. Would you like to go?"

"Can't. I told Jean and Bonnie I'd go with them. We're going out for dinner first. Sort of girls' night out. Maybe I can meet you there, and we can work something out?"

So why did you bring it up, I thought. "Maybe. I guess I'll go over with Roger."

"Sure, and maybe Roger and Bonnie and you and I can do something afterward."

She obviously knew about Roger and Bonnie long before I. "We'll see," I said cautiously. "But stop changing the subject. What was wrong in the movie tonight?"

"The acting was lousy, the story was trite and sentimental, the direction was shitty . . ."

"And I didn't buy you any popcorn. I know all about it. Come on, tell me."

"I don't know. I told you, it was stuffy in there, and I couldn't breathe. I had a couple glasses of wine before the movie, and I guess they got to me. I just didn't feel very well." She looked up and away and calculatedly shook her hair into place. I knew the look and I knew the move. Something was getting too close, something she didn't want to talk about, and she was going to hide out, put some distance between herself and whatever it was. She was going to be the beautiful lady, all cheekbones and detachment, and I was supposed to be intimidated and back off. I wasn't going to go for it. I was proud of myself for spotting it.

I decided to try Bogart-as-Sam Spade. It seemed to be the order of the evening. "Come on, sweetheart," I lisped, "come across. I want the goods, and I don't care how I get it. Them. If I have to play rough, that's okay by me. Now how about it?"

"Do you have ways of making me talk?"

"That's Richard Loo. I don't do Richard Loo. Don't confuse me. But seriously, folks." I knew I had her, and I pressed in for the kill. "What was wrong tonight?"

And I guess she saw I wasn't going to give in. "It seems so stupid now," she began, "but it was really bothering me. You want to know what it was? I thought the goddamn murderer was in the theater tonight. There. I told you it was stupid." It was the same way that she had confessed that it was her birthday the evening she came to my place.

"You dames," I said, and got down on the floor beside her. "If I live to be a hundred, I'll never understand you."

She smiled, laughed softly, and rested her head momentarily on my shoulder. I thought two things: if it was true that she had some feeling for me, it was never truer than at that moment; and I thought she was very close to tears, in spite of her laughter.

"I couldn't help it," she said. "I just couldn't help it. I told myself that he wasn't there, that it was just an ordinary movie crowd. When that didn't work, I tried to tell myself that it didn't matter. Even if he were there, he was just watching the movie. But it kept getting worse. I had these crazy, weird images of a man slinking through the theater with an ice pick. I don't know where that came from. I must have read it or seen it in a movie. Maybe it was the cover of a cheap paperback. That seems familiar. I don't know. Or I was afraid he was going to sit next to me, not do anything, just be close to me. When I talked myself into finishing the movie, I imagined that he was going to be next to me in that crush of the crowd leaving the theater. I couldn't stand that. I couldn't stand the idea of even pressing shoulders with him."

"Well, I don't mean to be morbid, but there's a fair chance you have already." The hell. I *always* mean to be morbid.

"God, I know. I know that's true. Some days I come home and say to myself, I've touched him. Sounds like a Broadway musical. I know I've touched him sometime during the day, somehow I've come in contact with him. And I can't stand that thought, that feeling. When that happens, I take a shower immediately. Jesus, I have taken a *lot* of showers lately. I am easily the cleanest person in Wanekia. And the most paranoid. Wouldn't you agree, Peter? Don't you think it's perfectly obvious that I am stark, raving mad?"

"I don't think I'm the best person to judge that. All that stuff sounds perfectly normal to me. Considering that nothing in this town is normal."

"It's abnormally normal?"

"I wouldn't go so far as to say that. It could be normally abnormal. It's hard to tell. One has to be cautious in one's judgments. Besides, even if you are crazy, isn't it great to know what's making you crazy? That's a privilege. And you know what's going to cure you. As soon as he's caught, you'll be un-crazy."

"You do make it sound beautifully clear-cut. Only I'm not so sure."

"Trust me."

She was returning to the good mood that she was in earlier in the evening. As she went to the kitchen, I thought about how I had been tempted earlier to say, when she said she was insane, "You think you're crazy? That's nothin'. You want crazy, *I'll* give you crazy." But only tempted. How this list of what I do *not* say grows.

Alexandra returned with the wine and put her head on my lap. She closed her eyes. It was all perfect—the beautiful woman in an attitude of adoring recline, her beau, the wine—like a kitschy ad in *Seventeen* magazine. And at that moment, I should stroke her hair softly and tenderly ask her if she will wear my Lane cedar chest forever.

She opened her eyes sleepily and asked, "Peter, do you want to do it?"

There was no pretending that the question did not surprise and shock me. "Do I—what?"

"Do you want to do it? Do you want to fuck, screw, make love—do it?"

"Is this a 'yes' or 'no' question or is it open for discussion?"

She was not particularly amused. "I just want to know because this wine is beginning to get to me, and I don't think I can stay awake much longer. But if you want to, I can certainly stay awake for that. Anyway, it's up to you."

"You believe in putting pressure on a guy, don't you?"

"What's the matter—can't you get it up?"

In fact, it was up already. And she probably knew, from the pressure at the back of her head, the answer to the question before she asked. I know it sounds odd, but it was remarks like the one she just made that caused me to believe that she might have some feeling for me after all. She must have felt she knew me reasonably well to be able to say things like that and not worry that I would be offended, frightened, intimidated, or insulted. Or perhaps she knew it was all right to say what the physical evidence contradicted. Or perhaps she simply did not care what my response was.

But truthfully, I did not know what to answer. Did I want to make love? Of course. Did I want it at that moment? Well, yes and no. The desire, the need was there. But I have this funny quirk; those things in life that promise to be most pleasurable, I put off, delay, for as long as possible in some vain hope of intensifying the pleasure. When I was a child, I opened last the biggest, and what appeared to be the best, Christmas gift. I ate cake in such a way that the bite with the most frosting was last. I still catch myself unconsciously eating sandwiches in peculiar (though once purposeful) patterns. I am continually delaying enjoyable experiences until the sunlight is right, until the wind dies down, until the acoustics improve, until my appetites achieve the perfect edge. As a result of this lifelong habit, I am often left opening a miserable, disappointing (though large) gift at the end of the evening, unappreciative of all those fine presents unwrapped earlier; or I am stuck with a too-rich glob of frosting in my mouth after a perfectly delightful piece of cake; in restaurants, people stare at the odd shapes into which I chew my sandwiches. Or, more often than not, I have missed out altogether, have passed on certain pleasures, waiting futilely for the fog to lift, the temperature to rise.

I read once that what distinguishes the middle class from the lower class is that the lower class seeks immediate gratification, the middle class always delays it. Given money, the lower class buys Cadillacs and color TVs; with a bottle of liquor, they drink it immediately; they engage more frequently in sexual activity. The middle class, on the other hand, puts its money away for college education and retirement, lards the liquor away until it turns to vinegar, and hoards its virginity for the marriage bed. (The upper class, presumably, gets its gratification both immediately *and* in the future.) I don't know if this division has any validity or usefulness; I do know, however, that by these lights I am hopelessly, irredeemably middle class.

And knowing this, one would think I would be able to correct the predilection, that I would *carpe* every *diem* I got the chance to. Not so. I keep holding out, continually gambling that at some time my delaying tactics will pay off, hoping that just once all the conditions can be manipulated into an experience that explodes into ecstasy, that is transcendent, that is "perfect."

So when Alexandra asked me if I wanted to "do it," that was the dilemma I was presented with—whether to take what I could get, there, at that moment, on the green-and-gold shag carpeting of the living room, or to wait. And what to wait for, I wasn't sure. I don't know exactly what my sexual plans for the evening were. Perhaps something erotically soapy as we showered together. Perhaps something slightly sordid on the kitchen counter. Perhaps something perversely gymnastic on the bed. As I said, I don't know exactly what I had in mind. But it wasn't the living-room floor. That was all right, but I thought we could do better.

So I looked at Alexandra and said, "Go ahead, take a nap. I can wait."

"I'm going to. Okay, buster. You blew it. You had your chance." My back was against the pillows that leaned against the wall, and she settled against me as though I were a pile of pillows. She smiled and closed her eyes again. "See if I give you another opportunity to refuse my favors."

And shortly, for the second time in a matter of weeks, days, I was watching Alexandra sleep. Her appearance was as sweetly appealing as before, but this time I kept my hands to myself and let her sleep.

There are times in life when, unexpectedly, regret washes over me. It happens as abruptly and surprisingly as if I were standing on a beach and out of rows of the ankle-high surf I am suddenly struck by a wave that reaches to my waist. Without my calling them, memories of stupid, embarrassing, painful moments come at me. I remember the ridiculous clothes I wore when I was under some mysterious spell and was convinced I wanted to be a fashion plate, and when it happens I see myself in the tight, pegged pants, the shaggy mohair sweaters, and the white snap-tab collar shirts that I wore for a while. Or I hear myself talking and my speech is sprinkled with some pseudo-hip jargon that I had affected to impress someone—a girl, no doubt—with how "with it" I was. I am capable of unwillingly remembering all the roles I played, the poses I struck, the lies I told. Or I remember the cruelties I committed, how I joined others in degrading and insulting those who were, in our eyes, "less fortunate" than we. (Not, of course, how we referred to them.) Or I remember the rocks thrown at dogs, cars, or windows. The petty thievery, the cheating, the memories of any of these acts are apt to come to mind without my bidding. These actions may seem to be a small matter—the communal property of embarrassing moments owned by everyone who has gone through the process of growing older—but for someone as self-conscious as I, the memory of them is particularly painful. It may be egotistical to think of it that way, I don't know. But I *do* know that anything I have done that is dishonest, foolish, humiliating, dishonorable, malicious, or idiotic is with me forever. And these things are plentiful and vivid enough so that if they were not submerged in memory most of the time, I would be gnashing my teeth in sorrow and regret all my waking hours.

And as Alexandra slept, and I looked at her, I knew that I had another moment of regret, of self-willed loss, filed away for the future.

So I left. I took minutes to slide myself carefully out from under Alexandra, trying to disturb her as little as possible and not to waken her. She continued to sleep, and I walked out quietly, making certain the door was locked behind me.

All the clouds had cleared off, and it was beginning to get cold. The yard and parking-lot lights between Alexandra's building and mine were out, so when I looked up I could see the stars perfectly. I walked slowly, hoping Alexandra would waken, find me gone, and call after me. She did not. I stopped before my building, and with the darkness and the adjustment of my eyes to the lack of light, the stars were more brilliant than ever. As I gazed upward, my neck already stiffening, the stars seemed to lower themselves, and the longer I looked, the more pinpoints of light I saw. It seemed for a moment that if I stood there all night long, stood there silently and watched the constellations wheel their great patterns, that I could hear them clatter across the sky. That's what happens. You stand out in the cold, feeling sorry for yourself, and you begin to think you can hear the movement of the stars.

21 April 1973, Saturday

*R*oger and I arrived late at Thelma's party—about nine o'clock. (His fault—he finds it impossible to be on time.) We had to park a block away since the narrow, bowered street in front of her house was solidly lined with cars. And the small house was packed. Thelma met us at the door, directed us to the food and wine in the kitchen, and excused herself. She was even more flushed than usual; strands of hair were beginning to creep downward toward her eyes, she looked harried, and the apron she wore did not seem intentional but something that, in the excitement, she had forgotten to take off. I helloed, bumped, and excused myself through the small living room, the even tinier dining room, and into the kitchen and toward the refreshments. Roger dropped off at the first group of conversation.

The kitchen was deserted. Everyone had, I suppose, grabbed his first drink of the evening and had gone on to "circulate." On the white-paper-covered table were two jugs of red wine and two jugs of white, a bottle of Cutty Sark, a blue plastic bowl of ice cubes, a quart of Coke and a quart of Seven-Up, plastic glasses, and assorted cold cuts, cheeses, and crackers in various circular patterns on two platters. I poured myself a glass of red wine and positioned myself in the doorway.

The few lights on in Thelma's house were low, dark-shaded table lamps, and the illumination they gave the room and the people in it was shadowy, eerie. When someone stood close to a lamp, his face was lit up from below, and the effect was exactly the same as when someone holds a flashlight to his chin: his features become distorted, often so distorted that he looks monstrous, satanic. And this is precisely what happened whenever someone stepped into a ring of light from one of Thelma's lamps. The effect, together with the room's general darkness, the sudden and huge shadows that were thrown when someone stepped between light and yellow wall, combined to make the gathering look like an unholy one indeed. I squinted, blurring my vision deliberately in order to give the room a pleasanter cast. When that didn't work, I stepped back into the bright, certain light of the kitchen.

Buzz Colmeco came into the kitchen with two empty glasses. Into one he poured two fingers of white wine; into the other he poured four slightly spread fingers of Scotch and plopped in a couple ice cubes. I was leaning against the sink, and Buzz hadn't seen me. "Howdy, Buzz," I said.

He jumped so sharply I thought he'd spill the drinks. When he saw me, he said, "Jesus Christ, Pete, don't sneak up on me like that. My heart's not that good."

"Sorry. I thought you knew I was here." Buzz Colmeco is another Wanekia native who went away to college and then returned. He went to the University of Wisconsin (on a hockey scholarship, but he never played; he hurt his knee in his first year), and I knew him there. Knew him very casually. We had two education classes together one semester, and we became slightly closer than just classmates when two other hockey players, Buzz, and I devised an elaborate scheme for cheating on the final exam in one of the classes. Then, when I came to Wanekia, I went out to the Ford dealer to get a part for my car, and I saw Buzz there. And why should I not, since it is Colmeco Ford and owned by Buzz.

(Of course, I should have made the connection with the name, but I guess I had forgotten about him completely until I saw him again.) It's not exactly true that Buzz owns the dealership, but he does run it. His father owns it. As soon as Buzz came back to Wanekia with his degree in business administration, dad plunked the business in son's lap and headed off for Arizona retirement. Buzz's wife, Elaine, is a substitute teacher at Wanekia High.

"What are you doing—hiding out in the kitchen?" Buzz asked.

I motioned to the table. "Just staying close, to the source of supply."

"Go slow. I bet Thelma doesn't have anything more to bring out when this is gone."

"I don't think Thelma is quite aware of our needs." I felt guilty as soon as I said it. I like Thelma and think of her as my friend. I certainly held more affection and loyalty for her than I did for the schmuck who stood before me wearing gray slacks, maroon blazer, black wingtips, and a white turtleneck that came up so high on his neck it looked as though he were wearing a neck brace.

Buzz said, "But you know, she's doing all right. This isn't a bad party—considering. Have you tried those little bacon-wrapped olive things? They're terrific." Then he's defending her. Jesus.

"How's Elaine? I haven't seen her at school for a long time."

"That's because I'm keeping her away. Christ, I don't want her around that fucking nut house. Besides that, she's knocked up. The kid's due in June."

I never knew quite how to respond to such an announcement. Especially when I'm not certain about the spirit in which it's made. "Congratulations. I guess." That seemed as though it would cover anything.

"Save it. Man, you don't know what it's like living with a pregnant woman. Or do you?" Then he laughed that high cackle of his that hasn't changed since college.

"Nope. Can't say as I do."

"I thought maybe. You know, young single guy like you gets around. Say, Pete, you got any new ideas? Heard anything new lately?"

"About what?"

"About the murders. What the hell else is there?"

"Haven't heard a thing. How about you?" I know the etiquette of such situations.

"Last week somebody said the cops know who did it, but since they got no evidence, there's nothing they can do. That's what I heard, but I don't believe it. Shit, if they haven't got evidence, how do they know? I mean, that's *how* they know, right?"

"That's right."

"Say, did I ever tell you about this old guy who works for me and thinks he's a goddamn detective?"

"You never did."

Buzz proceeded to tell me about Fritz (that's his name—so help me), an old German who works in the Colmeco Ford Body Shop. Fritz came to this country during World War II as a prisoner of war. He was imprisoned at Fort Lincoln in Bismarck, North Dakota, and after the war, he stayed in this country and eventually ended up in Wanekia. He is, Buzz says, "a regular Michelangelo with a rubber mallet but if you don't stay away from him he'll talk your ear off." One night, Buzz brought something to Fritz's house, and the old man invited him in to see his "crime corner." Buzz said that in one corner of the living room Fritz had set up a card table, a small filing cabinet, a bulletin board, and a map of the city. On the bulletin board, he had clippings about the murders and about any other crimes, no matter how minor. Different colored pins marked, on the map, the single location of the murders, sites of lesser crimes, and places where "suspicious things have been going on." In the cabinet, Fritz had files he had been compiling on "suspicious citizens." Buzz asked him if he had any theories from his research. Plenty, the old man said, but none he was ready to share. "Jesus Christ," Buzz said, "that's the first time the old fart *hasn't* wanted to talk about something."

"Maybe he's waiting for just the right moment to crack the case wide open."

"Yeah, and maybe he just doesn't know shit. That's more like it. I got to go, Pete. Don't spend the whole night in the kitchen."

There was a time when the strange, pathetic story of Fritz would have shaken me, moved me, puzzled me. Now, I nonchalantly tucked him away as only one more of our resident loonies, though, we could be grateful, a harmless one. In my parents' neighborhood there lived a woman who worked as an Avon saleswoman. She became so devoted to selling Avon products that it became her life, and she, somewhat like Fritz, I suppose, partitioned off a corner of her kitchen into her "Avon Office." Come to think of it, she had a map, too; hers was of her sales territory. I rather regarded Fritz in the same sad, curious way I thought of her. Hell, I even found myself pondering whether there might be some chance the old man might actually stumble onto something. Earlier, I would have wondered *why*, why an old man would devote himself to such a fanatic, lunatic pursuit, why he would concentrate the energies of his leisure time at a card table, sticking pins in a map, clipping clippings, filing files. Could it have something to do, I would have thought, with his prisoner-of-war experiences, with a Germanic passion for order, with some old, potent disgust with this country? But the thought that came to me as Buzz told about Fritz was, at least he's doing something, and in that respect he's got it all over me. I'm becoming jaded.

Two women and a man came into the kitchen to get fresh drinks. I didn't know any of them, but they were, I thought, prominent in local politics. Their faces looked familiar to me from last fall's countless campaign posters and television ads "paid for and sponsored by the committee to elect . . ." I guess Thelma's likability extends far enough to give her a wide circle of friends. I decided to wander, to see if I could find Alexandra.

I found her sitting on the stairs with Jean. Both of them were dressed in their out-on-the-town clothes. Alexandra wore a wool skirt and jacket and high russet leather boots that had some kind of strap around the heel. Everything fit her loosely but well, the effect, I guess, that fashion-conscious women strive for. I don't mean to ridicule her. She looked good; she always does. (Though if I had my way her shirt would have been buttoned one button higher.) I don't think it's just my prejudices showing, but Jean looked more—well—obvious. She was wearing a long, dark, shiny dress that had a small floral print. The sleeves were long, full, and flowing, and there was some kind of laced-up business in front. Jean had about half the laces done, so the low-cut dress was cut even lower. Jean reminds me of a celebrity, not a specific famous person, just a celebrity. She acts so haughtily, so condescendingly that she must think she is somehow removed from the masses. The result, of course, is that people resent her for her arrogance. I think she's a phony—mannered, pretentious, and artificial. Roger says I should be willing, as he is, to overlook these qualities. It should be noted, however, that he overlooks these qualities himself because he's been trying, for a year, to get in the sack with her. I tried to convince him that he was wasting his time, that she was, in an expression I once heard Dick Cavett use, a "daughter of Sappho." And I don't think she's attractive either, but it's not for a lack of trying. She's always carefully coifed, heavily made up, and extravagantly dressed. Part of the difficulty is that she tries too hard. But also she has an odd face; her jaw is a shade too large, her nose a tad too sharp, her eyes a fraction too widely spaced. Besides that, I don't think she likes me.

She and Alexandra were talking to—or listening to—two men, husbands of women who teach at the high school. As soon as Alexandra saw me approach, she excused herself and came down the stairs to greet me. Smiling, she put her hand elegantly on my arm and guided me to an unoccupied corner of the room.

"Tell me, Peter, did you have your way with me last night before you sneaked out?"

"I figured you could use some rest," I stammered. "I wanted to let you sleep." Since she did not seem to be angry, I decided that rather than be defensive and apologetic, I would try to shift the burden to her, to force her to be the one to say, "I'm sorry." She had, after all, fallen asleep in my presence, hardly the most gracious way to treat a guest.

"I was tired. But I told you, I wasn't *that* tired. Is there something you're not telling me? Is it my breath? Is my antiperspirant letting me down?"

"No, you don't have to worry about being close. It's me, I guess. I was in a funny mood last night."

"The old war injury acting up?"

"Just a mood. It's hard to explain."

She snapped her fingers and pointed at me like a comic book detective who had just seized upon a clue. "Careful, Peter, you're giving yourself away."

"Give me a break."

"Okay, I'm going to stop this in-depth analysis. But, Peter"—she became very serious—"we're going to have a long talk someday."

"Sounds all right to me. I'm flexible."

"I don't want you flexible. No, I'm kidding. Why don't you arrange something with Bonnie and Roger, and then after a respectable length of time we can break away. Now, I've got to get back to Jean. She'll kill me if I leave her alone with those two jerks. Let me know what we're going to do. And when." She squeezed my arm and walked away, going back to her perch on the stairs. Soon she was talking and laughing with Jean and the two men. If she did not want to be with them, she gave a convincing performance.

I continued to float through the party. In my wandering I noticed that Thelma *did* have more wine, which she dutifully brought out when the other jugs ran low. She also produced a half-full quart of Smirnoff's vodka, and as soon as she brought that out it was attacked like quinine in a malaria epidemic. Thelma continued also to bring out food, small,

bacon-wrapped wieners from the oven, boxes of crackers
from the cupboard, and more cheese and cold cuts from the
refrigerator. People kept drinking and eating. And smoking.
When I looked into the living room, a cloud of smoke hung
like a fog from the ceiling. And they talked, they talked
about sports, weather, politics. But mostly they talked about
the murders. As I walked through the rooms of Thelma's
house, I sat in on parts of the following conversations: I
heard it suggested—again—that school be closed until the
killer is caught. As the speaker said, there's no sense in
putting out a free lunch for him. In opposition, I heard that
school should definitely remain open, that there is little or
no chance of catching him outside of the school. Another
member of that group damned him for advocating that these
young girls, his daughter among them, act as decoys for this
vicious killer. I heard various punishments proposed, and
those who suggest specific punishments are rarely inclined
to be merciful. I heard, and had not known, that two people
had confessed, one after the first murder, one after the third.
Both were false confessions, as police questioning revealed.
As apparently is common practice in these crimes, some
small detail of the murder is not revealed; this information
is withheld to allow the real murderer to identify himself. I
heard someone else say that here the secret detail is the
particular arrangement of the victims' clothing. Someone else
said that this kind of madness (meaning murders) is an inevitable result of the generations of inbreeding that has gone on in
this region. I'm not very clear about what the woman who
sponsored this theory meant, but it's related, I guess, to the
fact that Wanekia is, and always has been, largely populated
by "insiders," people who have lived here all their lives,
whose parents, grandparents, great-grandparents also lived
here. That hypothesis is probably pretty fuzzy genetic thinking, but it does have some other interesting implications.
And I'm sure someone else believes that all of this community's troubles began when outsiders, such as I, came to town.
I heard all of these opinions, theories, suspicions, and
hunches—all of these and more. Thelma's reluctance to call

the convocation a "party" may have had some basis. The fact that so much of the talk was focused on one subject did give the gathering the feel of a civic meeting.

When I asked Roger if he was interested in skipping out of the party early to do something with Alexandra and Bonnie, he said that was fine. But whenever I returned to him to see if he was ready to begin the preliminary steps toward the door, he was either in the midst of a discussion or he was busy making sure that he was getting his ration of food and wine. Alexandra was not making any attempts to mingle, but anytime I saw her, still in the same place on the stairs, she was talking to someone else, as though all the guests made pilgrimages to her feet. Bonnie, I had not seen since moments after we came in.

At about eleven o'clock, people began to leave. And as soon as someone began the exodus, others followed fairly steadily. Soon the party was lessened by at least half. It was now possible to find a place to sit, even if it was floor space or the top of a radiator. And you could easily look from one end of the room to the other. Of course, that also meant that you could now see clearly the detritus of the party, the overflowing ashtrays, crumpled napkins, scattered toothpicks, and almost empty glasses. Roger was still animatedly involved in conversation with Rex Knudsen, a local studio photographer, and two women who looked familiar to me but whom I could not place. Alexandra was still on the stairs with Jean, and Bonnie had joined them. Also on the stairs was Byron Brassetere, the choir and orchestra director, and his wife. Thelma finally stopped scurrying around and sat down in an easy chair (which mysteriously emptied when she entered the room) and sipped a glass of wine. She also stopped setting out fresh food and drink, a message, no doubt, to the guests. I asked Roger again if he wanted to leave, and he said, "Soon. I'm going to finish my drink, destroy Rex in the argument we're having, and then I'll be ready to split." That could, I knew, still take awhile, and I decided to have another glass of wine. What little I had had to drink during the evening I had nursed slowly, consciously taking the smallest sips I could. What I wanted to do all evening was to bolt a few drinks fast, hoping to relieve or avoid the inevitable discomfort I feel at parties. But I had restrained myself because I didn't know what we would be doing later in the evening, and I wanted to be prepared. Now I figured, what the hell, I might as well get a little buzzed. As I walked to the kitchen, Alexandra shot me a questioning look. I mouthed the word "soon." What promise of a tawdry liaison!

In my last years of high school and first years of college I had a reputation as a prodigious drinker, one who could drink copious amounts and remain sober. The reputation was largely undeserved, but since it was an image I wanted, I did what I could to preserve and cultivate it. One of the first things liquor always did to me was to make me talkative. I would begin to pun incessantly and to throw out insults like a junior Don Rickles. I was usually quiet, and this behavior, my garrulity, was a definite effect of alcohol, but it only served to bring me up to the level of hyperactivity on which my friends usually operated. Later, as a drinking bout or party wore on, and I drank more, I devised certain tricks to give myself the appearance of sobriety. I braced myself against walls or furniture to prevent weaving. I positioned my feet in special ways to allow me to stand still and erect and to walk straight. I talked less and less as the possibility of slurred speech increased. I thought out sentences for minutes before I spoke. This caution made me serious just as others were becoming more and more frivolous, and again, I got credit for "holding my liquor." Much later, all that you needed to be regarded as a two-fisted drinker was the ability to remain more or less conscious and to vomit in the toilet rather than on your clothes. Neither were great problems for me. I so hated and feared throwing up that I would do anything to avoid it. As for staying awake, I never had to worry. Back then, alcohol seemed to have the opposite effect on me than on everyone else. Rather than make me drowsy, it stimulated me to wakefulness. Maybe it was like caffeine to me, or like the amphetamines given to hyperkinetic children to slow them down. By the last stages of a party, it was not even necessary to remain mobile. I remember once walking through a room, falling down twice, caroming off walls like a steel ball in a pinball machine, and finally flopping into a chair, and having a friend say to me, "Wow, you're still not even drunk." The amounts I drank were deceptive as well. If someone remarked that I once drank a fifth of bourbon at a party, what he did *not* mention was that the party very likely began at one o'clock in the afternoon and continued until two or three in the morning. Once allowances are made for carefully spaced drinks, spilled drinks, and drinks given to friends, consuming a bottle of liquor over a twelve- to fourteen-hour period no longer becomes such a remarkable feat. I always drank my liquor straight, sipping it slowly. (I could never drink much beer; I simply could not hold a great amount of fluid.) And I did have, and do have, an ability in the consumption of liquor that worked to my advantage. My drinking seems to go by very distinct plateaus. I feel the effects of alcohol fairly quickly, but then it takes quite a time, and quite a few drinks, before I progress (or regress) to the next level of drunkenness. And so it goes. I remain for quite a while at each level, and I can usually choose how and when I slip to the next plateau. But of course, the irony, the idiocy of it all, comes when you consider that while I was ostensibly drinking as much as I could, to get as drunk as I could, I was, simultaneously, trying to remain in control, trying to remain sober. It's a wonder I didn't herniate myself trying to reconcile that split in purpose. Ah, it was all so complicated. You can imagine my relief when drugs became popular. Instantly, matters were greatly simplified.

Now my experiences with alcohol are significantly different. No longer am I able, nor do I care, to drink as much or as often as I once did. Now I give myself more freely, more willingly, to the effects of alcohol. And I am very practical in my use of it. I explore its functional, its therapeutic properties. I use its tongue-untangling qualities (a fallacy, I know) to help me over the awkwardness I said I invariably feel at social functions. I use its potential as a sedative (I am grateful it no longer keeps me awake—just the opposite) to ward off insomnia, which I fear more than a pack of snarling, rabid dogs. (What could be worse than to lie sleepless at night, watching your life unreel itself before you like the endless reruns of the worst television situation comedy? The few bouts of insomnia I have had have shown me with what terror it is to be regarded.) In Thelma's kitchen, I gulped a glass of red wine and poured myself another. They were rewards. I had been very patient all evening.

I was so wrapped in my thoughts about my past and present drinking habits that I didn't notice that something was going on in the living room. And I don't know what caused me to notice finally, whether there was a sudden rise in the noise level or a sudden silence. But something *was* going on. As I walked out of the kitchen to investigate (slowly, I didn't want to appear to be one of the eagerly curious—which I am), I heard a low murmuring, the kind of sound people make when they are trying to restrain themselves but cannot, the noise the congregation makes when someone faints in church, the noise of the concert audience when the conductor's baton slips from his hand. In the living room, everyone was gathered, at a safe and respectable distance, around Thelma's chair. I maneuvered my way, around the back of the ring of people, and I looked over heads and shoulders. And the broken view I had showed Thelma bent over in her chair, her head in her hands and obviously crying. Beside her, seated on the arm of the chair, was C. L. Thorston, a local contractor; he had a comforting arm on her back. Kneeling beside Thelma, handkerchief in hand and an arm around Thelma's shoulders, was Bonnie. I could also see an overturned footstool by the chair.

I thought I heard Thorston say something like, "You might be wrong. It might not happen again."

As soon as he spoke, Thelma's head shot up. "My God," she said, sobbing. "That's just as bad. We'd have to wait the rest of our lives. Wait to see if it would happen again. My God. Who could stand that? Who could live that way?"

Her voice had risen almost to a shout and then it trailed away again. When she looked up, the tears that streaked her red cheeks made her look luminous, as if there were a light that shown on her alone in the room. I still did not know what was going on.

Suddenly, Alexandra was at my side, gripping my arm tightly. "Where were you?" she asked.

"In the kitchen. What the hell is going on? What's wrong with Thelma?" We stepped back from the others. Everyone else too was stepping back grudgingly.

"I'm not sure. I don't know if I heard everything. There's Jean. I think she knows how it started." Jean joined us, and Alexandra, as if to make room for her to stand by us, huddled closer to me, putting her arm around my waist and laying her head against my chest. Automatically, I put my arm around her shoulders.

"It was Knudsen," Jean said. "What a prick. What incredibly bad manners he has."

"What did he *do?*" I asked.

"He was talking to somebody—about *that*, about the murders—and when he reached for an ashtray he was standing next to Thelma. God, it was the first time she was off her feet all night. And he said very loudly, 'If it happens again . . .' And that was all it took."

I gave Jean a very puzzled look.

"Thelma heard him say it and she said to him, 'You don't mean *if*, you mean *when* . . . *When* someone is going to be killed again. Everyone knows it's going to happen again.' She got more and more hysterical and she started shouting. 'It's just a matter of time. We're just waiting for it to happen. It's past due already. It's got to happen soon. Do you think it'll be tomorrow? Monday? Tonight?' She was really shook."

Alexandra said, "She was mad, too. She kicked the hassock over when she first started yelling, and she slammed her wine glass down so hard it spilled all over the end table."

Jean went on, "Bonnie and Thorston went over to her right away to help her calm down. Then Thorston said . . ."

"Yeah," I said, "that's where I came in."

"Knudsen is such an ass. He's unbelievable."

"I don't think," Alexandra said cautiously, "you can really *blame* him. I mean, it's not one person's fault."

"Maybe not," Jean conceded, "but that's not exactly a suitable topic of conversation for a party." Where have you been, I thought.

Just then Thelma and Thorston walked through the room, and no one spoke. He had one arm around her, and with his other hand he held her forearm. He helped her upstairs, and as they walked by, everyone stood aside. People looked at Thelma the way they stare, at a funeral, at the widow of someone famous, with the same mixture of awe, respect, and morbid curiosity.

Roger and Bonnie came over to us. Before we could ask, Bonnie said, "She'll be all right. She's just really tired. If she gets some rest, she'll be okay." That sounded simplistic and naive to me, but I guess at such times there is a justifiable impulse to minimize matters.

In contrast to Bonnie's remarks, Roger said, "Wow. Old Thelma crackin' up. Who'd have thought it. Hope she pulls out of it all right."

"By the way," Jean said to Roger, with all the innocent interest that a mongoose takes in a cobra, "I saw you talking to Rex Knudsen. Maybe you can shed some light on what he said that upset Thelma so?"

"Not me, man. When I was talking to him, he was telling me about some arty photographs he's been taking lately, and we were comparing notes on how shitty this town is for selling work. I wasn't around when he said whatever he said that set Thelma off." The trap sprang shut; no victim in its jaws.

"Why don't we leave?" Alexandra suggested. "I don't think there's much of a party left."

Roger said, "Sounds good to me."

At that moment, Thorston came down the stairs and held

up his arms for attention. "I don't mean to be a party-pooper," he said, "but Thelma's going to sleep for a while, and I think we better call it a night for the party." As an afterthought, he added cryptically, "Maybe we can try again when things are different. Or at least better."

I asked Alexandra why Thorston was in charge, and why he seemed to be elected Thelma's chief nurse.

She looked unbelievingly at me. "They're lovers. They have been for a couple years."

I was surprised, but what struck me most of all was Alexandra's use of the word "lovers." It seemed an out-of-date term, but she used it so naturally, so unself-consciously, that I was charmed by it. Did she, I wondered, refer to us that way? Little chance of that. "Isn't he married?" I asked. "I thought he was married."

"He was. His wife died a few years ago."

Alexandra told Bonnie to ask Thorston if they needed any help cleaning up. When Bonnie reported back to us, she said, "Nope. His sister and her husband are going to stay." As we were leaving, it occurred to me that the last ten minutes of the party was the only time Alexandra and I had been "publicly" together.

I was not very happy about the conditions that attended our leaving. First, I felt bad about Thelma. I didn't think as Roger apparently did, that she had come completely unhinged, but neither did I believe, as Bonnie said, that she would be all right once she got some rest. Obviously, Thelma feels the tension that all of us feel; she simply reached publicly the point where she could no longer handle that tension. That it should have happened to her, to someone who is so sensitive to the image others have of her, is an injustice of the first order. Secondly, it bothered me to be asked to leave by Thorston. Not that he didn't do the right thing. But I felt as though I was at creepy little Johnny's birthday party, and after we depantsed (depanted?) Johnny, and he ran from the room, crying in embarrassment, Johnny's mother had to shoo us all away for our abominable behavior. Finally, and what bothered me most of all, was the fact that Jean came along with us. We decided, since we were going to do something together, that we'd take Bonnie's car. I thought "we" meant Roger and Bonnie, Alexandra and me, but as we got into Bonnie's big, old Chevy, Jean got into the back seat with Alexandra and me. I suppose she felt, justifiably, that she was invited to be a part of the activities, and since she did not have a car . . . Still, you'd think she'd see what the situation was and ask to be taken home.

Roger was driving and asked, "Where to?" When no one offered any suggestions, he said, "Well, I'd like to get something to eat. I didn't have any supper."

"You're hungry?" Bonnie said. "God, I saw you personally put away half the appetizers at the party. How could you possibly be hungry?"

"Easy. There's not much to those little wieners. And the cheese was cut so thin you could read a newspaper through it. And wine always makes me hungry."

Jean said, "I don't care where we go. If you're hungry, let's go someplace. I could use a cup of coffee. But what's open?" That's another thing I don't like about Jean; she has a tendency to take over.

"Highway Host," Roger said. "It's got to be the Host. The Trucker's Delight. Breakfast served twenty-four hours a day."

We rode in silence. Don't they always say that in novels? "They rode in silence, each of them alone with his thoughts." The thoughts I was alone with were of my first meeting with Thelma. It was a first-of-the-year faculty reception, and she politely sought me out and drew me into conversation. She asked me what writers, what books I admired. She asked me if I was interested in drama. Twice a year she went to Minneapolis to attend performances at the Guthrie Theater. (The last play I had been to was my high school's production of *Our Town*; since, I have been to Wanekia High's production of *Our Town*.) At that moment, the image of her that was with me was of her lying in her bed, cool cloth held to her forehead, her cheeks pale, and her apron still on. That was not the way she would want anyone to think of her.

We drove down Sixteenth Street, the rows of modest, middle-class homes on our right, the dark trees of the Lions' Club Municipal Park on our left. Then it happened. Do you know how it is that certain images become fixed in our memory? It is as if you were watching a movie, the film snaps, and one image freezes upon the screen, and similarly becomes frozen in the mind. The image may be of great or slight significance: of your grandfather lying on his death bed, his eyes beginning to glass over, his last breath crackling in the room like radio static; or the image may be of little more than the special slant of sunlight late on a summer afternoon. The point is, we do not know, until years later, that an image has become a permanent part of that visual baggage we carry through all our lives. But at that moment, driving down that half-lit street, the smell of Jean's cigarette as sharp as a knife in my nostrils, the wool of Alexandra's coat rough against the back of my hand, what I saw through the frame made by the windshield of Bonnie's car became such a part of me that already my memory of it is like looking at a photo in a family album, a painting in a gallery, an illustration on a book's dust jacket. There, in the light from the headlights, less than fifty yards from the car, a figure ran across the street. He came from the direction of the houses, and he ran toward the park.

Roger first touched the brakes, let up on them, then slammed to a stop in the middle of the street. Jean said what we all thought, what we all knew. "My God!" she shouted. "It's him!"

"Where did he go?" Bonnie asked. "Did he go into the park? He was running that way. I couldn't tell."

Alexandra said, "I think he did. Did you see him? Did anybody see his face?"

I was busy looking out my side window, trying to see if anyone was coming out from the houses, someone giving chase.

"All I saw," Roger said, "was a shape. Like a shadow.

Except for one thing. I thought he was wearing black tennis shoes. Christ. What a thing to notice."

I don't know if it was the power of Roger's suggestion or something I actually saw, but black tennis shoes sounded right to me as well. Also, I kept thinking "green"; maybe he was wearing an Army jacket. Like Roger's.

Jean reached into the front seat and rapped Roger on the shoulder. "Back up. Go into the park. Maybe we can still find him."

Roger obeyed, and we drove onto the narrow black-topped road that led down to the park, and the light from the street stopped quickly as the trees thickened and the road twisted. Roger drove slowly, and we all sat forward in our seats, straining to see something beyond the picnic tables and playground equipment that were close to the road. When the car moved around the curve, the headlights flashed ahead and the shadows made it seem as if the trees themselves were running figures. But we saw nothing. Once, Bonnie said, "There. I thought I saw something over by the tennis courts." And we all held our breath and stared intently. "I guess not," she said.

The more we drove the less the opportunity grew that we would see anything. All of us knew that though we did not say so. Then Roger said something that made that prospect—the prospect of not seeing anything—seem preferable. "Hey, Pete," he said. "What do you suppose he's using to cut up those girls' clothes? Something to think about, huh?"

It *was* something to think about, and when I thought about it, I thought of long-bladed hunting knives and of straight razors so sharp they could slice you to the bone before you knew you had been cut. Roger's remark was, I suppose, a way of reminding me of a wicked reality, of saying this was no lark, no glamorous hero play. It was the first time I had been frightened. That's not exactly so. Rather, it was my first experience with a certain kind of fear—the fear of physical harm. I had been scared, and the adrenaline had been pumping since I had first seen that shape in the headlights, but that was a sudden, reactive fear, the fear that causes you to jump when the wind slams shut a door, when someone sneaks up behind you. If any of the women caught the significance of what Roger said, they did not acknowledge it.

And something else, something queer, was tied up in what he said. Since murder so dominates our lives, we sometimes forget that it is a crime, a violence, a physical act. Instead, it becomes easier to think of murder as an atmosphere, a vague presence that is always there, part of the air Wanekia breathes. It becomes the thing that causes the small alterations in our lives. It is because of "murder" that we curfew our children, shop for groceries in daylight only, arm ourselves, dress conservatively, speak in respectful tones, make no loud noises or unseemly signs of mirth. And it is remarks like Roger's, crass references to weapons or to strangulation, that bring us back to murder's primary, brutal, physical fact.

Roger stopped the car at the dead end of the park road. By then we knew we were not going to see the mysterious running man, but we did *not* know what to make of what we *had* seen.

Roger put his arm on the back of the front seat, turned to us, and said, "Well. What the fuck do you suppose *that* was all about?"

"Turn on the radio," Jean said. "Maybe there's something on the radio."

Bonnie turned on the radio and tuned in WNKI (coyly pronounced "winky"), the local station. But as long as we listened we heard only standard radio fare: they told us the time and temperature, they told us where to buy cars and carpets, and they played the same songs that they play all day long.

"Maybe it was a kid," Bonnie said. "Do you suppose it could have been a kid?"

"It didn't look like a kid to me," Roger snapped. "I could be wrong, but I don't think so. And what if it was? So what? So what if it was?"

"I don't know. Kids are always getting into trouble.

Maybe he got caught window-peeping or stealing something."

"No one was chasing him," I said.

"No one we *saw*," Roger corrected.

For a long time, no one said anything. Jean lit another cigarette. Alexandra slumped in her seat. Roger reached into his jacket pocket, pulled out his Sucrets tin, waved it back and forth, and said, "Anybody want to do a number while we decide what to do?"

Like an admonishing mother, Bonnie slapped his arm down. "Don't. God, don't be stupid. I can see the headlines now, 'Teachers Parked on Lovers' Lane, Arrested for Possession of Dangerous Drugs.' That would be beautiful. You must have a death wish or something."

Jean said, "But don't you suppose we should do something? Call the police, maybe?"

It was probably a sensible suggestion, but because of my resentment of Jean, I couldn't let it pass. "And tell them what? Somebody ran across the street?"

"We can say it's probably nothing," Bonnie said quickly. "But they might want to know. Let them decide what to do. If it's stupid, at least we'll have reported it. What else can we do?"

"Don't look at me," Roger said. "I've made my suggestion."

"Okay," Bonnie said rather coldly. "I'll call the police. I don't mind doing it."

It was a good night for Bonnie and for her doing her duty. First, she had rushed to Thelma's aid, and now she was going to tell the police what we had seen. I think there's a good-citizenship award lurking somewhere in her past. Hell, there was no *harm* in calling the police; it was just that nothing was going to come of it. Just as nothing was going to come of our having seen a man run across Sixteenth Street. That realization was almost stunning in its frustration, but nevertheless, it was so. It reminded me of being at a sporting event, a football or basketball game, and seeing a spectacular play. But not fully seeing it, and longing for the countless, slow-motion, videotape replays of home television. That was the feeling I had. I wanted to rerun what had happened. It had all happened too quickly.

Roger started the car. Then he paused for a moment, took his hands from the wheel, held them up like a surgeon's, and looked at them. He held both hands out for our inspection. "Look at that." His hands were shaking slightly. I knew mine would too if I held them out. "Jesus, I'm still pumped up. Wow. I've got to get a grip." Turning to Bonnie, he asked, "Do you mind calling the cops from Highway Host? I still want something to eat."

"You are incredible," she said.

As we were driving out of the park, Alexandra sat up quite suddenly, leaned into the front seat, and said, "Rog, would you mind taking Peter and me to my place? I think we'll pass on the Highway Host tonight." It was the first she had spoken in a long time. She sat back and said nothing more. She did not look at me. What she said seemed, to me, like a public declaration of sorts, and it both pleased and embarrassed me.

"Sure thing, Alex," Roger said. "You're the boss." I thought I detected the hint of a wink at me in his response.

All the way to Alexandra's apartment I waited to hear from Jean. I expected to hear her say, "I'm not that hungry; why don't you drop me off at Alexandra's too." But she kept her peace, and as we got out of the car and slammed the door, I almost felt sorry for her, sitting alone in the back seat. Certainly all my unkind thoughts about her had vanished.

As Alexandra rummaged through her purse for her keys, she still did not speak. I, on the other hand, yammered on like a nervous schoolgirl standing at the door on her first date. "Some night, huh?" I said. "First Thelma and then seeing that guy in the park. That's a lot of action. I don't think I can stand so much excitement. Not all in one night." I *was* nervous; Alexandra was behaving strangely, and I was unsure about how I should be reacting. As we stood outside her door, someone, from the floor above, opened his door and then shut it again quickly. I did not see who it was, but I guess he was checking on who was in the building.

The second we stepped into Alexandra's apartment, the second the door shut behind us, before the lights were turned on, Alexandra had her arms around me. She did it so roughly and so suddenly, it was like an attack. "Easy," I said, and took a step backward. But she clung to me. I kissed her, less out of a sense of romance and more out of bewilderment, out of not knowing *what* to do. She pressed her lips so hard against mine that it hurt. She pushed her tongue into my mouth. When we came apart, I said, "Geez. Did you have something in mind?"

"Don't," she said, and put her hand over my mouth. "No jokes. Can't you just let this happen?"

Her remark embarrassed and shamed me. I was chastised and did not know what to say. "I can," I said. "I guess."

"Wait here." She went through the bedroom and into the bathroom. She did not close the bathroom door tightly, and I could hear the medicine cabinet opening, a pill container being popped open, then shut, water running, a glass being filled. Maybe it was nothing more than aspirin for a headache; still it gave me a bad feeling, as if she had to take something before being with me.

When she came out of the bathroom, she was wearing her white robe. To make it seem as though I could act spontaneously, I walked into the bedroom to meet her. We were, instantly, on the bed, and I began what I thought were the tender, gentle, almost tentative, preliminaries of lovemaking. I did not want to seem grabby, as though I were simply cashing in my rain check.

Alexandra would have none of it. Whatever urgency she felt at the door was still with her. She shrugged herself out of her robe, and in the dark room her flesh was as white as the robe, so when the white garment fell to the floor it was as if she had split herself in two. She unbuckled, unzipped, and unbuttoned me more quickly, more expertly than I could have done it myself.

What followed, as we pressed, ground, and thrust against

each other, made it seem, just as in a bad novel, as if we were trying to become one, as if we were trying to overcome all the separateness, the resistance of blood, bone, and flesh. What had seemed to me at first to be Alexandra's frenzy, a need almost violent, was, I knew, a tenderness that was beyond all gentle touching, all light stroking, all soft caressing, all modest rubbing. It was a lesson that was not of the mind. When we moved apart at last, I felt a chill come over me. It was caused by the evaporation of sweat, our mingled sweat, on my chest. I pulled the sheet up to my chin.

Alexandra turned on the light to get her cigarettes, and we looked at each other oddly. It was the look of strangers, but of strangers thrown together.

"Turn out the light," I said. I knew that the look we exchanged meant something, but I did not want to pursue it.

"I'm going to have a cigarette."

"It's bad for your health. It'll stunt your growth. It'll cut your wind."

"It's bad for me *not* to smoke. I *need* a cigarette."

"Okay, but turn out the light anyway."

"Can't." She got her cigarette lit, tilted her head back, and inhaled so deeply I could see her chest expand and her breasts rise. "I can't smoke in the dark. I have to see the smoke."

"Then if you were blind you'd be able to quit?"

She reached out and switched off the light. "There, baby. Are you going to sleep or do you want to talk?"

She did not mean that we might talk about the events of the evening. No, what she was referring to was "The Talk" that earlier she had promised me we would have. I was not ready for that. I knew it was inevitable, and I suppose I had already reconciled myself to it. But someday. Not at that moment. For that, I *was* too tired. "I am sleepy." I said pathetically.

"Okay. Some other time. Go to sleep. I'm going out in the other room to smoke. In the light."

I tried to stay awake. I tried to imagine what our talk was going to be about, and what my responses would be. But I could not "formulate a topic," as I am likely to say in the classroom, and as I stared out at the shaft of light coming from Alexandra's "smoking light," all I could think of was ways to say, no matter what subject might come up, "It's not my fault," or "What do you expect me to do?" or "I'm trying, I'm trying to do better."

I fell asleep and dreamed that I was in a huge, light-filled house—a mansion, complete with curving staircase and elaborate furnishings. I was on the main floor, in a spacious, window-lined hall, and inside that hall was another room, completely enclosed on all sides, a room within a room. Although I was never in that room, I knew it to be a brightly lit ballroom. It had parquet floors, orange chairs along the walls, a grand piano, and a huge chandelier. The room was jammed with people and I was supposed to be in there too. On all four sides of the room there was a door. I walked around the outside of the room and tried each door in turn. All were locked. A feeling of anxiety came over me because there was some urgency connected with my getting into the ballroom. I do not know what the urgency was, but I felt it keenly. It was not danger, and though I felt agitated throughout the dream, I was not afraid. The dream bothered me. It was so obviously symbolic that I was suspicious of it, and I did not care to spend any time in interpretation. Also, it was not a typical dream. A much more common dream pattern, for me, is this: I am in a house, and someone, something—whatever it is, it is to be feared mightily—is outside and it is going to try to get in. My task is to secure the house, to close and lock all doors and windows. On the periphery of danger, I hurry through the house, shutting down many possible means of entry, while others huddle as close to the center of the house as possible. Then, just as I'm certain my job is done and the house and its occupants safe, I remember a door in a far corner of the house that I haven't checked. Predictably, the door is ajar, and as I begin to push it shut, something on the other side attempts to push its way in. Its strength is far greater than mine, and just as I'm about to weaken, I wake myself rather than face whatever horror might tumble through that door. This is a recurrent nightmare. The dream of the ballroom is completely new.

When I woke, Alexandra was asleep beside me. By God, I think I've seen her sleep more often than I've seen her awake. As has become practice, I slipped quietly from bed, dressed, and left. My leaving early was a concession to Alexandra's fear that someone might see us in our late-night, early-morning comings and goings. Although I believed it was an unnecessary propriety, I wished to respect Alexandra's feelings.

As I walked to my building, it was just beginning to get light. I *know* I've seen more dawns in the last few weeks than I have in recent years. And I hate the dawn. What others find peaceful, calming, symbolic of a new beginning, I find tiring, false, and depressing. Maybe there are vampires somewhere in my ancestry.

My apartment was exactly as I left it. It was not right. I had been gone long and had been far. I had seen a decent woman crack up and had heard of a loony auto-body repairman. I had chased what may have been a murderous maniac through the streets. I had screwed myself into a fine sweat. I had dreamed, in a strange bed, that I was locked out of something grand. It had been a long night and nothing should have been the same after such a night. I was changed, so why should my books still sit so carefully upright in their shelves? Why should my furniture be in the same symmetrical arrangement? Why were the posters and prints occupying the same rectangles and squares of wall space?

22 April 1973, Sunday

Slept until noon today. Then I called Roger to see if Bonnie called the police and if anything came of it. Yes, she called, and the police thanked her for the information and said they'd send a car to check things out. Roger said the police did not seem particularly interested or excited by Bonnie's report. No, they did not want to speak to any of us; we had no value as witnesses unless someone was arrested.

Does this sound tired? I am tired.

Alexandra and Bonnie went to Thelma's today to help with the clean-up operation.

I think often of Alexandra lately. Have I mentioned that before? Is it necessary? And when I think of her, I try to project some future relationship with her. And I cannot. I cannot even fantasize about what we might do if we should see each other through the coming week. What bothers me as much as that lack of any projection of a future is the lack of a past. I've known her well enough to say hello for over a year, but we have only had a "relationship" (that dreadful, neutral word) for less than two weeks. It has become a source of irritation—no, more than that, of pain—that the past, the history that Alexandra and I share is, as a historical period, a past of murder. Once, I was more than willing to have her shoved into my arms by any circumstances, even those relating to murder. Now I wish it were not so. ("He wished it were not so." What a tone he takes, even with this subject.)

But why should it not be that way, why should Alexandra and I have a time, a history, that is not shared by the rest of this town? Time began here on January 29, 1973, the day Deborah Ann Munson was murdered. On that day, clocks began ticking, calendar pages began turning. On that day, chronicles began to be kept, citizens began to age, the seasons began their circular movement. (As you can see, I came to this record-keeping late.) The name of this new age that we live in is the Present. The Present is so strong it forces us to live only in its confines. It erases the past and keeps our heads turned away from the future.

I thought once that my own past belonged in these pages. I thought that I was lured here, that something in me responded to the magnetic pull of the place. Then, once here, the action began, and it was left to me to figure out what brought me here. I thought I would rifle my past like an attic, searching for the answer to what brought me and the violence of this time and place together. Why did we dovetail so neatly? Oh, I know these thoughts sound like little more than the crap of superstition. But I did intend to plumb my past, to go back to my earliest memories of my father, mother, and sister, to the play of my childhood, the friends of my adolescence, to my relationships with women, to every element of the equation that might add up to the sum of what I am. But I can't. The present here is too strong to allow the past to break through it. And certainly that applies to any speculations on the past that are so tentative, so groping.

So today, in that eternal now that is today, I followed what has become my new ritual of Sunday. I drove to Arrowhead Rexall and bought the Minneapolis and St. Paul newspapers. And in the car, and in my apartment, I made certain that the radio was always on. If there was a chance of any news, particularly news of our mysterious running man, I did not want to miss it.

Then, when I was through rummaging through the papers for any features on Wanekia (both the Minneapolis *Tribune* and the St. Paul *Pioneer Press* "profiled" the community in extensive Sunday feature articles after the second murder—but I guess three murders represent too much chaos, and now they stay with simple reportage—when there is something to report), I began to work my way through student essays, the essays I have put off reading all week and which must be returned tomorrow.

I made two neat piles on the living-room carpet: those easy to read which required a minimum of marking and would, no doubt, receive high grades; those difficult to read which I would put off until tomorrow morning just before class. I found, in pile number 1, a paper by Judy Langlin, a fat, blond, bright girl who is given to uncontrollable giggling fits. When she begins to laugh, she shakes, turns red, and tears run down her plump cheeks. The assignment was to define "obscenity" (I don't know how I come up with these gems), and Judy's paper was unlike her other work.

OBSCENITY

The dictionary defines obscene as "that which is repulsive to the senses" or "abhorrent to morality or virtue." But to me obscene has a special meaning and it has to do with the way people in this school and town are acting lately. The other day I heard some boy talking and one of them said, why do you think he's doing it? I knew what he was talking about, he meant the murderer. Another boy said he didn't know about the other girls but Debby Spencer probably got it because she was always twitching it in people's faces. Then he called her a name I can't say. A teacher at this high school, a man whose name I'm not going to mention, heard every word they said and didn't do a thing. I'm not saying, like alot of girls, that Debby Spencer was my best friend or anything but she always said hello to me and I felt terrible when she died. And I think it's obscene when someone says something like that and it's even worse when no one does anything about it. Girls are getting killed and I'm scared, so scared I can't sleep at night and lots of other girls feel the same way. But people make jokes about it. Teachers and ministers and parents and the police and everybody (the men especially I think) should be doing something. They should protect us too. But they don't and it makes me sick. It is *obscene!* When I graduate I'm getting out of this town and I'm not coming back. I don't think I'll ever even come back to see my parents.

Well. Judy Langlin is in Debate, and her papers are usually logical, structured, and carefully proofread. They are always typed. This one was handwritten and written sloppily. It would have been practically illegible, but as the paper went on her writing became larger. It was obvious that she wrote the paper hastily, without revision, and at an emotional peak. I know also how it happened that she "overheard" that conversation. We have all become, like John Turner, expert eavesdroppers, instantly attuned, as if we had antennae, to any talk of murder. I remember an occasion, a few weeks ago, when I was doing lunch duty in the cafeteria over the noon hour. From across the room, I heard Jerry Kugler, George Hall, Tommy Hindeman, Paul Mazzeo, and two other boys talking about the murders. I casually crossed the room to listen to what they were saying.

"I think he's picking the girls," Jerry said. "I think he's got it in for these girls. They probably did something to him, and he's getting revenge."

George was picking apart a styrofoam cup, bit by tiny bit. "Maybe not," Tommy said. "Maybe it's just random. He can't help himself and it just happens."

"He can help it," Paul said. "The sonofabitch can help it, all right. He's doing it because he wants to. The fucker."

"I don't know. Maybe," George said.

The conversation ended abruptly because no one, with few exceptions, wants these discussions to become arguments. And I walked away. I had—have—heard similar conversations. Everyone has. But what *I* heard asked nothing of me.

I did not know what to write on Judy's paper. I wanted to say, Judy, if I had heard the same conversation you did, I would have said something. I would have grabbed each of the boys, twisted their arms behind them, and told them they were as bad as the scum who murdered the girls. But I know I would not have done that. I would have done as that other teacher (Roger? Gary? Turner? Carl Becker?) did; I would have pretended to ignore it, and I would have walked away, so glowing with shame that it would seem I could light up dark places.

23 April 1973, Monday

I'm not coming back," Alexandra said.

"What?" I knew what she was saying, but I resisted it; I had to hear it again so it would sink in. I didn't want to understand what she was saying. I wanted to be *made* to understand.

"I'm not coming back. I turned my contract back in and said thanks, but no thanks."

We sat in Alexandra's Mustang, on a hill just outside of town. Earlier in the day, Alexandra had asked me if I wanted to go for a drive after school. I thought her invitation had something to do with the fine spring day. After three days of gray skies and drizzle, today's sunshine and warm temperature seemed like a golden promise, enough to emerald the lawns and put the final, full bloom on the lilacs. She asked me to drive, and I headed out toward the highway. I planned to drive to a stretch of wide, straight road to the east of town. There trees line the road, and I imagined we'd roll down all the windows, and, driving as fast as we safely could, let the wind whip through the car, let the sunlight flash through the trees onto us, dappling us, making our smiles, all our gestures, seem like the jerky movements of home movies. But I hadn't driven long when Alexandra asked me if I could park someplace, someplace where we could talk.

"We're supposed to talk about that?" I said peevishly. "It doesn't sound like a subject for discussion. It sounds like an announcement. It sounds like all the decisions have been made. Subject closed."

"Come on, Peter. Don't be that way about it. I want to talk to you about it so you know *why* I'm doing it. I want you to understand."

Does it make sense if I say I both was and was not surprised by what Alexandra was telling me? Her announcement stunned me; it came as unexpectedly, as shockingly, as some violation of nature, as some freakish upset of a natural order. I was looking out the car window, watching a bird flying in widening circles above a pine tree, and it seemed that I should concentrate on that bird, that if I watched the bird in its flight, I could avoid Alexandra's announcement. If I did that, I would not have to think, my God, she really is leaving; she will not be around any longer. On another level, I said to myself, right, of course she's not coming back. And on that level, I included myself as part of her decision; somehow, it was *because* of me she was not coming back. I didn't want to talk about these things; I did not even want to think about them. And as a way to keep it all superficial, to avoid going into the ramifications, I kept the quarrel going. It was also a way to stall for time while I waited for the bleeding to stop.

"Okay," I said. "I want to understand. I want to understand *when* you reached this decision. It wasn't recently, was it?" (Notice I say I want to know "when," not "how"; "how" leads into much deeper waters.)

"It wasn't sudden, if that's what you mean. I decided recently, but I've been thinking about it for a while."

"You couldn't talk it over with me? Or you didn't want to?"

"I didn't want to." Then suddenly she became angry. "Jesus, Peter. I don't want to say things like that to you, but you drag it out of me. You beg for it. Do you want me to play the bitch? Do you *want* me to say hurtful things? That's not the way I want it. I want you to know how I came to this decision. And why. It matters to me. I care about having you understand. But if you're going to be a prick about it . . ."

"I just want to know why you wouldn't talk about it with me . . ."

"Because I was afraid you'd try to talk me out of it. Or because I was afraid you *wouldn't* try. Okay?"

"Okay." Her anger settled me. Or made me feel, at least temporarily, less emotional, less wounded, and more objective.

She put her hand on my shoulder. "So can I go ahead?"

"Yeah, go ahead." I looked straight ahead. It seemed important, both for her telling and my listening, that I not look at her.

"Now it's going to seem funny to say it. It's so obvious. You know what it is. Mostly. It's this place. It's this crazy *goddamn* place. You know, sometimes it hits me—very suddenly and very unexpectedly—that I live *here*. In this place. At this time. In the town that's getting written up in *Time*. And I can't believe it. It's totally incredible. It does a lot of other things to me as well, but in one way, it just seems so unbelievable." She paused, slowing herself down. "Well, living here might be unbelievable, but to stay here is absolutely insane. Especially if you don't have to."

All along I presumed that she meant she was going to leave next summer, as soon as school was out. But the way she talked now gave me the sudden feeling that she was talking about leaving sooner. Like tomorrow. I had a vision of her sparsely furnished apartment, and how quickly she would be able to clear out.

"So when are you leaving?" I tried to sound calm and matter-of-fact, but it didn't work very well. And I guess she heard some concerned catch or shift in my voice and was touched by it because she smiled very warmly, very affectionately at me.

"As soon as classes are over. I made some discreet inquiries about the possibilities of getting out earlier, but it's just not possible. Anyway, we're out the twenty-fifth. That's a Friday, and before the weekend is over, I expect to be gone."

I did not want her to go. That was the plain, simple, but quite desperate, fact of the matter. I did not want her to go.

She sat sideways, facing me, one arm across the back of the seat, one leg folded beneath her. In that attitude, bent toward me, she seemed to be composed of crazy angles. Her skirt had ridden up high, exposing her thighs. And through the unbuttoned gap at the top of her blouse, I could see that palest portion of her bosom, that area that still had a border of tan from last summer's sunbathing. Those areas of flesh, the inside of her thigh, the soft rounding of her breast, seemed as pale, as white as the moon. And the glimpse of that moon-flesh pierced me with a pain that was as sharp and sweet as loss can ever be. It was as if those slight, narrow strips of Alexandra's skin were tortures specially concocted to accompany this conversation. With them, came a voice that said, do you think you won't miss her, look at that, that's a small sample of what you will miss. I started to reach for her, to touch her in those teasing spots particularly, to reassure myself that they weren't lost to me forever. And just as quickly, I pulled back, knowing that to touch her was going to prove nothing and would insure nothing.

I did not want her to go.

I also knew that as lovely as she looked in the flesh, as touchable, as seductive, that was not what I would miss most of all. This scene, the two of us together in her car on a hilltop, was quite sufficient. Even to exchange these wounding, quarrelsome words was better than *not* speaking to her. I was willing to pledge, at that moment, that I would never touch her again, never lay a hand on her, if I could be assured that she would always be available for talk that was even as painful as this.

I did not want her to go, and I knew I had to say something.

When I was eight years old, my family was scheduled to

vacation in Florida, to visit my mother's sister in Miami. We were going to fly, our first trip not in the family station wagon. I became convinced, out of some tangle of eight-year-old logic, that if we attempted to fly, the plane was certain to crash. I tried everything to get the trip canceled. I bad-mouthed my aunt and Florida. I feigned illness, each day complaining of a new symptom—sore throat, earache, headache, stomachache, dizzy spells. When nothing worked, the day before our scheduled departure, I finally said to my father, "Dad, let's not go. I got a feeling we're going to crash." He replied impatiently, "Cut it out. We're leaving tomorrow and that's that." Confronted by Alexandra's announcement, I felt that same desperate need to avoid what appeared tragic and inevitable.

"What if he's caught?" I thought switching the basis of the argument might be an effective strategy. After all, she had mentioned the murders, not our relationship, as the reason for her leaving.

"Oh, Peter. Come on. You know better than that. That's not it. Not anymore."

"Why not? He's going to get caught sooner or later. It can't go on forever."

"But that's not going to make everything all right. This place is never going to be the same. It's tainted or poisoned or infected or something. And whatever is wrong with this place is getting to the people who live here. Or has gotten to them already. You want to know something else that's happened to me? Something besides the fear, the paranoia—all that shit?"

"Sure."

"I feel guilty. I feel guilty all the time, and I don't even known why. Maybe it's because I'm alive or because I'm not doing anything. Maybe it's because I'm still sane. And I am. I know that. I might be shaky but I haven't completely lost my mind. Anyway, I don't like it. I hate it. I don't want to be afraid and I don't want to feel guilty. I don't like any of the things this place has done to me. And I'm not going to let it happen. I can do something about it. I can leave. And that's exactly what I'm going to do.

"And besides, why are you arguing with me? You know I'm right. You know I am."

It's true, I did. But I was not ready to concede, even if she was convincing. Perhaps my argument was feeble, maybe even irrelevant. And though I did not have another argument ready, I was not about to give up. I decided to bide for time.

"Where are you going?" I asked. "Have you decided?" In the back of my mind, I hoped that it would be someplace near. Minneapolis, maybe.

"I'm going to stay with my brother. At least for a while. He lives in Malibu."

When she said that, I knew I had her. She had revealed a fallacy, a flaw in her logic. "You mean you're leaving here because it's too weird, and you're going to fucking southern California? Which is only the haven for every kind of crazy in this country? That's a goddamn zoo out there!"

She shrugged in a way that said she didn't care, that she was not bound by the rules of logic. "I don't know, maybe. But when I last talked to my brother—that was the night I was late for the movie. I was late because I wanted to talk to him as soon as he got home from work. When I talked to him, he said things were very quiet out there. Particularly where he lives. He's got a small, sort of isolated place close to the ocean. Anyway, it's not permanent. And it's not *here*."

"Maybe not. But it's California. *Southern* California, for Christsake. They've got religious cults out there that make human sacrifices. And pray to granola. Is your brother married? Is he older than you?"

"He's divorced. And he's two years older. Why do you ask?"

"No reason. I'd just never heard you talk much about him before." It's nice to pretend that I am untouched by something so mundane as jealousy, but I'm not. I could imagine her single brother having parties, parties at which Alexandra would be very much in demand, and I could imagine him introducing her to all his bronzed, sun-bleached friends. I had hoped that he was married, with about three children for whom Auntie Alexandra could baby-sit.

As time went on, as we talked, my position, my hope of saying something that would keep her here, became increasingly untenable. And the number of things I could say was dwindling.

So I blurted out, "I've got cancer."

"What?" she asked, laughing.

"Cancer. I've got cancer of the—uh—of my internal organs. And I've only got six months. Wouldn't you like to be near me for my final days?"

"Peter," she said softly, "are you trying to tell me something?"

"Yes, I'm going blind, too. I've got even less vision left than life."

She stared at me. "Yes?"

"And heart disease."

She said nothing but waited.

God, she was persistent. She was, I guess, determined to wring it out of me. And perhaps she had not weakened in the course of this discussion, but I had.

"What about us?"

"What *about* us?"

"I don't want you to go."

"You don't? Why not?" I knew what she was doing, what she was asking, but I was having more and more difficulty.

"Because. Because I like being with you," I said haltingly. "Because I care about you. Because if you leave that'll be it for us." (Was it difficult to say that? Yes and no. Is it difficult to pour paint from a bucket? No. But occasionally it will take can openers, screwdrivers, chisels, and hammers to get the lid off.)

Alexandra let herself fall backward, as if she were exhausted in victory. "I'll be damned," she said sarcastically. "You said it. You finally said it. I've been waiting a long time to hear something like that from you."

"You don't have to be smug about it."

She sat up quickly and grabbed my arm. "I'm not kidding. This isn't some kind of fucking competition where I threaten to leave just to make you say certain words. You mean something to me too. But you *know* that. You know I love you and need you. Without my saying anything. I don't have to. Not with you. I had a pretty good idea that something was happening between us, but I couldn't be sure. There were times when I thought, right, we're going good. We're getting closer. We're really hitting it off. Then at other times you're so goddamn cold I think you wouldn't give a shit if the earth opened, swallowed me, and closed up again. I don't get it. I don't know why you're like that."

I had absolutely no idea of what I should say. She posed questions to which I had no answers. At some time, a time that lay outside the reach of my memory, I had acquired the odd, the twisted notion that to reveal one's emotions, perhaps even to *feel* certain emotions, was undesirable, unseemly, maybe even unmanly and unattractive. But I have no idea how I came by this attitude. I do not remember my father and mother telling me to dry my tears, that big boys do not cry. Neither do I remember falling under any cultural spell that said I should emulate Clint Eastwood or Charles Bronson and stay cool at all times, shrug off the affections of women, bear pain stoically and let the blood trickle quietly from the corner of my down-turned mouth. What Alexandra said was true but I could not account for its origins or its continued operation.

Every day of our lives, every minute, every second, forever over our heads are the mysterious waves or beams that carry television images from the senders, the studios, to receivers, our home television sets.

Traveling over us are Ed Sullivan; Vince Lombardi; Kukla, Fran, and Ollie; Milton Berle; Hopalong Cassidy; Johnny Carson; Pinky Lee; the Smothers Brothers; Howard Cosell; Mary Tyler Moore. How these images fracture themselves, metamorphose themselves into invisible impulses, dots, and microwaves, then reassemble themselves before our eyes is absolutely incomprehensible to me. All of the electronic, electric, mechanical marvels of our age—telephones and golf carts, computers and vacuum cleaners—are as baffling to me as anything magical. But because I don't understand them does not mean I deny them. Likewise with my own nature. I do not understand my lifelessness, my reluctance to reveal my feelings, my lack of desire to demonstrate affection or hatred. But this *is* a part of my nature. It is a part of me as undeniably present as Walter Cronkite's appearance on the CBS evening news.

Still, in spite of the truth of what Alexandra said, her words hurt, and out of that hurt, out of a desire to cover my exposure, I said to her: "You're criticizing me for being cold. Jesus. You're as capable of being as chilly as anyone I've ever known." It was a weak, spiteful, unfair thing to say, and I knew that our cases were different. Nevertheless, I said it.

Without hesitation, she said, "Self-defense."

"What?"

"Self-defense. You're right, I do withdraw at times. I do get cool and go inside myself, but it's only a matter of self-defense. It's automatic. I do it so I can go on living in this place. I'm doing it right now. I do it so you won't get to me. Ever since I decided to leave Wanekia I've been hoping that you'd do something, or say something, to make me want to change my mind. But truthfully, I can't imagine your ever making a commitment."

For a long time, I was silent. I lacked both the energy and the conviction of righteousness to defend myself. I finally said, "You know, just because I don't demonstrate my feelings doesn't mean I don't have them."

"Does a tree falling in the forest make a sound?"

That remark, as faulty as the analogy might have been, totally disarmed me. What I said about myself, I believe to be so. I believed that I felt love, hate, anger, sorrow as keenly as anyone. Perhaps I felt them more strongly, and I hid these feelings to prevent my being constantly buffeted by their display. But this new thought, this idea that by foregoing a demonstration of emotion, I was suppressing the emotion itself, was new. And I had to adjust to it. I wanted to take this theory and lay it over my life, to examine my life through it, to see what it would explain. And yet at the same time, I was afraid of the conclusions I would come to.

"Tell me," I said weakly, "is this 'The Talk'?"

She looked sympathetically at me and nodded.

"I don't know what to say," I said.

"You don't have to say anything. These were things I wanted to say. This was my 'Talk,' remember?"

"And nothing I say is going to make much difference, is it?"

"Make a difference how? Am I still going to leave, you mean? Yes. But saying some of these things may have some other, I don't know, usefulness. But I *am* leaving. I've got to. I'm not like you. I don't *want* to be here. I don't like what's happened to me already."

"Are you saying *I* want to be here?" She had thrown it out so casually, I almost failed to pick up on it. She said it as if it were a fact of which everyone was aware; as if it were a verity of our lives.

"You know you do."

"The hell, I know nothing of the sort."

"Oh, Peter. Forget the bullshit. You know you get off on living here. It's no big thing. I understand. It affects a lot of people that way. I can feel it, too. It pumps you up. It's almost like a funny kind of high. It hypes you up and numbs you at the same time. And stop pretending you're mad. You're not. That's part of the problem. But don't act angry and don't act as if what I'm saying isn't the truth. You know it is." She seemed to be getting tired and closer to the edge of impatience. I knew that if I pushed matters further, I would not help my cause.

This is what amazed me. It was not that she knew these things about me, these things that I thought of as dark secrets. It was that she knew them, and *they made no difference.*

"You really know me. I think better than I know myself."

"I've been paying attention. I've been watching you very closely."

It was my turn, but nothing was going to come out.

Alexandra finally spoke. "So let's go get something to eat. I've starving." Although she favors intimacy more than I, she too knows there are limits.

We drove to the Hi-Ho Drive-In, Home of the Minnesota Burger (known elsewhere as a California Burger) and the World's Greatest French Fries (quartered wedges of potato, deep-fat fried). We waited a long time for service, since Cap Starnes, the proprietor, has difficulty now in hiring car hops (what parent—or what girl for that matter—would want a job in which she walks alone to what might be a stranger's car?); Cap has a sign permanently in his window that says, ominously and tactlessly, "Girls Wanted."

The only other car in the lot was Kenny Foote's super-charged black Pontiac Firebird. Kenny and another student, Martha Keller, paid far more attention to each other than to their food. That could not be said of Alexandra and me. It was a day in which I added to what has become my great, growing store of words unspoken, gestures unmade. And right to the end of the day, I knew, I knew exactly, what words I should have said. But they lay on my tongue like ashes, and I could not get them out.

24 April 1973, Tuesday

We had a faculty meeting today, the first in weeks, ever since all after-school activities were discontinued. We met in one of the study halls, and Roger, Alexandra, Bonnie, and I sat in the back row; Alexandra doodled cartoons throughout the meeting, and Roger cracked under-his-voice insults about whoever happened to be speaking.

There were three primary reasons for the meeting. First, Proctor wanted to clarify the School Board's position on paying those teachers who had contracted for helping with extracurricular activities. Since these activities—athletics, drama, debate, band, orchestra, choir, and others—have been canceled, certainly it would not be right to reimburse faculty for not rendering a service; nevertheless, since contracts have been signed, and many staff members have justifiably counted on this income, it was agreed that faculty would be paid half the amount that the extra-service portion of their contract specified.

Second, Proctor said that there were serious problems in the school with the great numbers of rumors that were circulating constantly. (We all leaned forward, hoping to hear some of the more sensational examples; none was forthcom-

211

ing.) If any of us should hear anything that clearly belonged to the category of rumor or gossip, we should report it to either the principal's or vice-principal's office. The school's administration wants to act as a clearinghouse for these rumors. Many of them will be reported to the police for "standard investigative procedures."

Third, and last, we were told that, as we are keeping our eyes watchful, we should especially be aware of couples (male and female) in the school. Investigators have the theory, Proctor said, that the killer may be luring girls into "isolated situations" by some "means of seduction." His operating in such a manner would account, police have speculated, for the marked lack of a struggle, for the fact that no screams have been heard, and for the girls' appearance of having been so "neatly disrobed."

I have my doubts about this hypothesis. It sounds too exotic, too Bluebeardian. And it also sounds like a somewhat desperate idea, like straw-clutching.

But it is disturbing in another way. I don't like *having* to be a policeman in the place where I work, and I particularly object to having to "watch" those boys and girls who lounge at each others' lockers, who, holding hands, walk each other to class, who seize every opportunity to press against one another, who fondle, nuzzle, stroke, and kiss each other in the halls, in the parking lot, in the lunch room, and at assemblies. These people may be guilty of indiscretion, of tasteless public displays, but I don't want to have to suspect them of anything worse.

Roger summed it up aptly, as we were leaving the meeting. "How about that?" he said. "Now we have to watch out for people in love. Ain't that the shits?"

25 April 1973, Wednesday

Miss Retternmund sent me on an errand today. When she asks, no one dares refuse. She is the school's official blue-haired old lady, a fixture in Wanekia's school older than the plumbing. She's past sixty-five, mandatory retirement age, but no one has the courage to tell her she has to retire. And I am certainly not one to go against her. She is the unofficial head of the English Department, and she rules us, the English, Drama, Speech, and Journalism teachers, in a spirit of absolute tyranny. Besides that, she scares the hell out of me. She's sharp-tongued, impatient, belligerent, and thoroughly intimidating. The telling detail about Miss Retternmund occurs when she teaches and she gestures constantly with the clawed fingers of her right hand. The turn of that hand, with the talons toward her face instead of in the threatening direction of the class, is the only sign of mercy about her. (I've often thought, when I've seen her in action in the classroom, that if that hand slipped out of control she could scratch out her own eyes.) Her students do learn; it's just that as a result of the process they become emotionally scarred.

"Mr. Leesh," she said to me (she calls everyone "Mr.,"

"Mrs.," or "Miss"—she has the stereotype down cold), "since we are beginning our unit on Shakespeare this week, would you bring our model of the Globe Theater out of storage? It's one of the few visual aids that I find useful. You should find it where the Playmakers' props are stored."

I don't particularly care to teach Shakespeare this year. I'm scheduled to do *Julius Caesar* and *Macbeth*, and the bloodiness of each play seems risky to me. But I would never dare suggest to Miss Retternmund that these plays are inappropriate. I know what she would say. "Mr. Leesh, we have been teaching these timeless classics for many years. We will teach them this year as well." Miss Retternmund does not recognize the murders. That's how she deals with them; she refuses to acknowledge the existence of these killings.

As I said, she intimidates me. I obeyed instantly. And since I brought the Globe Theater out of storage last year, I knew exactly where to look.

The props are kept in a maze of small, dark, cold, cement storage rooms and closets beneath the stage and the auditorium. But the Globe Theater was not kept where it was last year. That's probably a Wanekia High tradition: never store the Globe Theater in the same place.

I began my search. The storage areas are, to me, a very unpleasant place. The air is filled with the smell of paint, canvas, and mold. Stacked against the walls and scattered on the floors are canvas backdrops and flats, slats and two-by-fours of pine, half-empty paint cans, lighting equipment, and all the discarded props of old productions; overstuffed chairs, two wagon wheels, some pillars that were supposed to bring to mind Greco-Roman times, a sign that said "Aloha, Bill," a short section of picket fence, a Confederate flag, and various other items, all once put to use by the school's thespians.

Something happened as I was hunting for the Globe Theater. It was as sudden as a gust of wind and as irrational as a dream, but I thought—no, that's not strong enough—I became *convinced* that I was about to find a dead body, the nude, strangled corpse of a young girl. Maybe it was the sight of one of the headless, costumed mannequins that made me think I was going to stumble upon a real body. I don't know. But I do know that my conviction, no matter how mindless it was, was very real. I became paralyzed, unable to move because I was sure that if I looked behind a flat or under a drop cloth I would see not the Globe Theater but the staring, sightless eyes of a murdered girl. The temptation to run was very strong, and what kept me from giving in to it were two things: I knew that this seizure was just that, and without rational base; and I knew I couldn't tell Miss Retternmund that I was sorry, but I just couldn't find the model of the Globe Theater.

So slowly, hesitantly, I continued my search. But when I turned over a flap of canvas or pushed aside a stack of crumpled newspaper, I did it so gingerly that I could have been expecting to find a rattlesnake, coiled and ready to strike. You see, though I knew that my obsession with finding a body was irrational, I could not shake it. Consequently, I altered my search slightly. I began looking for a body first, and only distantly, remotely, a model of an Elizabethan stage. I did not want to be *surprised* by a body; I knew I could not face the sudden horror of that.

So, as I looked through the maze of small rooms, I was alert, most of all, to a glimpse of flesh, to any color on the spectrum that was pale, tan, pink, white, or even faintly blue. My eyes were adjusted for any sight, no matter how slight, of a stiffened limb or a strand of hair. The Army has developed, mostly for night jungle fighting, a special infrared sight. It keys on heat, and in some way lights up and reveals the warm body that is giving off that heat. One of the peacetime uses of this device is almost as grisly as its combat function. When someone, alive or dead (more often the latter, as it usually turns out), is lost in an uninhabited area, forest, desert, mountain, or swamp, this infrared scope is used in an attempt to pick out a still-warm body from the cooler masses of trees, tall grass, rocks, and sand formations. As I walked through the storage areas, I felt as if my eyes had become as sensitized as that special scope. And my eyes too were sensitized for any appearance of still-warm flesh.

The longer I looked, the more excited I became. Since I knew I was going to find a corpse, I was eager to get on with it. As the adrenalin began pumping, and as I began ripping through bolts of canvas, overturning props, costumes—anything large enough to conceal a body—my heart beat faster and faster. I became flushed—it seemed my temperature was actually rising. The blood pulse was loud in my ears. My breathing became the loud, labored panting of physical exertion. I had only one room left to look through, and that room was, if one believed that setting was as important in life as it is in art, the most likely, indeed the *perfect* place for a body to be hidden.

That room is little more than a large closet, and it is directly below, but oddly enough in no way connected to, the stage in the first-floor gymnasium-auditorium. To get from the prop rooms to this room, you go down a cement ramp (you go down bent over—the ramp is tunnel-like with a low ceiling), and the only light you get is what filters down from the prop rooms—the ramp is unlighted.

As I walked hesitantly down toward the room, I smelled something strange. It was a smell that was quite distinct from the damp, musty, moldy, cellarlike odor that was a natural part of the place. This smell was sharp, pungent, something like vinegar. And in my attempts to determine what that smell was, I inevitably linked it to the object of my search. In the room I was approaching was a dead body, and what I smelled was that body giving off its smell of death—the mingled aroma of the sweat of a final struggle, of excrement, perhaps even of blood. It had to be.

With that smell in my nostrils, and with the conviction of what the smell was in my mind, I stopped, and I stood up so quickly that I bumped my head on the low ceiling. The excitement of the search collapsed—collapsed into fear. The physical symptoms, pounding heart, shortness of breath, sweating, the taste of brass, were all the same as before, but the association now was plainly with terror. And there was a new dimension. I felt a tightening in my genitals. I don't know what caused that, but I suspect it had something to do with the knowledge that the body I would find would be a nude girl, and I was afraid of how that might affect me sexually. Or afraid that it *would* affect me sexually.

I backed slowly up the ramp. As I did, my crablike motion allowed a bit more light to creep past me into the room. When I noticed that, I stopped and, bending over, I peered down into the room, trying to see the pale outline of a body, trying to confirm by sight what I knew in my mind to be there. I could see nothing, and I decided to move forward again.

(I'm uncertain now, but one of the elements that may have propelled me forward was a hope of heroism. Each discovery of a murder victim leads to a few days of celebrity status for the "discoverer." They become the ultimate insiders for a brief period of time. Such thoughts may have been on my mind. Certainly I know by now that I am not above that kind of thing.)

When I finally entered the room, the smell was stronger than ever. With my shaking hands, I groped along the low ceiling for the one bare bulb and the chain that would turn it on. Each step forward I took was also groping. I touched each foot forward tentatively, as if expecting to step into a bottomless pit. Actually, I was afraid I would stumble over a body, a body whose whiteness I could not see but which may have been hidden under a dark drape.

I finally found the light, and as I switched it on, I spun around the room, wanting to see quickly what was there before it could surprise me.

The room was empty. No dead body. No Globe Theater.

I take that back. Not quite empty. There was one object in the room, and that object was the source of the smell.

In one corner was a large earthenware crock, and in the crock was a greenish-golden, briny liquid. I guessed that it had to be a feeble, foul-smelling, long-ago-abandoned attempt at homemade beer. Apparently, some students had been planning a grand coup; brewing beer right in the school. There were probably cannabis plants in some other remote corner.

I walked back up the ramp on weak, unsteady legs. The muscles in my legs felt as though they were close to cramping. I had been so tense that now, now when I was able to relax, my muscles would not cooperate. And my chest ached, I supposed from a combination of muscle tension, pounding heart, and heaving breath. Back up in the light of the prop rooms, I sat down on an old, rolled carpet to catch my breath. I took a few deep breaths and hung my head down between my knees.

There, in that position, ready to faint, vomit, anything the situation required, I had a new fright, but this scare was of a different nature. It was another horror of self-discovery. I realized what I had been afraid of as I searched through these rooms. I had been afraid that I would find a dead body; I had not been afraid that someone was dead. The distinction was an important one. My fear was totally self-centered. I could have discovered the body of another Debbie, of Judy Langlin, of Bonnie, of Alexandra. That thought now was harrowing enough. But my fear had not been that someone, perhaps someone close to me, someone so recently alive, someone's daughter, lover, friend, was now dead, and dead of a violent and agonizing struggle. And I had not been afraid (as I had been when we saw the man run into the park) of possible physical harm. This killer, who strangles women, girls, is not threatening to me, both because I am not likely to be on the victim list, and because, since he weakly and cowardly chooses women, he seems my physical inferior. (I know these consolations are both arrogant and stupid. I cannot help but cling to them.) No, I had been afraid of stumbling across dead flesh, of finding a lifeless tangle of chilling blood, gristle, and bone.

In my life I have seen five dead bodies (probably close to the national average for a person my age), all of them in the artificial, wax-fruit, open-coffin world of churches and funeral homes. They are: one grandfather, one grandmother, one uncle, two fathers of friends. With none of them did I receive the impression that they were only sleeping. My grandfather did not wear his glasses when he slept. With none of them was I willing to step within reach.

In college, I roomed for a while with Tim Muir, whose father taught in the Biology Department. One day someone came to take Tim to the gym, where his father had had an accident playing handball. The "accident" was a heart attack, and by the time Tim got there his father was dead. He asked for and received permission to be alone with his father for a few minutes before they took the body away. So there, in the tiny four-walled, high-ceilinged cubicle of the handball court, Tim, he told me later, said good-bye to his father. His father was sitting on a corner, and Tim laid him down. He removed his father's handball gloves, kissed his father on the forehead, and left.

The story touched me, in more ways than one. I was impressed with Tim's feeling for his father, but in spite of my love for my own father, I knew, and know now, that I could never touch him in death.

None of my apprehensions about the dead come from any mystical, ghostly, horror-show feelings or superstitions. And certainly the dead do not ask anything of you, not the way the living do.

I take that back. They do ask something of me, something far greater than simply covering their lifeless bodies, sealing their sightless eyes, or closing their gaping mouths. They ask me to feel something for their passing.

Which I resolved to do.

Then and there, surrounded by all those objects of falsity, all those instruments of make-believe, I decided to resurrect the dead, to parade them before my mind's eye, to survey them until they called forth in me those feelings that I would not show at their leaving.

I bent over further and resolved not to leave the prop room until tears began to splash down onto the sawdust by my feet.

Ah, it was a madness, a madness that I cannot begin to approximate in these pages. My knees began to quiver, and I felt light-headed, close to collapse.

But the parade began. I saw my grandfather who had come so close to dying in the back bedroom of my parents' home. I saw my grandmother, her heavy veins collapsed in death. I saw my Uncle Julian. I saw Tim Muir's father. I saw the three girls who have been murdered in this school, all of them streaming brown hair as if they were trailed by dark fire. I saw a friend who killed himself in high school, his tight, grim mouth showing his anger at me for not saving him. I saw my father's sister, so starved by cancer she could not support the weight of her own bones. I saw Lee Schuster. I saw Gene Rowell, the father of my childhood best friend. I saw them all clearly.

The tears they asked for were slow in coming, but the pain they brought was quick and sharp, as if my heart, suddenly unbound from a tight wire wrap, could not handle the expansion of release. And once the tears began, they came freely.

In fact, they came too easily, and I was afraid they would not stop. When I tried to squeeze them off, my throat constricted and jumped as if I had hiccups.

I do not want to write of it further. If I go on, I will become embarrassed and begin to make cheap, easy jokes. I composed myself by walking back and forth across the room, sniffing to dry my running nose and wiping my eyes on my shirtsleeve.

When I began to climb the stairs, still *sans* Globe Theater, I imagined that I was going to be greeted when I got back to the main floor. I had a vision of a crowd of friends, acquaintances, students, colleagues, even strangers waiting for me at the top of the stairs. Proctor, Gary Clubb, Miss

Retternmund, John Turner, Carl Becker, Thelma, Bonnie, Roger, Alexandra—especially Alexandra—would all be there. They would put their arms around me and wordlessly would welcome me to them.

The halls, of course, were empty, as they should be when classes are in session. Still, one could do worse as visions go.

26 April 1973, Thursday

*L*ast night—this morning, I should say—about three A.M., I awoke, certain that someone was in my apartment. I woke fully, without a trace of the difficult and foggy transition from sleeping to waking.

Motionless, I listened, and I heard nothing, but that did nothing to lessen my conviction that I was not alone. I stared at the bedroom doorway, waiting for a shadow to darken that rectangle of dim light that came from the living room.

The longer I lay still, and the more fearful I became, the more acute my senses grew. I could see the outline of any shape—dresser, chair, door, lamp, clock. My muscles were so tensed, so straining for release, that my entire body felt like a spring. Then, I heard sounds. First, what could have been the crinkle of a paper bag. As I listened to this rustling, I finally determined that the sound came from my own foot, moving back and forth slightly between the sheets. Then I heard breathing—and just as quickly I realized that too was my own. My breath chuffed in and out between the folds of my pillow, and in the spaces between inhale and exhale, I could hear no one else's panting.

After a long time—minutes—I knew rationally that no one

was in my apartment. A murderer would have had time to enter the room and strangle me, shoot me, or slit my throat. A burglar would have had time to make off with my TV, stereo, and anything else of value he could find. Still, I felt the presence of someone, something. In an effort to quell that feeling, I got up and walked through the rooms. In every room I turned on every light, as if, no matter what were present, that much illumination would certainly reveal it. I almost called Alexandra to tell her of my strange experience.

When I returned to bed, I became frightened again. I was no longer afraid of any imminent danger, of any intruder. But I was afraid for my sleep, my rest. In the weeks since the first murder, no matter how anxious, how agitated, I might be during the day, I have always been able to rely on the escape of a night's sleep. But I felt that what woke me last night, what invisible hand shook me awake, was free to do so again. And again and again. I felt as though I had been found out, discovered in my sleep, and I was no longer free to rest undisturbed.

27 April 1973, Friday

*T*his morning, at approximately ten thirty, during third period, Jackie Kuntz, a senior, was pulled into the third-floor darkroom that is next to the Journalism room. Her assailant held a hand over her mouth, kicked the door shut, and as he pulled her backward into the pitch-dark room, he knocked over a tray of developing fluid and a stack of film canisters.

Herman Wahl, the janitor, heard the noise and knocked on the darkroom door. "Is something wrong in there?" he asked in his thick accent. No one answered, but now Herman thought he heard some scuffling sounds coming from inside. Herman tried the door, but it was locked. Again he thought he heard something. Finally, using his master key, he opened the door, and said, "All right, what's going on in there?"

Just as he opened the door, someone pushed Jackie Kuntz into him, and Jackie and Herman tumbled backward, crashing into a row of lockers. Jackie immediately began screaming hysterically. Up and down the hall, doors opened, teachers tentatively peered out, and students, up from their desks, pushed the teachers from behind, trying themselves to see what was going on.

Meanwhile, Herman got up and ran after the figure who had run from the darkroom after pushing Jackie out.

Soon the hall was filled. Hesitantly, teachers and students moved over toward Jackie. Two friends of hers asked her if she was all right. She couldn't stop crying long enough to say. Most of the buttons were ripped off her blouse, one of her shoes had fallen off and been kicked down the hall, and she had a bump on her forehead that was swelling rapidly. Her lipstick was smeared around her mouth where her attacker had held her to keep her from screaming.

Everyone looked at her in awe. Here she was, a human artifact; she was one of the girls attacked, but she was alive, sobbing as she sat on the cold tile floor.

By this time, word filtered down from the third floor, where the incident took place, to the first floor, where I was teaching. I first noticed people going by my door, some walking, some running. I thought there might be a fire, and when I stepped into the hall, I saw John Turner.

"What's going on?" I asked him.

"A girl was attacked up on the third floor. I heard they caught somebody."

My class heard what Turner said, and before I could stop them, or even slow them down, they were by me and on their way to investigate.

It's over, I thought. It's over, it's over. That thought came to me neither as something joyful nor as something sorrowful. It was simply a conclusion that I came to: something that has been happening here in Wanekia is now finished. I let myself be caught in the drift of the crowd, and I soon found myself, along with what seemed to be everyone else in the school, on the third floor.

I stood off to the side, looking for Alexandra or Roger. I could not see either of them, but while I was scanning the crowd, Herman returned.

He came up the end stairway. He was red-faced and sweating so hard his glasses kept slipping down his nose. "I couldn't catch him," he said, in response to the inquiring looks everyone was giving him. "I chase him for two blocks but he's too goddamn fast." (That was, I thought, the only time he's going to get away with swearing in front of students without a reprimand.)

Proctor was on the scene now and was taking charge. "Did you see who it was, Herman? Did you see who you were chasing?"

"I saw him, yah. But I don't know his name."

"I do! I know who it was!" It was Jackie Kuntz speaking. She was still on the floor, but she had begun to compose herself and she had found voice. Someone had draped a coat around her shoulders, and someone else was giving her a cup of water. "I know exactly who it was!" she shouted."It was George! George Hall!"

"Yeah!" Herman seconded. "That's who it was—the football player."

When the name was announced, there was, at first, a loud, disbelieving, shocked gasp from the people standing about. Then I heard one girl scream. Then someone else said, "Not George! It can't be!" From someone else came, "That sonofabitch!" Then everyone was repeating, "George Hall, George Hall, George Hall, George Hall."

I hung my head and closed my eyes. Everything before this moment, all my suspicions, theories, and fantasies of who the killer might be, became games, the mind-toys of someone removed from reality, from the reality of this moment. I never would have known, I thought. I could not have guessed that George Hall was the one. Logic would not have led me to that conclusion. Reason, rationality would have been of no use. Nevertheless, here it was: the truth. The Great Truth everyone had sought for months.

Then I had an image of George's hands, his large, long-fingered, javelin- and discus-throwing, football-player's hands. It was a haunting vision, as if something that I had noticed in the past, something everyday and benign, had taken on a murderous, demonic dimension. At that moment, I did not think of George Hall committing those crimes; I thought of his hands committing them.

"Did you know him?" someone said.

It took seconds before I realized that Carl Becker was speaking to me.

"What?" I said.

"Did you know him? Did you know George Hall?"

"I knew who he was. That's all." It was a lie. George had once been a student of mine. I remembered him as shy, hardworking, solemn, and as a practitioner of that awkward, but heavily adorned, prose style. And before, I may have treasured the fame, the notoriety, of any "intimate connections" with the murderer, but now, like Peter of the Bible, I wanted to deny, deny. Besides, what Carl wanted to know was, did I know George as, in any sense, a possible murderer?

"I was hoping it wouldn't be one of us," Carl said. "Somebody from the school. I knew better, but I kept hoping."

Just as I heard the sirens, coming from far off but getting closer, two policemen, one uniformed and one in plain clothes, came running down the hall. I suppose they drove up in silence, hoping not to frighten off the killer. I wondered who had the presence of mind to call the police.

The officers pushed their way through the people. They kept asking, "Where's the girl? Where's the girl who was attacked?"

When they reached Jackie Kuntz, they ushered her off quickly and brusquely into an empty classroom.

No one left the hall. In fact, more teachers and students, those who had been in classrooms in the further reaches of the building, continued to arrive. A girls' phys ed class, the girls still dressed in their shapeless, one-piece, green gym uniforms, showed up. One girl carried a volleyball. It was a strange crowd. The scene reminded me of pictures I had seen of World War II Britain; then, when the air-raid sirens sounded, everyone stopped what he or she was doing and ran to and gathered in an underground corridor.

Proctor was standing on his tiptoes, waving his arms, and shouting, "Could I have your attention! Could I please have everyone's attention! The police have everything under control. There's nothing for us to do. I know we're all excited and upset about what happened, but there's nothing for us to do. Let's go back to our classrooms and stay there. When the bell rings, do not go to your next class. I repeat, do *not* go to your next class. There will be an announcement when it's time to do something. Teachers, I want you to take a very careful roll. I want to know *exactly* who was here today and who wasn't."

I returned to my classroom, and eventually, grudgingly, so did my students. "Just take your seats," I told them, "while I take roll. Then I don't care what you do. As long as you stay in the room." Then, with the roll taken, I stationed myself by the door, watching hopefully to see if Alexandra would go by. She did not. Perhaps she had not allowed her students to leave the room.

Finally, after fifteen or twenty minutes, the PA system crackled, the room hushed, and Proctor began to speak. He had, by now, regained his slow, heavy, authoritarian, Rotary Club-speaker voice: "As most of you know by now, we had something unfortunate happen this morning up on the third floor. A girl, one of our seniors, was accosted. She is all right. She is not harmed. She has been taken to Holy Cross Hospital for observation. The police have the situation under control. We are going to dismiss classes for the day, but please, go directly to your homes. These are the wishes of the Police Department and I concur with them. Unless notified otherwise, classes will meet tomorrow at the regular time. We hope we can get things back to normal around here. Thank you."

And the school did clear. No one ran, rejoicing, from the building, as if the day were a holiday, as if it were the first day of summer vacation. Rather, they filed out slowly, steadily, the way they leave school when they are on a fire drill. And they glanced about constantly, the way they do on a fire drill, trying to catch a glimpse of smoke, trying to see if the fire were a real one. But today they were trying to see if the police were handcuffing a suspect. Those students who had ideas of loitering about the parking lot were shooed away by the police.

The faculty too was expected to leave. Some of the teachers hung around the halls, and some headed for the lounge, all hoping to hear more of what was going on. But the police wanted the building vacated completely. In spite of the fact that their suspect ran from the school, they still wanted to lock the building and conduct a thorough search.

I ran into Alexandra at last as I was leaving. I asked her if she wanted to go get a cup of coffee or something.

"I can't, Peter. I promised Bonnie I'd go with her and help her."

"Help her? Help her what?"

"We're going to the hospital first to make sure that girl is all right. Then we're going to find some way to make ourselves available to those girls who need to talk to someone."

"Need someone to talk to? Today? I don't get it."

"I know it sounds strange, but Bonnie said that it's very common for people to begin to break *after* a crisis has passed. I guess they've held on for so long that the release is too much for them. She said one girl already came up to her in the hall, asking if she could talk. We might set up in the basement of the First Methodist Church. Will you be home?"

"Yes."

"I'll call you as soon as I know where I'll be, okay?" She put her hand lightly to my cheek, and then she was gone. I envied her having someplace to go and I envied her usefulness.

I did go home. My apartment looked strange, but I guess it was just the light. The curtains were drawn, and since I am so rarely there at that time of day, the half light, half dark of noon made the rooms seem unfamiliar, as if I had walked into the wrong apartment. I turned on the radio and the television.

The information that I have of the events of the rest of the day is pieced together from many different sources. There were light, sketchy, news reports on radio and television and in the newspaper. Later, I went to Candy's to meet

Roger for a drink. The bar was crowded, and everyone there had some fragment of news that he was eager to plug into the larger puzzle. Roger, in fact, was an excellent source. John Rausch, Roger's friend and sometime tennis partner, lives next door to a police sergeant. And when Alexandra called (from the Methodist Church), she too had accumulated a few random bits of information.

These, then, are the things I learned.

The police, in force, went to George Hall's home. They surrounded the house, evacuated the dwellings on both sides ("secured the area," as one of the patrons of Candy's put it), and then anticlimactically knocked at the front door.

Yes, George was home, his mother said. He was upstairs in his room. Since he had come home from school in the middle of the day, she assumed he was sick. The police removed her from the home (for her own protection), and then, with guns drawn, they proceeded cautiously up the stairs to George's room.

The door to the room was closed. The police went in quickly. George was sitting quietly on his bed, waiting. Two of the officers grabbed George, threw him face down on the bed, and handcuffed him. He gave them no resistance, but said, "I did it. You've got me. I did all of them, and you've got me. I'm glad it's over. I couldn't stand it much longer. I'm glad you've got me." The police had to shut George up so they could inform him of his rights.

Once they got George down to the station, he continued to talk freely. No, he had no use for a lawyer; he wanted to talk to the police, he wanted to unburden himself. Yes, he had attacked Jackie Kuntz this morning, and yes, he had attacked and killed Deborah Ann Munson, Laura Irene Dobe, and Debra Helen Spencer. Although he had not raped any of the girls, in each case he had intended to. However, he became so frightened during the attacks, so afraid that someone would discover him, that he did not have intercourse with the girls. To do so would have put him, as he said, "in a compromising situation with [his] pants down," and he would not have been able to effect a fast getaway if he had been found out. All of the girls undressed themselves and neatly folded their own clothes. He convinced each girl that he did not want to hurt her; he only wanted to see what she looked like without any clothes on. (Jackie Kuntz confirmed this fact of George's "approach." She said that when he grabbed her, he said, "Be quiet. I don't want to hurt you. I just want to try something. If you let me, I won't hurt you." Jackie said she thought she would be all right if she let George do anything he wanted; it was her impression that the other girls were killed because they would not cooperate. As she lay in her hospital bed, she said she knew how wrong she was to believe that—that George could not allow any girl to go free, able to identify him as the attacker. At the time, however, she was only able to do what she thought would keep her alive.) It was funny, George said, that he did *not* rape the girls, because that was the motive—sex—behind the attacks. He had nothing against those girls. He only chose them because they were pretty and because they were alone in the school at certain times. When he choked them, he only thought of squeezing his hands together, as if he were wringing a sponge.

George used his "weapon"—a carpenter's knife—to cut the girls' clothes. He didn't have a reason for doing that, for cutting up the clothing, but he thought it might "throw people off the track." He thought that if he did something like that, something unpredictable and illogical, that the police might key on that and that it would lead them into "unproductive areas of suspicion." (In this, and in other analyses of his actions, I think George's interpretations are not always the most reliable, that he is not able to understand very clearly what he has done or why.)

George is an only child, and his mother and father went to police headquarters to find out why their son had been arrested. They too heard rumors but they received no confirmation from the police. They were only told that George was being questioned. Later, after George had made and signed his statement, after he had confessed, after he was charged with three counts of first-degree murder, then Mr.

and Mrs. Hall were told why their son was in custody. Reverend Gunnar, minister of the Presbyterian church which the Halls attend, heard of the arrest and went to the jail to be with the Halls. Ed Bender, George's football coach, also went down to the station to see if he could be of any help to George or the Halls.

These were the major events of the day. I have omitted that material that I thought would be of little interest. I have not mentioned, for instance, that when I returned to my apartment this evening, there was the distinct smell of cooking cabbage coming from one of the other apartments. On every Friday, that smell permeates my building. I have also not mentioned that the weather today was exactly as it was yesterday: high clouds, temperatures in the low sixties, light southerly breezes.

And I have not mentioned how Peter Leesh reacted to the events of the day. But how could I? Peter has no time to react. He must remain the chronicler, the archivist, the one who records the way the clouds stack up in the sky, the one who marks the bitten, tearful faces of those around him, the one who measures the length of the fingers on a murderer's hand.

15 June 1973, Friday

Mark down this entry as the last effort of a compulsively tidy mind, as the loose-end-tying, mopping-up entry.

George Hall has not yet come to trial. His lawyer, a young, inexperienced man from the Twin Cities, applied for a change of venue, and it was granted. And the court, the prosecution, and the defense all want extensive psychiatric tests. There have been preliminary hearings, motions, counter-motions, continuances, and numerous other delays. I don't pretend to know all the legalisms involved but I suspect that it will be at least another month before the trial.

The reaction in the community has been strange and mixed. There are, predictably, those who want to see George strung up from the nearest tree. After months of hating, fearing, and cursing an anonymous killer, there's no reason to believe that they would feel differently now that there are a name and face as a specific object, a focus for all that terror and loathing. Why should they suddenly become merciful now that someone has been arrested? But what *has* surprised me is that there has been an astonishing amount of understanding, tolerance, and even, to a limited degree, forgiveness. No one condones what George did and no one excuses it, but since so many people knew George for so many years, cheered him on in his athletic career, pointed to him as a model for their own sons, they find it difficult to switch off their fondness for him and now despise him. (But they no longer say, "I can't believe it." For the first few days after the arrest, they couldn't believe it. They believe it now.) A typical attitude was expressed by Mrs. Anthony Bates, a neighbor of the Halls: "For years George delivered my paper, mowed my lawn, and shoveled my walk. I just can't hate him."

And how does Peter Leesh feel about George Hall? I'm not sure exactly. I feel tolerant, generous, pitying. But I do not understand him, and I do not want to. George Hall is, unquestionably, awash in madness. And I want that madness to remain as a wide, unbridgeable gulf between George, and all the George Halls of the world, and me. To understand him, to know how and why he did what he did, is to come too close to what he is. That is why I no longer want to know why. That is why I no longer read newspaper accounts of these or any other murders. That is why I turn my back on any conversation about George. That is why I have shed, like an old coat, my curiosity about murder, about the pathology of it, the reactions to it. I am content with this distance of ignorance between George and me. I do not recommend it to others but I am satisfied with it.

The Hall family has also fared reasonably well at the hands of the community. No crosses have been burned on their lawn, no rocks heaved through their windows, no tires slashed, no anonymous threats, no tar and feathers. Pity and awe seem to be the prevailing emotions. George is an only child, and he has been semiorphaned since the arrest. George's mother left town a few days after his confession. She simply could not handle what had happened to her life, and she left town. Permanently. She lives now with her sister in Seattle, and she has no intention of returning to her husband, her son, her home, or this town. She is unavailable for comment. George's father, a tall, quiet, Standard Service Station operator, has, however, remained loyal to his son. He does not protest George's innocence but says only that his son needs him now more than ever.

Herman Wahl, the janitor, who was as responsible as anyone for George's capture, was finally given the reward this week. Herman says he is going to use the money to buy a boat.

We did have to make up the canceled days of school. But it was done in a sly and painless way. It was simply announced that school would be in session on certain Saturdays; however, students were not encouraged to attend those Saturday sessions (and neither were teachers).

At commencement ceremonies, there was a moment of silence for those who could not be present. Richard Mantor, who gave the valedictory address, and Harold Dingle, president of the Board of Education and keynote speaker, both alluded to our "recent unpleasantness" in their remarks, but in the true spirit of political, religious, and graduation speeches, they preferred the general to the specific, the abstract to the concrete.

And this town does not seem to me to be much different from the town it was before the murders. On still June nights, such as the ones we've been having lately, if you stand outside and listen carefully, you find that the quiet is filled with noise. Mosquitoes hum, June bugs clatter against the screen, crickets chirp, nighthawks cry out in their hunting, and frogs croak back and forth in a guttural chorus. If, on such a night, you step out onto the porch and into the darkness shout "STOP!" your command will be obeyed. For a few seconds, the frogs, birds, and insects will stop, and the only sound that will come back to you will be the echo of your own voice. Then, as suddenly as it stopped, the noise will begin again, completely and without missing a beat. That is what this community's resumption of normal activities reminds me of. It's as if there had been an annoying interruption, but now the gently subdued clamor of the town and its business can begin again.

But I know that appearance of normalcy is a deception, that despite the continuation of casual, ritual life, this town and everyone living here has changed and changed profoundly. When Jenny Gerhardt is considering whether or not to buy a new halter top, part of the consideration may be, is this too provocative? Could it attract the twisted attention of someone like George? When mothers spank their misbehaving children in K-Mart, mothers may ask themselves if such public punishments are part of what turns children into adolescents like George. When Mr. Loftis, owner of the Loftis Book and Card Shop, stocks his magazine shelves with *Playboy, Penthouse, Cavalier, Stag,* and *Saga,* might he wonder about the effects of these fleshy publications on such minds as George's? When Dr. Loos, a local pediatrician, member of the School Board, and chairman of the PTA, drives his light blue Lincoln through town, he might wonder if he has done all he can to serve as an example to the community's young people. Might not many fathers of teenage girls cross themselves when their daughters leave the sanctity of home? Hundreds of citizens of this town might lie sleepless in bed at night, trying to trace back their lives to mark each point of contact with George Hall, and they might blame themselves for not having noticed something "strange" about the lad. In other words, although the quiet, smooth surface of life has been restored, although the downtown merchants are holding their annual Crazy Days Downtown Sidewalk Sale as usual this week, although the Elks Club is again having its Summer Madness Carnival, although Bob's Bar has returned to its "Thank-God-It's-Friday-Nickle-Beer-Night," although Mrs. Dohr has gone back to walking her poodle every evening at six o'clock, although Broomie is still sweeping the streets, nothing here is the same and never will be.

Something else. Without the frame of murder around the tableau of our lives, a friendly disorder has returned. In an obvious way, no longer are our school schedules and our leisure activities regimented by fear, by having to be home before dark, by always having to be in the company of two or more. But there is more than that. Somehow, while the murders were going on, everything, every thought, every gesture, was related to murder. Now that's gone. Now nothing is related to anything else, and everything we do is characterized by a pleasing randomness, by a relieved lack of connections.

And of course an observable change, observable particularly to me, is Alexandra's absence. True to her word, she left on Monday, May 28. I helped her pack. She sold her television, shipped her books, gave away her furniture, and what little else was left—clothes, her stereo, and some boxes of "personal belongings"—we managed to squeeze into her car. When she drove away, her car was piled so high with boxes, suitcases, and bags that I could not even see the back of her head as she pulled out of the parking lot. My last glimpse of her was of her arm, which she stretched out the window and waved while driving away.

Her leaving was very hard for me. She left early, about six thirty, and we were both tired. We had packed the car the night before, and then she spent the night with me (for the practical, if not very romantic, reason that she no longer had a bed). Since it was our last night together, we drank a lot of wine and then tried for one final, dynamite lovemaking session. Which turned out to be something more frantic than fitting as a farewell. We tried again about five thirty with slightly more success. Then Alexandra showered and she was ready to go. Outside, we both busied ourselves with the car, trying not to look at each other, trying to keep the occasion light and official. When she got in the car, and we made each other promise to write, I kissed her casually (a husband's peck to a wife on her way to the office), and then she was gone.

I stood in the parking lot for a while, watching the sun dry the dew, waiting to see if she had forgotten something, waiting to see if she would simply return. She did not.

But it got worse later that day. I had promised Alexandra that I would clean her apartment after she was out. There was little to do; she had lived there very lightly. But I vacuumed, defrosted the refrigerator, puttied the nail holes, and washed the floors. Then, as I was leaving, closing the door for the last time, the fact of her leaving hit me. And it hit me physically. I couldn't swallow. I couldn't breathe, and I felt a crushing sensation in my chest. When you stand close to a jet revving its engines or close to the amplifiers of a loud band, you can feel your chest vibrate and thrum; it feels as if your ribs could shake loose from your sternum. For a moment, I had difficulty convincing myself the pain was from grief and not a coronary.

At the end of the *Wizard of Oz*, when Dorothy is about to return to Kansas, when she is saying good-bye to the Tin Woodman, the Cowardly Lion, and the Scarecrow, the Woodman says to Dorothy, "Now I know I have a heart because it's breaking." As I took Alexandra's key to the manager, I kept repeating the Woodman's farewell. It became my mantra. Throughout the day, I mouthed those ten words, holding on to them, clinging to the sentimental ending of a children's movie as a way of keeping myself together.

I did receive a postcard from Alexandra. It was a picture of the Pacific and said, "Beautiful and quiet here. The ocean is lovely. Three times bigger than Lake Kinnewa [a small lake outside Wanekia]. Love, Al." Each day I intend to write, but so far I have not. Unless it's for money, I'm lousy at letterwriting.

Roger also is gone. He has friends who have some land near Missoula, Montana, and he plans to spend the summer with them. He did not say whether he intends to return in the fall or not, but I suspect he has left Wanekia for good. He gave up his apartment and took everything he owned in a small U-Haul trailer. He told me he's going to store his possessions in the garage of his parents' home in Chicago. In spite of his popularity with students, I don't think Roger was cut out to be a public-school teacher; he somehow does not have the proper sensibility. Whatever that means.

Although his departure saddened me also, it was not as bad as Alexandra's leaving. For one thing, I expect to see him again. I expect to see him periodically throughout my life. For no particular reason, I expect Roger to turn up on my doorstep, wherever that doorstep might be, at more or less regular intervals throughout my life. I can see him showing up, every five years or so, Sucrets box in hand, and saying, "Hey, Pete. How's it going?"

Bonnie is still here. She has another year left before she has enough money saved to go to graduate school at the University of Michigan or Colorado or wherever the hell she wants to go. After Roger left, Bonnie and I got together one night. We had a few drinks, each trying to console the other, and we finally ended up in bed. It was not wholly satisfactory. Nothing overtly inept, nothing embarrassing, no obvious examples of incompetence or incompatibility. But as far as I was concerned, something was not quite right. Although I don't care to make comparative studies, I couldn't help myself as we lay in bed together. When I put my arm around her, I noticed how much thicker she was through the waist than Alexandra. I noticed how looser, how wetter, her lips were. How fuller her breasts, how darker her skin. These were things I could not help noticing, and although she was not aware of my observations, I felt nevertheless as if I should be apologizing for having made them. From now until the first of July, Bonnie is attending a Counseling and Guidance Workshop at St. Cloud State College.

And what are my plans? What have I decided for my own future? Before I reveal that, let me say what has gone into the decision-making progress. (Since we no longer have any suspense in our lives, I guess I feel obliged to create some.)

First, I read through this journal of days. How strange it was to read through this record. (And how strange it has been not to write in it each day. At first, I missed it, missed it desperately. Each day, I felt as though I had forgotten something. I felt guilty, as if, by not recording each day, I was committing a great sin, letting that day slip away and be forever lost. Then, when the guilt went away, it felt good.

It felt good not to have to hold onto each hour, each minute, each event, of the day, just for the purpose of cataloging. It felt good to let the days slip and run together, to return to some continuum of time. I was free of anticipation, too.) But to read through these pages was to hear the sound of my own voice. However, though I knew the voice to be my own, it did not seem familiar. It was like listening to a tape recording when you know it is a reproduction of your speech, but you simply cannot believe it. Oh, no, you say, that clotted, nasal, shallow, wavering voice simply cannot be mine. But it is. And the words on these pages, no matter how cracked and faraway those words may seem, are mine. And somehow, reading the words and hearing the voice were revelatory.

Earlier this week, when the hot and humid weather was at its peak, we had three consecutive days of tornado and severe thunderstorm warnings. Through those warnings, I thought of Alexandra and her fear of natural disasters. Then on the third day, late in the afternoon, the sky darkened, and the heavy blue-green clouds came down so low it looked as if they were lowering themselves just to get ready to drop a funnel cloud. If Alexandra were here, I thought, she'd be going crazy. Each long roll of thunder would cause her to jump. Each flash of lightning would cause her to flinch. If only she were here, I thought. I'd call her and tell her that I'd be right over to hold her hand, that we could go find a basement together. Selfish, no doubt, but that was my wish, to have her close enough for me to protect.

That was the second thing that contributed to my decision.

Next to my apartment building is a baseball diamond, and from my living-room window, I have a perfect view of kids' games. I can hear, even with the window closed, the bat hit the ball, and the slap and thump of the ball in the glove. I can hear them yell—their clumsy swearing and their infield chatter. Yesterday afternoon, I was watching some boys—they were about twelve years old—play baseball. Six of them played listlessly in the heat. They were too few for

even a decent game of work-up, and their boredom probably contributed to what eventually happened.

A small kitten kept running out onto the field, and anytime the ball was on the ground, still or in motion, the cat
was at it as if the ball was there only for the cat's play. The
boys tried everything to get the kitten off the field. They
threw rocks, which it dodged skillfully. They removed the
kitten, dumped it over the fence, but it always returned.
Then one boy, older and bigger than the others, picked up
the kitten by the scruff of the neck, and in the other hand,
picked up a bat. Then, as casually as if he were hitting
fungoes to the outfielders, he threw the cat high in the air,
and when it came down, he hit it with the bat. He swung
with both hands, upward and hard.

By then, the other boys were standing around, staring at
the kitten. It lay in the dirt, and it must have been partially
paralyzed by the blow, because it was kicking frantically
with one back leg; that action succeeded only in spinning
the kitten in a dusty circle.

Before I knew what I was doing, I jumped up from my
chair by the window and ran from my apartment. I ran
toward the diamond yelling, "Hey! Hey! Hey!" When the
boys saw me coming, they scattered in all directions. "Hey,
Chicken Shit!" I yelled. "Come back here and finish what
you started!"

But they were not about to come back, and by the time I
got out onto the field, what they started *was* finished. The
cat was dead. Which was just as well, because I don't know
what I would have done if it were still alive. Its eyes were
closed, and its body was not misshapen or marked by blood.
I picked it up by three of its legs and carried it off the
diamond. I dropped it in an adjacent field in some tall grass.

And as I was walking through that high grass back to my
building, I looked up at my apartment window, the window
behind which moments ago I was sitting. It will sound
strange, I know, but the sight of that window, as blank as
dark water, jarred me. I don't know what I expected to see.
Perhaps I thought I would somehow continue to see my

face, my form, in that high window. Not my reflection, but some shape that actually was mine. This is all beginning to take on a metaphysical significance that it doesn't deserve. At any rate, it was the emptiness of that rectangle of glass that seemed so unsettling.

So what do these three seemingly unrelated occurrences, the reading of a journal, a series of storm warnings, and an unfortunate bit of brutality on a baseball field, have to do with my reaching a decision? I don't know. There may be no connection at all. I only know that after these incidents, I reached, without seeking, pondering, or meditating, a decision. And this may be a classic example of the *post hoc, ergo propter hoc* fallacy. I don't care. I am no longer interested in analyzing my own life. I leave it alone, able to find its own shape or its own chaos.

And what is the decision?

I am quitting my job, vacating my apartment, selling my goods, and going to California. "Lighting out for the territory," as they say.

I have Alexandra's brother's address and telephone number, but I'm not going to get in touch with her until I get to California. Then, I still won't call (unless I can't find the house); I'll simply show up.

Among my many reasons for going there is my eagerness to see the ocean. I have not seen the sea since I vacationed with my parents, and even then, even when I was a jaded, difficult-to-impress child, the sight of that expanse of blue water awed me.

Of course, fascination with the sea is a condition that is ageless and well documented. In Whitman, for instance, the sea is a symbol of both life and death. But since I don't intend to continue teaching, I no longer have any use for symbols.

Even before the ocean comes into view, you can hear it. The sound of it, like someone breathing in your ear, is at first subtle, and you can never be certain when you began hearing it. As you move closer, the sound becomes more distinct, as if you threw open the doors of an auditorium and released the noise of a crowd, hundreds of people, all cheering wildly in one great voice.

So this is good-bye to Minnesota, to its woodlands, lakes, and fields, to its frigid winters and its torpid summers. And good-bye to these pages, to this record of the spring of 1973. Good-bye. Good-bye. Farewell.